if this was a movie

if this was a movie

A Falling into Fame Novel: Book One

by

Ginna Moran

ISBN 978-1-942073-71-0 (soft cover)
ISBN 978-1-942073-73-4 (ebooks)

This is a work of fiction. All of the characters, organizations, and events portrayed in this novel are either products of the author's imagination or are used fictitiously.

Cover design by Silver Starlight Designs
Cover images copyright Depositphotos

For Inquiries Contact:
Sunny Palms Press
9663 Santa Monica Blvd Suite 1158
Beverly Hills, CA 90210, USA
www.sunnypalmspress.com
www.GinnaMoran.com

For Jan Moran,
This book wouldn't have existed without you. Thanks for being the
best mother-in-law in the entire world. Love you!

chapter 1

🌴 The World of 90210 🌴

THE BLUISH-GREEN Pacific Ocean ripples beyond me as the plane hurtles forward to land at LAX. I clutch my backpack against my chest, never taking my eyes from the window. Watching the world zoom below me makes this feel more real. I didn't have to leave my home back in Austin, Texas, but it just didn't feel like home anymore since Dad died. I'm not even sure how I survived as long as I did under Cecilia's care. She probably danced the moment I left her at security in the Austin-Bergstrom International Airport.

Cecilia was my stepmother, but the moment she realized she didn't have to raise someone else's kid, she turned into a step-monster. I still can't believe Dad's gone, but he didn't think about me for one second when he signed a will leaving everything to Cecilia after they first married. Dad's ashes hadn't even arrived before she turned me into a modern-day Cinderella.

She took away everything—my computer, my cable, my phone—and told me she wasn't going to pay for a worthless moocher. If it weren't for my best friend, who had won the lottery when it comes to having an amazing step-mom, I don't know how I would've made it this long. I can still hear Cecilia's words resonating through my mind about how this is all some precious life lesson to learn from, like Dad wanted me to rely on no one but myself. But I refuse to believe that was the truth. He intended for us to remain a family after he was gone. If only he wasn't too sick to realize everything before it was too late.

A brunette flight attendant touches my armrest, drawing my attention away from my morbid thoughts. "Hey, hon, you need to stow your backpack and put your seat in the upright position for landing."

I jab my finger at the button until I'm sitting straight. The flight attendant smiles, tilting her head to the side, but I only turn my gaze back to the window. Hazy air clouds the sprawling city of Los Angeles as the plane descends toward the runway. I clutch my armrests and think about the first and only time I had visited Aunt Jen in Beverly Hills.

It was the summer before Dad had met Cecilia, just a year after Mom had passed away from a freak accident where she'd tumbled down some stone steps at her office downtown. Aunt Jen bribed Dad to bring me, said I could use some new surroundings, and she was right. I'll never forget all the touristy stuff she took me to do—like window shopping on Rodeo Drive and strolling down the Hollywood Walk of Fame. She even let me explore her neighborhood on my own, where I found a house with life-sized animal statues that looked like a fake zoo. I begged Dad to let me stay for the summer, but he said no. All these years later I know it was because he was afraid to be alone. *Look where you left me, Dad...*

Touching down on the runway, the plane bumps and shakes. I close my eyes. I didn't realize I was afraid of flying until we took off from Austin and by then it was too late. I take a deep breath and relax as the plane slows, and the pilot navigates us toward the gate. This was the longest three hours of my life. I think about how my old life is gone, tears clouding my vision at the thought. How I had to say goodbye to my best friend, Taylor, and how I'll be finishing my high school education in the world of 90210 while living in the less famous 90211 zip code.

Hoisting my backpack over my shoulder, I wait for the crowd to mosey from the plane. My nerves bunch in my stomach when I exit into the terminal and peer around. This is my first time traveling alone, and everything is just so new and foreign that I wish I had taken up Aunt Jen on her offer to fly to get me so we could travel together. I wanted to prove that I'm not the same girl I was the last time I saw her at Dad's funeral before the start of summer. Cecilia made sure of that.

I push thoughts of the monster with small square teeth, beady eyes, and deep wrinkles into the corner of my mind. She only makes me angry about my dad, and I can't let her soil the few good memories I have left of him. She doesn't deserve even a second thought.

"Nora! Over here!" Aunt Jen swings her arms over her head, a huge smile on her plum-colored lips. Her sandy brown hair sits on top of her head in a messy bun, and she wears black yoga pants and a hot pink tank top. It's a big difference from her usual pantsuits, low bun, and neutral makeup.

"Welcome home! You don't even know how happy I am to have you here. I've missed you." She pulls me into a hug, pressing her delicate chin to my shoulder, and I squeeze her back.

I laugh when she doesn't let me go. "I've missed you more than you know."

She pulls away, a flicker of sadness in her eyes, but she doesn't stop smiling. "Come on, let's get your bag."

Aunt Jen pulls into the driveway of her quaint home, smaller than my old house back in Texas but probably a million times more expensive, on Clifton Way. The green trim pops against the white paint and bougainvillea bushes surround her walled-in patio. She pulls her sleek, black Lexus GS F into the two-car garage and shuts off the engine.

She doesn't move to get out. "I didn't want to decorate your room for you, so it's pretty basic. We can go shopping tomorrow if you like. I took the next two weeks off."

I unbuckle my seatbelt. "I have everything I need."

She touches my arm. "You have two suitcases. Is Cecelia shipping the rest?"

I climb out of the car without answering. I'm embarrassed that I gave away most of my belongings and donated or threw away what others didn't want. I have enough baggage to carry already. It lessened the load. Hopefully I'll forget Cecelia, and it'll be like she never existed.

Aunt Jen lets the subject drop. She opens the door to the house, motioning for me to stroll ahead of her. A small Yorkshire terrier skids across the gleaming wood floors from the hallway, yapping as it jumps up and down on my leg. I reach down and let it sniff my fingers before petting his floor-length fur.

"Jasper likes you," Aunt Jen comments while scooping the dog into her arms. She crinkles her nose as Jasper licks her cheek, and then holds him out to me.

He rests his paws on my shoulders, sniffing my chestnut-colored hair. "He's so cute. When did you get him?"

Aunt Jen motions me to follow her. "A few months ago. Julian's landlord complained about Jasper's barking and threatened to evict him if he didn't get rid of the dog. I warned Julian that it was a bad idea to rent a duplex with his landlord as the neighbor." I've only heard about Julian through stories, but Aunt Jen swears he's the world's best assistant.

I cradle Jasper in my arms. Aunt Jen swings open the door to what used to be the guest room. The pale gray walls are the same color I remember them being, but she moved all her knick-knacks and framed paintings from the walls. On top of a dresser is a small flat-screen TV, and a new corner desk and computer sit near the sheer-curtained window.

I place Jasper on the dark purple comforter of my new bed. "You got me a computer?"

She steps into the room and runs her finger along the pristine desk. "I missed your birthday and thought you could use one."

I blink tears from my eyes. When Dad was alive, we always shared a computer. It was never a big deal because he always worked late at the River View Hotel where he was general manager. It's where he met my step-monster. Everyone used to always laugh when Dad explained how they met. Cecilia was nick-named the nightmare client after she asked to switch rooms three times because something wasn't up to her satisfaction. Dad would tease that she appeared at the front desk so often that she grew on him. Cecilia would roll her beady eyes and add it was only because she liked him. It makes me gag just thinking about it.

"Nora? You okay?" Aunt Jen studies me for a moment.

I realize I'm hugging myself, not doing much of anything except staring at the laptop. I don't even know how long I've been lost in my thoughts. She probably thinks I'm crazy.

I lick my lips. "Yeah, I'm fine. I really appreciate the gift. I haven't had a computer in a while. Taylor always lent me her laptop when I needed it."

Aunt Jen shows off her perfectly straight teeth in a smile though her eyes don't crinkle in the corners like usual. "I bet it was hard leaving. You're welcome to invite Taylor to stay with us anytime."

I nod even though I doubt Taylor's parents could afford to send her out here, and Taylor is saving for college with the income she makes from her part-time job at the H.E.B grocery store. I've come to terms with the fact that I probably won't see my childhood best friend until we're both in college—that is, if our friendship survives the long distance.

Silence falls between us. Aunt Jen glances around the room before looking at me again. A line forms between her arched brows, and the corner of her mouth twitches like she's contemplating what to say next.

I shift on my feet, feeling more awkward than I should in front of the woman who swooped in to save me when I felt like I was drowning in the desert.

I do the only thing I can think of, and I hug Aunt Jen, breathing in the scent of her warm perfume. She squeezes me, digging her chin into my boney shoulder. Slowly easing away from her, I drop my hands to my side. "I'm going to take a shower and rest for a bit."

She furiously bobs her head like it's the best idea she's heard all day. "I'll grab your suitcases. When you're ready, I'd like to take you out to dinner, if that's okay."

I sit on the edge of my bed. "Sure." My nerves bunch together so tightly in my stomach that I'm not sure I can eat, but I'll force myself to try. I shouldn't be so nervous. This is a dream compared to the nightmare I've been living.

Aunt Jen leans in the doorway. "You remember where the

bathroom is?"

"Down the hall on the right," I answer.

Her lips curl up into a small smile, then she exits and shuts the door behind her. Jasper whimpers from the bed, and I cradle him like a baby in my arms. His stubby tail wags, and he stretches his neck to try to lick me, but I keep him just out of reach before I move to sit down at my desk.

I wiggle the wireless mouse on my laptop. It's ten times better than the old PC Cecilia kept as her own. At least it's something. I can only hope she gets a million viruses since she's the least tech savvy person I've ever met. I'll never forget when she tried to use the status box on her Friendconn page to search "ingrown hair removal on butt cheek." I had a dozen of my friends share screenshots of her status before Dad had the chance to delete it. It was worth the weekend grounding.

I log into my video chat and wait to see if Taylor connects. It's already nine o'clock her time, but she should be awake for a few more hours. She sleeps with her phone glued to her hand and would probably answer even if she did fall asleep.

The video box appears in the middle of my screen, and Taylor's room pops into view and blurs, spinning with her movement. "Hold on, Nora. I'm putting on my night face."

I rest my elbows on my desk. "Trying out the grapefruit mask?"

Taylor hums along to her low music. "Mmm-hmm."

She took most of my beauty supplies, apart from my small makeup bag with my favorite products. I had a whole bin of all sorts of skincare stuff because Aunt Jen is a legal advisor to Eva Devereaux, one of the world's most iconic models, who recently signed a huge deal with the giant beauty brand Tilly Pop. It was like Christmas in June when I got the box in the mail. It wouldn't fit in my suitcase, though, and I knew Taylor would try anything once.

After a long minute, I sigh. "You're not supposed to use the whole jar, you know."

She laughs, the sound bursting through my speakers like she's saying ha-ha-ha-ha really fast. The noise is contagious, and I laugh because of it.

The video display bounces and moves around her room again. She pops into view. Her shiny skin reflects light from her bedroom lamp. I can't help but smile seeing my best friend's face, even though it's only been a few hours since we said good-bye at the airport.

Her dark brown eyes sheen over, and she blinks. "God, Nora. I can almost pretend you're a few blocks away."

"This whole situation sucks, but I couldn't stay with Devil Woman any longer. You saw how she treated me." I don't need to reiterate how terrible the last few months have been, but I like what Taylor tells me every time I mention it.

She glares at her camera. "Karma's going to kick down her door and toss a lifetime of bad luck in her face. You'll see. And if she doesn't, I'll figure out how to do it myself."

I snort. "Why do you have to be a million miles away?"

"At least you're somewhere amazing. I can only dream of

living somewhere so glam."

"I promise the streets aren't encrusted with diamonds."

She holds her finger up to her lips. "Shhh! They are to me."

A loud banging noise echoes over our video chat, and Taylor rolls her eyes. She brings her phone closer to her face so I can only see her light tan lips and crooked smile. "Call me back later," she whispers, fogging her camera over, making the video turn hazy.

"You better be up."

She laughs as she clicks off the video chat. I rock back in my desk chair and stare at the light fixture in the center of my room. It's a blown-glass, gray-and-white dome, and reminds me of a full moon beaming its silver-white light onto me.

My nerves settle as the day finally sinks in. I'm no longer with my step-monster, and I won't have to worry about her ever again.

At least, that's what I hope for.

chapter 2

Add Connection

I PULL MY hair into a top knot and stare at my reflection in the bathroom mirror. I haven't found motivation to leave the house for anything other than eating out with Aunt Jen, which she does a lot.

I can't help it, though. I used to spend so much time out of the house to avoid the step-monster that I'm okay with turning into a shut-in. School doesn't start for another week, so I'm enjoying the rest of my summer vacation doing absolutely nothing.

"You dressed, Nora?" Aunt Jen asks from outside my door.

"Yeah."

I peer down at the black yoga pants I borrowed from Aunt Jen's drawer and the screen printed T-shirt Taylor bought me as a going away present at the airport with the slogan, *Keep Austin*

Weird, scrawled across the front. She reminded me that I shouldn't hold a grudge against the whole state of Texas because of one person, and I told her she should consider studying Psychology in college because she'd make a great therapist.

Aunt Jen swings the door open and stands in the doorway with her hands on her hips. She's in a similar pair of black yoga pants, but her hair cascades down her back. In this light, it's almost the same exact color as mine, and she reminds me of a younger, more delicate version of my dad.

"I'm going to the local farmers market near City Hall. You're coming with me." She kicks my sneakers to me. "And we're walking."

I swing my legs from my bed. "You're serious." I don't ask. Her smirk is enough to confirm my suspicions.

After sliding my socked feet into my shoes, I stand up and check myself in the full-length mirror that hangs on my door. If I were back in Austin, I'd have changed, applied makeup, and let down my hair in case I bumped into someone like Eric Dawson, the hottest boy at Bowie High. I don't know anyone here, so it doesn't really matter. My giant sunglasses mask my face enough that I don't care. I'm nobody here, anyway.

Aunt Jen grins while she hands me a canvas tote bag with the name *Julia, Julia* stamped on the side. It's a brand I've never heard of, but I'm sure she'll tell me all about it if the conversation halts.

"Don't look like I'm forcing you to scrub the walls or something. It'll be fun." She loops her arm through mine and drags me out of my room and down the hall to the front door.

Hot sunshine engulfs us as we step onto the walled-in patio. The morning traffic hums by, with people heading out on their fun-filled Sunday adventures. I plop my dark sunglasses on my nose and consider turning around to go back inside to change into some track shorts. While the weather isn't as hot and humid as Austin, it's still on the warmer side.

Aunt Jen leads the way, strutting down the concrete path to the sidewalk like we're about to start a marathon. She walks in place for a moment before turning toward me. I hover at the edge of the shade, eyebrows nearly touching my hairline, and I blow air through my teeth.

I step into the blinding sunshine. "You said we were walking, not racing."

Laughter bubbles from her throat. "Come on, Nora. I won't go too fast." She marches forward at a pace twice as fast as I usually walk and heads toward the end of the block that'll take us in the direction of City Hall.

Trailing behind her, I drag my feet forward. She peers over her shoulder, shaking her light brown hair in the warm breeze, and then draws her focus back in front of her. I stay a good twenty feet behind her all the way to the intersection of Rexford Drive and Santa Monica Boulevard.

Perspiration beads on my forehead, and I wipe it off with the back of my hand. My damp T-shirt clings to me, and I regret not changing into shorts. I blink through the sunshine glaring off the car windows at the stoplight. Dozens of palm trees, the tallest I've ever seen, decorate a small park area. A block away, a fire truck blares its siren as it leaves the station.

It's not until this moment that the thought sinks in. I'm in Beverly Hills. I'm starting a new life most can only dream of, but why do I feel so bad about it? *Because of what you went through to get here.*

I touch my cheek even though the sting and red mark of being backhanded has long since faded. It was the moment I decided not to stand for Cecilia's awful treatment any longer. I wonder what Dad would think if he saw her now.

Following Aunt Jen across the street, I gaze at the hustle and bustle of this new-to-me city. A double-decker tourist bus squeals to a stop outside the library, and I wonder where all those people have come from. Like me, they don't really fit in, and it's obvious from their cameras and cell phones recording every single step they take.

Aunt Jen slows down and pulls me in the direction of the Beverly Hills Library where a temporary bright yellow sign announces the farmers market. We take a side street and pop into the closed off area lined with white-topped pop-up tents. Crowds mosey around, checking out each booth, and the scent of food wafts through the air, making my mouth water.

A small child rides on the back of a pony, and chickens cluck from a petting zoo stationed on the fringes of the market. Women push children in strange looking strollers, and some people chat on their cell phones. It's the most life I've been around in days, and it's overwhelming.

Aunt Jen taps my arm. "Here, take this." She hands me two twenty dollar bills. "Explore a little, buy something. Enjoy yourself."

I hover behind her, watching her browse the fresh produce of a few stands before I get bored. I wave as I walk off in the direction of the music. Soon I find myself in front of a band playing cover songs from when I was born. I stop by a cluster of shaded tables.

I order a fresh, organic smoothie from a vendor with a brightly painted sign and plop down at a plastic table. Searching the crowd, I spot Aunt Jen filling a tote bag with fresh flowers. With the smile lighting her face, she looks like she's in the candy section.

The chair next to me squeaks. Someone sits down, but I don't turn my head to see who it is. This place is crowded enough that you sit where you can, and it'd be impossible to claim a table for only myself.

"I picked up a similar shirt when I vacationed in Austin last fall. It's a pretty cool city, but it rained the entire time I was there. The weather sucked." A masculine voice draws my attention away from Aunt Jen.

I swivel on the chair and meet the golden brown eyes of a boy my age. His dark brown hair reflects strands of caramel in the hot sun, and sweat curls the ends around his ears. Ray-Ban Aviator sunglasses hang from his plain black T-shirt, and I catch my embarrassing reflection in them.

I pull at the hem of my shirt and peer down even though I

know what it looks like. "At least there is weather there. I like the rain and thunderstorms." I sound so lame, like I'm actually offended by his comment about the weather in a city I grew to hate.

I struggle to come up with something more to say to make me sound less weird, but nothing comes. I've never been great at holding small talk with strangers, and I'm especially awkward when a hot boy catches me off guard and I don't have time to prepare.

He stops things from becoming uncomfortable by asking, "Then what are you doing here?"

The corners of his lips tilt up in a smirk. His playful question sends a cold shiver over me, and I try to laugh it off.

I hold my cup up to him. "I heard the smoothies were amazing. Had to find out for myself."

His smirk turns into a full blown grin, his white teeth peeking through his full lips. "So you're just visiting, huh?"

I shrug. "Permanently."

His laughter sounds over the music, and I can't stop myself from smiling. He smiles back at me, and I bet we both look kind of stupid to anyone watching us. Heat blossoms up my neck as our conversation dwindles into nothing but flirtatious banter.

I sip my smoothie, scouring my brain for something else to say. When nothing comes to mind, I slide from my seat and stand up.

I stick out my hand to him and regret it. Seriously, what is wrong with me? Taylor would die laughing if she saw me now. "It was nice meeting you."

He wraps his fingers around mine, but instead of letting go, he hops to his feet still holding my hand. His bold move surprises me so much that I don't pull away.

"Let me give you a tour," he says, dropping his gaze to stare at our hands.

I close my eyes for a split second and suck in a breath. "I don't even know you."

"That can be changed." He tugs on my hand. "I'm Eli."

"Nora," I say, the sound of my voice lost to the thudding music. I tug my hand from his and grip my smoothie cup between them.

"Do you have a last name?"

I raise an eyebrow. "Do you?"

His shoulders shake as he laughs. "Evans."

"Well, it was nice to meet you, Eli Evans. Maybe I'll see you around." I spin on the balls of my sneakers and move into the crowd. As much as I'd like to stay and hang out with Eli, I have no idea if Aunt Jen would be cool with it. The last thing I need is for her to get angry because I ran off with a stranger—even if he was cute.

I peer over my shoulder and catch Eli grinning at me, and I wave my hand, beaming my biggest smile at the boy who made my fresh start a little lighter.

I find my aunt buying three small containers of salsa and a bag of chips at a tent near the end of the market. She motions for me to come over, and the vendor offers me a sample. The spicy salsa coats my tongue, and I savor the burst of flavor.

"I saw you made a friend," Aunt Jen says, not meeting my eyes as she hands the man a twenty.

I press my lips together to keep from smiling. "Sort of."

"Well, I'm glad. You should make more." She laughs.

I roll my eyes. "I have friends."

"I meant here. You should get out of the house more."

"Are we really discussing my lack of a social life?"

She hands me one of her tote bags. "No, but people are starting to talk."

My mouth drops open.

She chuckles. "It's all over the tabloids."

I bat her arm. "Fine, I'll get out more."

She wags her eyebrows. "Good."

I sit at my computer and do the only thing I can think of. I enter the name Eli Evans into my search engine and watch as dozens of pages pop up with information about people with that name. I add in Beverly Hills to the search and click on the first link, which directs me to Friendconn, the social media site I haven't been on in weeks.

Eli's smiling face greets me from his profile picture, and I hit a dead-end since his profile is set to private. I rest my head on my curled fingers and lean my elbow on my desk. My mouse hovers over the Add Connection button, and I click it, closing my eyes a moment later, like it'll somehow calm my heart from racing in overdrive.

My eyes glaze over the longer I stare at my screen. I can't take the waiting. I don't know why I'm obsessing over a boy I met for all of ten minutes. What if he thinks I'm stalking him instead of just doing a little internet investigating? I won't go as far as Taylor would, like the time she ended up on Jonathon Locke's ex-girlfriend's brother's best friend's profile after he had asked her out.

I run my hands over my face. Why doesn't Friendconn have a cancel button? What if Eli denies my request? *Who cares?*

I put my laptop into sleep mode and turn away from my computer. I need to get out of the house before I go crazy.

Shimmying out of my *Keep Austin Weird* shirt, I pull out the only cute item of clothing I have from my closet. The ivory, eyelet sundress brushes my knees, and I slide into a strappy pair of sandals I borrowed from Aunt Jen. I grab Jasper's leash from my desk and click the hook until I hear Jasper's nails tapping the wood as he races toward my room.

"Wanna go for a walk?" I ask, reaching down to pet him on his chest. He wags his nub tail, shaking with excitement, and I pick him up to clip the leash to his collar.

Aunt Jen peeks out from her office. Her black-framed glasses sit on the tip of her nose. "I just walked him."

I wrap the leash around my hand before I set Jasper down. "I need to get out."

She smiles. "Take my cell."

I nod. "Can I call Taylor?"

She waves her hand at me. "Call Switzerland for all I care."

I laugh and head to the front door. Pinks and oranges paint the sky from the setting sun in the distance. The balmy air warms my cool skin, and I take in the quiet neighborhood now that the street traffic has dissipated.

Jasper sniffs every plant we pass, and I hold Aunt Jen's phone to my ear and listen to it ring once before the line clicks and music erupts in my ear.

"This better be Nora," Taylor says into the line.

I'm surprised she even picked up for the strange number, but I guess she knew the 310 area code. I thought I'd have to leave a message or text her to get her to pick up.

"The one and only." I pause at a stop sign to make sure a Mercedes won't blow through and run me over. "Anything exciting happen?"

"Nope. I doubt anything exciting will ever happen again with you gone." Taylor whimpers into the line, sounding like Jasper when he wants on my lap.

I cross the street and stare at the hedges of a walled-in mansion. I can't get over how different each house is, since I grew up in a cookie-cutter neighborhood where all the houses looked alike.

I adjust the phone on my ear. "You can live through me. I met someone to—"

Taylor squeals. "Tell me everything about him."

I cover my smile with my hand, hiding my face from a shirtless man in basketball shorts jogging in my direction from the next street over. He whistles for me to get out of his way, and I tug Jasper's leash so he doesn't jump on the man's leg as he blows past us.

"His name is Eli Evans." I pause. I have nothing more to say about him.

"And?"

"And…"

Taylor huffs into the phone. "Oh, come on, Nora. You need to call upon your inner Taylor and stop being shy."

Heat warms my cheeks. "I requested him on Friendconn."

Static bursts through the line as she moves. "I'm logging on in your name."

"Taylor!"

She giggles. "You shouldn't have saved your password."

I stop at the next stop sign and plop down on the curb. I shorten Jasper's leash so he can't wander into the street. "Enjoy it now because I'm changing it tonight."

She hums for a moment before saying, "He's hot, Nora! And popular." The tap of keys clicking sounds through the line. "Oh, my God. He knows Alexander Montgomery."

I twist my lips to the side. "He accepted my request?"

"Oh, my God. He's messaging you right now!" Taylor screams without answering my now obvious question.

"Taylor, don't say anything stupid," I beg.

She doesn't answer, but I can hear her typing.

"Taylor?" Annoyance purses my lips. "I swear if—"

"He knows I'm not you, don't worry."

I let out a breath, getting to my feet. "I'm heading home now. You have five more minutes to talk to him, and then I'm locking you out."

"Give me ten, and I'll know everything you need to know about this boy."

I roll my eyes. "Talk to you later, Taylor."

She makes kissing sounds in the phone. "Love you."

I hang up and head back in the direction of my house. When I get there, Aunt Jen sits in her car in the driveway and waves for me to get in. I glance between her and the house where I desperately want to lock myself in my room, but I know I can't get out of getting in the car.

"You were right about going out. Let's grab a bite to eat and go shopping," Aunt Jen says through the opened window.

I force myself to nod. "Okay, let me just put Jasper away."

I stare longingly into the house as I take Jasper's leash off but turn around and head to the car. I guess I'll have to wait another few hours to talk to Eli, that is, unless Taylor scares him away. *Only you can do that, Nora.* I just hope I don't.

chapter 3

I GLARE AT the private message box between Eli and Taylor. She erased everything except for his last line, which said, *Tell Nora that I hope to see her soon.*

I should've said something to him last night, but Aunt Jen wanted to watch a movie, and we both fell asleep on the couch.

After a few more seconds of glaring, my speakers ding, and I realize that Eli messaged me again.

Eli Evans: Up for the exclusive tour yet?

I suck in my bottom lip before typing.

Nora Novak: I've already been to Rodeo Drive.

Eli Evans: I guess that's a no.

I tap my fingers on my desk.

Nora Novak: It's a, "Take me somewhere that isn't Rodeo Drive."

Eli Evans: Address?

Nora Novak: Meet me at Whole Foods on North Crescent in an hour.

Eli Evans: **See you soon.**

I spin in my rolling chair, throwing my head back to smile at the ceiling. I don't know where I summoned my bravery from, but I've never been out with someone I didn't know from school.

Butterflies flutter in my stomach, and I stare at the bags of clothes Aunt Jen bought me from a trendy boutique on Robertson Boulevard. The two sundresses, pair of jeans, and cotton skirt cost more than my entire wardrobe combined. I offered Aunt Jen some of my savings from the last two summers I spent working at the hotel with Dad, but she refused. I'll have to see about getting a job here. Cecilia made sure I'd feel guilty about asking for anything from anyone for the rest of my life.

I pluck a sleeveless, Chambray mini-dress from the bag and hold it up to my chest to view it in the full-length mirror hanging on the door. It's casual enough that I won't seem overdressed, but a step up from my *Keep Austin Weird* shirt. I rush to change, slip on some nude strappy sandals, and add some lip stain to my cheeks and lips.

Jasper jumps on my leg when I step into the hallway, and I find Aunt Jen bending over a steaming cup of coffee on the kitchen counter. She blinks a few times, her eyes puffy with exhaustion, and then she notices my new outfit.

"You're going out with that boy from the farmers market,

aren't you?" she asks, standing straighter.

I smile. "If that's okay. He's meeting me at the grocery store."

She reaches over for her purse, tipped over on the bar. "Here's some money and my phone. I swear I'll get you your own one of these days. I just hate going to the phone store."

"It's not necessary. You've done enough."

She fake glares at me. "Come on! Let me spoil my favorite niece. Your dad never let me before..." Her voice trails off as some memory of Dad pulls her away.

I clear my throat. "Can I borrow a purse?" I need to change the subject before the thought of Dad brings me down.

She bobs her head. "Hanging in my closet."

Fifteen minutes later, I'm strolling up North Crescent Drive, heading in the direction of Whole Foods. It's the only grocery store within walking distance, but I've only been inside once when Aunt Jen needed me to get some sugar for her coffee.

A line of cars turn into the parking structure next to the building, and I enter Whole Foods through it, walking up a ramp, past a dozen buckets of fresh flowers. Cool air wraps around me, drying my damp skin, and I peer around the crowded store.

I purchase two bottled waters and head back to the front to meet Eli outside. I'm a few minutes early, so he should show up any minute...hopefully.

I shift on my feet, wishing I had worn more comfortable

shoes. I hand some change to a man holding a sign wishing me a great day and meander to the end of the building where an empty table and chairs sits next to a window covered in photographs of farmlands. I plop down on a chair under the green canopy and stare at the time on Aunt Jen's phone.

He's ten minutes late. Maybe he's not coming after all.

I sigh, sipping my water, and then after another five minutes, a car honks its horn, and I turn in the chair to see Eli wave from an espresso-colored Range Rover. He slows, turning into the parking structure, and I head in to meet him.

He parks in an empty spot and rolls down the window. "Sorry I'm late. They had Santa Monica blocked off for construction." He doesn't get out.

I shift on my feet. "I thought we could walk."

He cuts the engine, smiling at me. "Well, that's a first."

I adjust my purse on my shoulder and step back so he can open the door. I hope he doesn't think I'm crazy, but I can't help being cautious about who I let into my life. Cecelia shoved enough horror stories down my throat that I have trust issues. I can't help it. Dad should've taken a lesson.

He clicks the alarm button on his key fob, and the beep echoes through the concrete parking structure. We stroll next to each other, our shoulders grazing together every few feet, and I glance at Eli in my peripheral vision and catch him studying me.

He smirks. "I have to be honest with you."

My heart pounds against my ribcage. I hate whenever anyone starts a sentence like this. "Yeah?" My voice cracks. I think of the million things he needs to be honest about. What if he asks me more about Taylor? *Ugh!*

He shoves his hands into his pockets. "I'm a little nervous because I know nothing about you. Your Friendconn page barely even gave me your last name, Nora Novak."

I puff a small breath through my lips in relief. My cheeks flush, and I consider how to explain the fact that I deleted the last three years of my life from my profile because so much of it included my dad. I couldn't help it. I was so angry at him for leaving me—still am. This is the kind of information that'll send a boy running in the opposite direction. I know that because it happened with Cesar Flores, who I thought totally liked me.

"What do you want to know?" I ask instead of explaining myself.

He guides me to the end of the block where we turn left onto Dayton Way. "What brings you to Cali?"

I press my lips together. Why do people always have to start off with the hard questions? I consider lying but decide to go with a half-truth instead. "My aunt asked me to live with her." *There. That wasn't so hard.*

"My mom would flip if I just up and moved away to live with her sister," Eli says. "She hated when I was gone for a month and a half at the beginning of summer."

We turn right onto the next street, heading toward the Rite Aid Pharmacy, and I spot the cute little bakery Aunt Jen loves to get French macarons from. We cross the street, and I steer him in its direction.

"Where'd you go?" I slow down as we near the bakery.

"Savannah, Georgia."

"Oh, okay." I want to ask why he was there, but the scent of sugary pastries halts me in my tracks. "Mind if we stop?"

He grins. "I feel like you're leading the tour."

I shrug and smile back at him. "Maybe I am."

White tables and chairs sit on the sidewalk, and a fake white tree sits in the corner of the enclave the store front is tucked in. Stickered on the window, a woman in a lotus pose holds out a cupcake, and the words French Pastries draw my attention to the white tiered wedding cakes on the other side of the glass.

He holds open the door to the bakery, and I catch his ever-happy expression in the glass. It's like he's amused by every little thing. I wish I could bottle up his attitude to carry with me whenever negative emotions plague my thoughts.

His brown eyes flick to mine, holding my gaze for a second. He touches his hand to my back to guide me to the counter where a woman in a black apron with the bakery's logo embroidered on front stands next to a display of French macarons in every color of the rainbow and more.

The woman lifts a glass lid from a silver stand. "Try a sample of our red velvet cupcakes. They're amazing."

Eli plucks a square piece from the cupcake wrapper and pops it in his mouth, leaving the wrapper behind. He closes his eyes while he savors the bite. "I'll take two."

"And I'll have the baker's dozen. Just pick a variety." I point at the French macarons. "My aunt loves these."

I pull out my wallet from my purse, but Eli shakes his head. "I got it."

I hold an even expression as he pulls two twenties from a stack of at least ten bills from his wallet. I've never seen anyone my age carry around that much cash unless they were planning on buying something expensive that they'd saved for. I definitely need a job.

I touch his arm. "Thanks. I'll buy next time." I think about what I just said, my heart fluttering. I've only been hanging out with him for less than an hour, and I'm already assuming there will be a next time.

He swipes the white paper bag from the counter, sliding the silver roped handle over his wrist. "Sure. I'd like that."

I release a breath. "Wanna sit here?"

He shakes his head. "I have a better idea."

A five-minute walk later, Eli guides me to a table near a trickling fountain in the middle of Beverly Canon Gardens next to the Montage Hotel. Black wire tables sit on a stone foundation. The buildings surrounding us cast shade through the courtyard, cooling the air just enough that I don't sweat, thankfully.

Eli unwraps his white-frosted, red velvet cupcake. "So, how do you like it here?"

"It's nice," I say, playing with the wrapper on the second

cupcake.

He laughs. "I meant living here."

"I haven't been here long. Haven't left my house much, either. Jasper can only handle so many walks." I take a bite of my cupcake. Frosting coats my top lip, and I lick it off. "Jasper's my aunt's dog."

"We'll have to change that." He pushes back from his chair and stands. "Come on. Let's eat and walk. There's a lot I want to show you."

I scoop up my purse and adjust it over my shoulder. He carries the bag of French macarons on his arm and polishes off his cupcake before we even reach the opposite end of the gardens that will take us to North Beverly Drive.

"Elijah Rousseau!" A feminine voice yells from the entrance to a swanky restaurant that looks more expensive than all the money I have in my savings account. "Elijah!"

A girl with blond, beachy curls in a tight-fitted dress struts from the restaurant with two other girls. They're all smiles and saucer eyes, keeping their attention solely on Eli like I don't even exist.

"You lied about your name," I say, trying to hide the confusion and hurt in my voice. Why would he do that? Why would he have his Friendconn page as Eli Evans? I don't understand.

The blonde cuts between Eli and me, forcing me to take a step back, and the other two girls, both brunettes, surround him like a flock of seagulls attempting to steal your last hotdog.

Eli smiles at them with the same smile he gives me, and I can't stop the jealousy from snaking up my spine to circle my chest and squeeze my heart in a death grip. I should've known better than to assume I might be the only girl he's offered to show Beverly Hills to. I bet he does it all the time.

The blonde giggles, tossing her beach waves over her shoulder, and I whiff the scent of fruity perfume. She stands on her tiptoes and whispers something into Eli's ear, and I cross my arms over my chest and wait for him to tell these girls that he's busy. I expect him to introduce me at any second, but he only glances my way, his now annoyingly stupid grin still plastered on his face.

I take a deep breath, feeling like an outcast among beautiful people. Aunt Jen's cell rings from my purse, and I dig through it and answer it when I see Taylor's number flash across the screen. Pressing the phone to my ear, I turn my back on the scene unfolding between Eli and the girls.

"Thank God you called. This is a nightmare," I say into the phone.

"What's up?"

"I took Eli up on his tour of the city, but he was stopped by these three girls, and I don't know what to do. It's like I'm not even here."

"Leave. If it's like you're not even there, no one will notice," she says without even pausing to think about it.

I peer over my shoulder at Eli, and he's now taking a picture with the blonde. *Seriously?*

"You're right." I turn away and speed walk back in the direction we came from. I'm still close enough to home that I know my way around. I don't have to accept this form of torture from a boy I've just met. "I'm already walking home."

Taylor breathes into the line. "Sorry your date didn't go as planned."

I keep my gaze on the ground. "He even lied to me about his name. The girls called him Elijah Rousseau. I don't know what I was expecting."

"His loss, babe." I wish I could hug my best friend right now. I've never felt so embarrassed in my life.

"Thanks, sunshine." I'm back on my street in a matter of minutes. "I'll talk to you later, 'kay?"

"I'll call you tomorrow."

I hang up as I enter the house. Tossing my purse on the couch, I plop down on the barstool next to Aunt Jen, who is probably on her second pot of coffee. She doesn't smile or ask how things went because I'm sure my feelings are as clear as glass on my face.

"Want to order in and binge watch TV?" she asks.

I nod. "Boys suck."

She laughs. "I'll save the plenty of fish in the sea speech for later."

chapter 4

Second Chances

I'VE IGNORED THE sixteen messages Eli sent me through Friendconn. Didn't even read them. I can't help it. I'm a glutton for punishment, I guess. I'm afraid he'll talk his way out of how he treated me with flirty banter and dimples, and I refuse to be treated like that again.

Plus, I don't have time for those worries. Aunt Jen had an emergency at her office and invited me to tag along. Julian, her assistant, asked me if I'd like to help him out, and now I have a part time job that'll make me feel less guilty about my living situation with Aunt Jen.

I stand at the office printer and watch as at least a hundred pages fly onto the paper tray. I never realized how long legal documents could be, and I'm really glad I'm not the one having to read them. I can already feel my eyes glass over as the printer whirls out a few more papers before falling silent.

I scoop up the papers and neatly stack them in a pile, clipping them together with the biggest binding clip I've ever seen. It could probably snap my finger off if I accidentally pinched myself with it.

Strolling down the gleaming, wood-floor hallway, I glance at the expensive artwork hanging on the warm tan walls and the opaque glass office doors with names etched into the glass. I check the light near the keypad to make sure Aunt Jen is free and pound in my four-digit pass code before entering. Aunt Jen leans over a stack of papers, a pencil sticking out from between her teeth. She smiles when she glances up, and I drop the stack of papers into a wire metal basket on the marble counter under wall-to-wall cupboards.

She stretches her arms over her head. "Want to grab a bite to eat? I need to get out of here."

"Let me check with Julian." I start to turn on the basic black heels I borrowed from Aunt Jen's closet.

She hits a button on her intercom. "Hey, Julian. I'm heading to lunch with Nora. Want to join us?"

"Give me five," her assistant says.

She smiles at me. "Perks of being the boss."

I lean back in the booth of Panera Bread and gaze out the window that overlooks the busy street. South Beverly has quickly become my favorite street because of the vast variety of shopping and dining without the touristy feel of Rodeo Drive.

"God, I could marry this sandwich," Julian says as he tears into a sandwich that looks like someone dumped a salad onto it and called it a day. "We should come here more often. Once a week isn't enough."

I raise my eyebrows but don't say anything. Maybe if Panera Bread was new to me, but Taylor and I ate at one in Austin together all the time.

Aunt Jen nods her head. "Just keep me away from the desserts."

I shake my head and nibble the potato chips that came with my boring yet delicious grilled cheese. Aunt Jen and Julian laugh about something that happened at the office before I moved here, and I tune them out, losing myself in my thoughts.

"Nora? Earth to Nora?" Aunt Jen pokes my arm. "Are you all right?"

I drop the empty bag of chips on my plate. "I'll be right back. I need to use the restroom."

I slide from the booth and wander past the window that looks into the kitchen and where the servers grab trays of food. I hit the button for the elevator and ride it up to the second level where the restrooms are located. The elevator ride up is slow, and it takes forever for the door to open. Fear trickles through me at the idea of getting trapped, but just before panic sets in, the door chimes and slides open.

I freeze in my tracks.

Eli stands a few feet away from the door with one hand in his pocket. His aviator sunglasses hang from his dark blue shirt, and he stares at his phone in his other hand. I step out and walk past him, hoping he doesn't notice. I figured if I ignored him long enough, he'd forget about how I ditched him out of jealousy.

He clears his throat before I have a chance to run into the bathroom. "I see how it is."

I cringe. I hate confrontation. I'm better at just disappearing. I turn to face him, anger building in my chest. I narrow my eyes. "Excuse me?"

A smile plays on his lips, and I want to smack it off. "You've been ignoring me."

I lick my lips. "I've been busy."

"After you abandoned me to the wolves on our date."

My mouth drops open. "What? I didn't abandon you."

He steps closer. "You did."

I place my hands on my hips. "Well, you lied, Elijah *Rousseau*."

His shoulders slump, and he scratches his chin. "Is that why you're ignoring me?"

I shift awkwardly. Aunt Jen's going to wonder where I am or think I'm having stomach troubles. I take a step back. "One of the reasons. Now, if you'll excuse me."

I spin and run into the bathroom, but he follows me in. I glare at him as he stands in front of the door. I consider yelling out, but he doesn't move or threaten me. He just stands there with round puppy dog eyes and looks like I just told him to sit out in the rain.

I blow out a breath and enter the last stall, shutting and locking the door. "If you don't mind, I'm on my lunch break and don't have time for your excuses."

His shoes squeak on the tiles. "Please, Nora. I'd really like to explain."

I place a seat cover on the toilet and sit down. I'm way beyond the point of impressing him. "Go on."

"In here?"

"You're the one who followed me into the bathroom."

He laughs, his voice echoing over the low music humming through the speakers overhead. "Elijah Rousseau is my pseudonym. My agent thought I should go with a name that reflected my French heritage. It's my mom's maiden name."

I flush the toilet without responding and exit the stall. He faces the exit like I need privacy to wash my hands. I still don't respond until I've run my hands through the hand dryer and allow him to open the door for me.

"You have an agent?" I ask. I don't know why I'm surprised. Beverly Hills is next to Hollywood, and a lot of people come here to pursue their dreams of stardom. I guess I've grown used to hanging around people like my aunt—the ones who work as lawyers and doctors and CEOs. I haven't even seen a familiar celebrity since I arrived.

"And a manager and publicist and—"

I lift my hand. "Okay, I got it. But you could've told me."

"Would you have thought differently about me?"

I don't answer because I don't know if I would've. I don't

know if I do. I've never heard of Eli Ev—Rousseau, so it's not like he's a big deal to me.

I fiddle with the ends of my light brown hair. "You never gave me the chance to decide."

His smile fades. "Give me another chance. I really do want to get to know you better. I swear, next time I get recognized, we'll run, okay? It doesn't happen that often. My movie doesn't come out until late winter."

He takes my hands in his and pleads with his warm eyes. Serious looks adorable on him, and I can't help nodding my head. Life is about second chances. I should know this. This one's mine. I just hope it's not a mistake.

"Under one condition."

His face lights up like the flash of a camera. "Yeah?"

"I want to know everything about you."

"Deal."

The elevator dings, drawing our attention away from each other, and my aunt steps out. She glances between Eli and me. "I thought you had gotten lost."

I pull my hands away from Eli. "Sorry."

She holds out her hand. "I'm Jen Novak, Nora's aunt."

He shakes her hand. "Eli Evans."

The corners of her lips tilt upward. "I know."

He shifts nervously like he wants to bolt into the still opened elevator instead of enduring the half-curious, half-protective stare my aunt bestows on him.

"I should be going. My cousin might think I ditched her."

Eli turns to me. "Can we talk more later?"

I bob my head. "Sure. See you around."

Eli leaves me standing with Aunt Jen outside the bathrooms. I let him go first instead of riding the elevator down with him to save him from any more awkwardness that might arise. I told my aunt about how much of a jerk he was and how he ignored me when the girls—who I now know were fans—basically demanded his attention, and then she catches me holding his hands.

She raises her eyebrows. "I guess you've made up."

I throw my hands out. "I don't even know. Come on. I'll tell you on the way out."

chapter 5

 The Spotlight

WHEN ELI ASKED to talk more later, that's exactly what we did, though not in person. We've been messaging back and forth on Friendconn because I can't let his stupid, lovable smile sweep me away for the millionth time.

My speakers chime, and a message box lights up in the top corner of my screen. It's him.

Eli Evans: Busy tonight?

I smile.

Nora Novak: Why?

Eli Evans: Do you realize you answer my questions with questions?

I laugh to myself.

Nora Novak: Yeah. ;)

Eli Evans: So?

Nora Novak: Pick me up on the corner of Clifton and Palm.

Eli Evans: Give me ten. :D

I roll away from my computer and hop from my chair. I'm still wearing the dress clothes from work, and I'd rather not wear them out with Eli. I dash to my closet, throw a few things from the hangers, and finally decide on an A-line, high-waist Herringbone skirt, a semi-sheer, long-sleeved cropped top, and peep-toe wedges.

I apply my favorite brown lipstick, fluff up my hair and spritz in a little hairspray, and in five minutes, I'm out the door.

I text Aunt Jen with the phone she bought for me when Taylor decided to call her phone ten times early in the morning. My best friend forgets I'm no longer in the same time zone. Aunt Jen had to work late at the office and left me to fend for myself.

Eli pulls up to the stop sign in his Range Rover and gets out to open my door. Smiling, I climb in the front seat and trail my gaze over the gleaming dashboard and pristine seats and floor. Taylor never failed to have a backseat full of clothes, school books, and trash, so it's kind of weird for me. Eli hops behind the wheel, grinning at me like he can't believe I'm here.

The sun sets the sky ablaze, the night pushing the day away. A car honks behind us, and Eli startles in his seat before accelerating through the intersection where he turns left on Oakhurst. I think our bathroom conversation knocked his confidence down a peg because he seems especially nervous. It makes me feel ten times better. It's actually kind of adorable on him.

I fold my hands in my lap. "I'm glad you asked me to hang out. Aunt Jen's working late, and I wasn't sure how much more boredom I could handle before I started my online investigation about you." I promised Eli I wouldn't scour the internet to find out more about him.

He tilts his head back a little while he laughs. "What would be the fun in knowing everything everyone else already knows about me?" He taps his fingers on his steering wheel. "Half of which is probably made up lies."

I turn a little in my seat. "Then tell me something no one else knows."

Dimples peek out on his cheeks, and I press my lips together to stop myself from smiling. It's hard not to around him. I can't explain it, but it's like Eli is the first breath of fresh air after sitting in a dusty room for hours. His presence and charm fight off the negativity I've been drowning in for months. And I kind of like how he makes me feel, though I'm afraid of another disappointment.

He fidgets with the radio without answering me. After he finds a song he likes, he turns it down to the point where I can no longer hear it.

He keeps his eyes trained on the road. "Can't you start with something easy? What happened to asking about my favorite color?"

I release an overdramatic sigh. "Eli Evans, what's your favorite color?"

He chuckles. "Burgundy. My stylist says it brings out my eyes."

I snort. "You have a stylist?"

"Only for events." He pulls his Range Rover to the curb, and I notice this street doesn't have permit-only parking like the ones around my house. We're far enough into a residential area that it doesn't matter. "My turn for a question."

I lean back in the seat. "My favorite color is indigo."

He touches my knee. "You can't answer your own questions."

I peer into his dark eyes. The reddening sky sets his golden skin aglow. His stylist was right about burgundy bringing out his eyes. I could stare into them until night makes it impossible to see.

"I just did."

"Nora..."

I laugh. "Fine. Ask away."

"What's the real reason you left Austin?"

The smile falls from my lips. "What happened to asking easy questions?" I grab the door handle. I need air. Being so close to Eli almost makes me want to spill my guts to him, but I don't want to bring him down. When people find out about my past, they can't stop from pitying me. I don't want their pity. I want to forget.

He follows my lead. "You're right. How about you tell me whether or not you've been to the Witch's House?"

"The what?"

"Come on. I'll show you."

Eli wasn't lying about the Witch's House. On the corner of Carmelita and Walden lies a house straight out of a storybook. With a dark brown, pointy roof and yellowish-tan, almost wavy walls, the house looks like one you'd imagine a green-faced witch would live in. The wooden shuttered windows sit unevenly and at random in the frame, and a light glows from within. A fence made from smooth, whimsical stakes lines the property, and the foliage grows enough to obscure the path to the door.

"This is the Spadena House."

"It's impressive and creepy and random," I say.

He chuckles. "I know."

I snap a couple of blurry pictures with my cell phone to send to Taylor, and Eli offers to take one of me with the house. A moment later, he spins around and snaps a picture of the two of us, and I laugh at my startled expression. I won't dare share this one with anyone except Taylor.

"Give a girl some warning next time," I say, tucking the phone in my handbag.

He reaches out and laces his fingers through mine. "Not a chance."

He tugs me along, our fingers curling around each others, and my heart flutters in my chest. We head back to his car, and he navigates Beverly Hills like he's lived here his whole life—which he probably has.

"Are you getting hungry?" he asks, turning onto Wilshire Boulevard. "I know of this great restaurant."

I press my lips together. "I don't have a lot of money on me." And by not a lot of money, I mean I have ten bucks because I don't want to ask Aunt Jen for any. I was paid today, but I need to go to the bank, and now it's too late.

"Did any of your boyfriends in Texas ever pay for you?" he asks, smirking.

Warmth flushes over me, and I'm grateful the sun set or else Eli would see how red I'm turning.

I shift in the seat. "You say that like I've had a ton." I'm a professional at redirecting questions away from me.

His smile falters. "I didn't—I mean—"

I rest my hand on his knee. "I'm kidding, and yes, I've let other people pay for me." Just maybe not boys. Taylor and I took turns paying for each other all the time.

He lets out a breath. "Thank God. I thought you were going to make me take you home, and I'm really starting to like you."

Tingles rush through my stomach and up to my chest at his words. I knew he liked me, because if he didn't, we wouldn't be hanging out, but it's exhilarating to hear him admit it out loud. I rake my teeth over my bottom lip and slide my hand into his. His thumb rubs along my index finger, and we smile at each other.

"I like you, too, Eli."

We sit in the corner booth of a small diner in West Hollywood off La Cienega Boulevard. I haven't ventured outside of Beverly Hills much except to go to a larger grocery store than the one down the street from my house. I can't stop the excitement fluttering through me even though all we're doing is eating burgers and sharing a plate of fries.

Eli's knee touches mine. He insisted we share one side of the booth, and every once in a while we bump elbows because he's left handed. We could switch sides, but we don't. I like facing the street to people watch, and Eli likes sitting on the outside.

I wipe my mouth on my paper napkin. "This is amazing."

He scoops up a fry and waves it at the rest of the diner. "It's one of my favorites."

"Hey, Eli!" An older woman, wearing an apron over a pair of jeans and a T-shirt, calls out. She flies through the swinging door from the kitchen. "Why didn't you pop in to say hello to your godmother? Forget about me already? Silvia mentioned you were here."

He slides from the booth and hugs the woman. "I'm on a date, Gigi." He motions to me.

I smile at Gigi.

She smacks Eli's shoulder. "And you brought her here? We're not exactly fine dining."

He laughs, jumping back. "Not every place is special to me, though."

Gigi's thin eyebrows peak into her bangs, and she pats Eli

on the shoulder. She leans over, whispers something into his ear, and he nods as he watches my expression. I'm nervous she won't like me. I haven't even said anything, but I can't help my palms from sweating.

Gigi pulls away. "It was nice meeting you, dear. Keep my Eli out of trouble, okay?"

I force my lips to smile. "Yes, ma'am. It was nice to meet you, too."

Gigi turns away, and Eli takes his place at my side. I absently stare at the few fries left on the plate without saying a word. Eli nudges my shoulder with his, and I raise my gaze to meet his dark eyes.

He leans closer. "We should leave."

I frown. "Why? Does Gigi not want me here?"

His breath tickles my ear. "That's not it. She overheard a few people in the next booth over. They recognized me."

I turn to look at him, pulling back just enough to put inches between us. My heart pounds in my ears, and his intense eyes bore into mine like he's reading my thoughts. He tucks a strand of my brown hair behind my ear, and I imagine kissing him, though neither of us moves.

The audible sound a camera phone makes when it takes a picture resonates through the room, pulling my attention away from Eli. I suck in a deep breath, meeting the eyes of a few teens sitting at a table in the middle of the room. A blond girl holds up her smart phone to us, and I glare daggers at her. She has a lot of nerve snapping a picture of us.

Eli squeezes my hand. "You look like you're going to jump out of the booth."

I clench my teeth. "I want to."

He chuckles. "Come on. Unless you want to be famous for attacking a stranger, we should probably just go."

I close my eyes. He's totally right. I don't know how famous Eli is, but I know he's recognizable, which means people who follow celebrity gossip will know who I am if I continue to see him. If I continue... I'm unsure of how I feel about being in the spotlight.

Eli takes my hand, and we stroll past the group. He smiles and shakes the hand of a red-haired girl and tells her we're in a hurry so they don't ask for a picture.

When we reach his Range Rover, I lean my back on the door, and he stands in front of me. He reaches out and takes my hands in his. His fingers warm my cool skin, and I wish I had brought a sweater. The crisp air clings to me, and I shiver.

"Eli," I say. I press my lips together. I need to figure out how I'm going to express my feelings. "I'm not sure how I feel about all this."

His smile falters. He tugs my hands, pulling me closer, and then he wraps his arms around my shoulders. I rest my cheek on his chest.

"I know it's not exactly ideal, but this is my life. I love it. I've had small roles the last few years, but the movie I have coming this winter—they expect it to be a hit." He hugs me tighter. "It'll change my life."

"And that's why I think we should take this slow." I pull back to meet his gaze. "My life has been the downhill portion of a rollercoaster and things are just starting to even out. I'm not sure I can survive another drop."

He bobs his head. "I can respect that. I'll follow your lead."

He opens the door, and I climb into his car, buckling my seatbelt. I promised I wouldn't internet stalk Eli, but curiosity is killing me. Maybe I'll have Taylor do it for me instead. She's awesome at that kind of thing.

Eli starts the engine. "Should I take you home?"

I link my fingers through his. "Wanna hang out there?"

He smiles. "I'd like that."

chapter 6

Home of the Normans

I CAN'T BELIEVE summer is already over, and I'll be forced inside a stuffy classroom for the next ten months of my life. I thought the last two weeks of freedom could go on forever, but then Aunt Jen reminded me that we have to wake up way too early to head to Beverly Hills High School.

The one good thing I've discovered is that Eli will be waiting for me on the front steps near the cement sign when I arrive. Part of the deal to start his acting career early was that he had to finish high school like a normal teenager even though he's far from normal.

We're out the door half an hour before school starts and fifteen minutes later, Eli greets Aunt Jen and me exactly where he promised near a cement sign with bold black letters that spell B.H.H.S. Beverly Hills High School, home of the Normans, has a backdrop of a dozen or so skyscrapers of Century City and is about half the size of my high school back in Austin. Tall, triangular windows decorate a white, two-story building with a reddish-brown roof, where I'm guessing classrooms are located.

We enter the main building, and Eli guides us to the counselor's office. Students stand in clusters, some near lockers and others heading toward wherever their first class is located. I smile at whoever looks my way, and when we're finally in the reception area, I release a breath.

"I'll wait outside to show you to your first class," Eli says.

I nod, my hands trembling as I clutch my book bag, which is one of Aunt Jen's large designer purses. He hugs me long enough for me to relax before heading to the exit. Going to a new school feels like freshman year all over again, but at least in Austin I had a bunch of friends already. I'd probably be even more petrified than I am if it weren't for Eli.

Aunt Jen waves to Eli before turning to me. "You nervous?"

"I think I'm going to throw up."

She laughs and pats my shoulders. "You've been through worse. I'm sure you'll love it here."

I roll my shoulders, forcing them to loosen up. "I've had the same kids in my class my entire life. What if I don't fit in here?"

"Then you stand out. Isn't that what kids your age want?"

I adjust my bag. "Not at Bowie High. I wish Taylor were here."

Aunt Jen squeezes my arm. "Just breathe."

A moment later, a man in a dress shirt and tie comes out of one of the doors. He heads in our direction and greets Aunt Jen with the biggest smile I've ever seen anyone give her. They shake hands, and Aunt Jen wraps her arm around my shoulder.

"Nora, meet Mr. Singh. He's a good friend of mine."

I shake my new counselor's hand. "Nice to meet you, sir."

He beams a smile. "Come on in. Your aunt told me some of your history, and I think you'll enjoy what Beverly Hills High has to offer."

Mr. Singh brings us into his office, and I stare at all his college degrees hanging on the wall, along with a few pieces of art that students probably made. He informs me that I'll be a little late to my first class, and my nervousness turns to panic when I realize I have to walk into a classroom late. Just what I wanted.

I slide my cell phone from the pocket of my jeans and text Eli not to wait for me. He responds with a simple OK, and I hide my phone, making sure to turn it on silent.

After forty-five excruciating minutes past the second bell, Mr. Singh shakes Aunt Jen's hand again, this time in front of the Beverly Hills High School Alumni Hall of Fame, which is an entire wall of the faces of notable people who graduated from the school.

I grip my schedule and student handbook with the map of the campus printed on the back and watch in despair as my aunt abandons me to figure out how to survive a new high school on my own. Most people would be glad to see their guardian leave, but Aunt Jen is the least embarrassing person I know. It helps that she's only twelve years older than me.

"I'll see you to your first class, Ms. Novak, and Fae Yzarra, one of the best student ambassadors at B.H.H.S will meet you after class to show you to your next. She'll also give you an official tour after school." He motions for me to walk next to him.

We come to a hallway with lockers lining the walls. The floors gleam under the rectangular fluorescent lighting. My expectations for the high school might've been slightly higher than they should've been. It looks like any ordinary school. Taylor would be disappointed.

He stops in front of a locker. "Your combination is on your schedule."

I don't bother opening it. I don't have any books yet, and I'd prefer to carry my bag for now. I nod, and he waves me to stroll alongside him once more. We reach my first class, which my schedule says is English, and Mr. Singh knocks on the door before opening it.

My heart pounds in my ears, and I swallow the lump forming in my throat. All eyes fall on me, and a man with a clean shaven face, a bald head, and wire-rimmed glasses resting on the bridge of his wide nose greets me with a smile instead of the frown I expect for interrupting his first day of school speech.

Students fill the front rows of desks, and I spot a few empty seats scattered throughout the room. It's quiet enough to hear the humming of the laptops and tablets my peers have opened on their desks, apart from a handful of kids who prefer a regular notebook. At least I'm not alone in that aspect.

"Ms. Novak, your seat is the empty one over there. I assign seats alphabetically until I learn everyone's name." He motions to the third to last seat in the row two over from the door.

I adjust my bag and shuffle down the row to my seat. Mr. Goldberg hands me a syllabus and a copy of Don Quixote. I pull my notebook from my bag and set the syllabus on top of it. Mr. Singh waves from the door before disappearing, and Mr. Goldberg starts where he left off before I interrupted him. The class turns their attention back to the teacher, and I slide lower into my seat and watch the clock tick until the bell rings.

A girl with black hair pulled into a tight bun, wearing skinny jeans, sneakers, and a tight-fitting quarter sleeve top struts into the room and heads straight to Mr. Goldberg. He catches my gaze and jerks his neck for me to come to his desk.

I slide from my seat and stroll up to where he and the girl stand. She must be Fae Yzarra, the girl who's supposed to show me around.

Mr. Goldberg tells us to have a good day, and Fae beams a brilliant smile at me, one big enough to light up her entire face and crinkle the corners of her eyes.

"Hi, Nora! I'm Fae. Welcome to Beverly Hills High School, where our motto is a *Today Well Lived.*" Her voice chimes over the loud mumbling of students heading to their next class. It sounds like she rehearsed her introduction a thousand times.

I shake her hand. "Do they force you to say that?"

She laughs, rolling her eyes. "I told Mrs. Rodriguez that the intro was lame."

"Only a little." I shift my bag and pull out my schedule, opening it up to read.

Fae snatches it from my hands and gazes at it for a minute before handing it back to me. "We have three classes together, so my day got a whole lot easier. Our next one is TV Production with Ms. Valentine. I'm surprised you got in. It's one of the most wanted classes besides Drama and Stage Design."

I shrug. Mr. Singh basically picked out my schedule for me. He wanted to put me in drama, but I told him I'd die if anyone made me get on stage. "My aunt is friends with my counselor."

She bobs her head. "It's nice having connections. Networking is everything." It sounds like something my aunt would say.

Linking her arm through mine, she guides me through the crowded hallway. We make small talk, and she waves and introduces me to a few of her friends. I forget their names the moment after they say them.

When we reach the TV Production room, I take a seat and glance around the walls with hundreds of pictures of students handling camera equipment, computers, and more. What looks like a newsroom set-up sits in the back of the room, and a projector casts a TV broadcast filmed in this exact room.

Fae motions at the screen. "We run a weekly news show. It actually plays on TV."

My brows scrunch together. "Really?"

"On the local access channel."

I grimace. I hope there are a lot of behind the scenes stuff I can participate in. Back in Austin, I spent the last three years in Journalism, so maybe I can hand off my stories to someone else.

After a moment, I pull out my cell phone from my pocket and notice two texts from Eli, asking what my schedule is. I snap a picture of my schedule and send it to him, and a moment later, he replies that he'll meet me after class because we share the next one together.

I smile at my phone. Today's looking a lot better than I expected. Fae taps my desk with her pen, and I hide my phone when a woman strolls into the room and drops her bag at a desk with three monitors on it. She wears a pencil skirt with a blouse and looks ready to smile at the camera with her perfectly curled brown hair and made up face.

She peers around the room. "Looks like we have some new faces this year." She points at me. "Tell the class your name and what you like most about what's portrayed in the media."

My mouth dries at being put on the spot. "Um, I'm Nora." I take a deep breath and stare at my hands. "Well, everything that isn't sinister."

"Which is?"

I cross and uncross my legs. "Entertainment, I guess." I don't know why I say it. I actually prefer science and technology and travel pieces. I lick my lips to change my answer, but Ms. Valentine scribbles something on a clipboard.

"Good, you can pair up with Fae and Anthony," she says.

Fae wags her eyebrows.

Ms. Valentine moves on to another person, and I'm all but forgotten.

Fae turns to me. "Working the entertainment segment is the best. I promise."

I smile without saying anything. I hope she's right.

Fae clutches my arm as Eli waves at me. "Don't look and keep walking."

My eyebrows furrow. "What? Why?"

"Elijah Rousseau is one of the most cocky, annoying people alive. The only people who like talking to him are those trying to break into the industry." She pulls me a few steps.

I'm probably about to ruin my chance at a friendship with Fae, but nothing gets under my skin more than someone forcing their opinion down my throat and expecting me not to have one of my own.

I tug my arm away. "I don't know who Elijah Rousseau is, but Eli Evans has been nothing but nice to me since I moved here."

Her eyes widen. "I—I—" She takes a breath. "I'm sorry, Nora. I didn't know you were friends."

Eli reaches us and slides his hand into mine, but I pretend to need my hand to adjust my bag, and then I cross my arms. The look Eli gives me makes me feel horrible, letting Fae's unwanted opinion get under my skin.

I smile, playing it cool. "I'll catch you later, Fae."

She nods, her cheeks deep red with blush, and then she spins on her toes and pushes through the crowd.

Eli tries to take my hand again, but I shake my head. "It's my first day. I want people to get to know me for me not for the people I hang out with. You understand, right?"

His ever-present smile falters before he catches himself. "Yeah, totally. I get it."

I don't think he does, and I feel like a jerk for it, but I want to play it safe. Fae's reaction was enough to have me thinking about everything outside of whatever is happening between Eli and me. This is supposed to be my fresh start at a new school, and I want to fit in as much as everyone else. I want to make friends so I don't have to hide in my room, wishing Taylor were here every day. I want to stop missing Austin and my old life.

I stroll next to Eli close enough that our arms brush. He guides me to our one and only class together, Economics. He doesn't say much on the walk over, and I meet the gazes of the people we pass. And I swear everyone is looking. I'm not sure if it's because I'm new, but there have to be more new students than me. The entire freshman class is new, and I doubt I have some invisible sign I can't see that everyone else can that reads *New Senior*. People are staring because of who I'm with, but it doesn't feel like it did when we were out and about. This is foreign territory, and I don't speak their language.

I nudge Eli's arm with my shoulder. "I have to ask you something."

His jaw tightens, and his lips twitch. "I think I know what

it's about."

"I expected different is all," I say.

He pulls me to a stop and looks into my eyes. "I knew I should've warned you. I was just hoping things would've changed this year."

"What happened?"

He shifts his eyes away. "Can I tell you later? I don't want to be late."

With those words, he cuts off our conversation and motions me into the classroom.

The rest of the day continues without issue, and I do my best to keep an open mind about what could've possibly gone wrong with Eli to feel like I'm being judged for hanging by his side. Fae pretends she didn't tell me to avoid him and even invites me to hang out with a few of her friends on Saturday.

When the last bell rings, I text Eli that I'll see him later because Fae is giving me a tour of campus. He replies that he'll call me.

Fae rushes me through campus, and I'm relieved when Aunt Jen calls to tell me she's here to pick me up. I wave to Fae as I get into Aunt Jen's Lexus and hide my face in my hands the second she pulls away.

I have a feeling this awkwardness is just the beginning, and there's nothing I can do about it.

chapter 7

Nothing is What it Seems

THE LAST COUPLE of days have gone by in a blur, and Eli still hasn't told me about his past at school, though I haven't really bothered him about it. I can't. I don't want to have to discuss anything to do with what happened after my dad died. He doesn't even know I'm an orphan. One of us has to give, and it's not going to be me. I shudder at the thought.

I meander toward my locker to put away my Chemistry book. I promised to meet Eli outside on the lawn where the nutrition carts serve a la carte food for those who don't want to go into the cafeteria.

"Nora! Wait up," Fae calls, rushing in my direction. A girl with deep chocolate locks keeps pace by her side, and the reason I remember her name is because she's named after a fruit. "Come eat lunch with me and Cherry."

Cherry rubs her wine-painted lips together. "You shouldn't be hiding every time you leave a classroom." I didn't think anyone noticed when I wasn't around.

I shift on my feet. "Maybe tomorrow, okay? I promised to eat with someone else."

"Elijah." Fae drops his name like holding it back leaves a bad taste in her mouth.

"Yeah, Eli, unless you're okay if he sits with us, too." I don't turn my gaze away from her. "You know, I don't know exactly what he did that has him on a lot of people's bad side, but I wish y'all would just get over it."

Cherry snickers but doesn't say anything.

Heat blooms up my neck, spreading into my cheeks. I ignore her and turn to Fae. "I'm starting to think this has less to do with Eli and more to do with jealousy."

She elbows Cherry. "Don't mind her, Nora, and if you want to ask Eli to eat with us, too, we can all get over it."

I puff air through my lips. "Thank you."

"I'll save you a seat in the cafeteria." Fae yanks Cherry away and leaves me standing by my locker.

I pull myself together and head out the front entrance and spot Eli waiting for me, two sandwiches and water bottles in his hands. He beams me the biggest smile. I drop my bag at my feet when I close the distance and gaze up into his dark eyes. Sun haloes him in golden light from behind, and I have to squint to clear my vision.

"Where to?" he asks.

I suck in air through my teeth. "The cafeteria. Fae invited us to eat with her."

Eli lowers his brows, his lips turning downward like I told him we were going to Boringville. Maybe I just did. I don't know.

He reaches his hand up and tucks strands of my hair behind my ear. My dangling earring tickles my neck as it jiggles, and my knees weaken the longer he stares into my eyes with a slight pout on his lips. I consider stretching up on my tiptoes to kiss him, but I don't want him to think I can persuade him with kisses, especially since we haven't had our first one yet.

I've thought about it a million times, but it just hasn't happened. Now doesn't feel like the right time either.

He rocks back on his heels. "Would you be sad if I said no?"

It's my turn to pout my lip. "A little, but if you don't want to, we don't have to."

He shakes his head. "I don't have to. I really did hear what you said about not having my presence mess up your first impression."

"Eli..." My voice trails off. Why couldn't he be the guy every person swooned over at this school? I thought I was going to have to worry about meeting expectations of the girl who won the attention of Eli Evans.

He cups my face. "It's okay, Nora, really. You can fill me in on all the gossip. I'm sure Fae has a mouthful to say about me."

I sigh. "Okay, I'll go, but I want you to join me next time if I like eating with them."

His nose crinkles. "Really?"

I laugh. "Yes, really. It shouldn't be so hard to fake a good time anyway. You're an actor."

He rubs his fingers over my arm. "And you're something else, Nora."

I sit between Fae and a girl with her dark hair twisted into a side braid. She watches me in her peripheral vision, and I try to pretend I don't notice her while I eat the sandwich Eli picked up for me.

"So, what do your parents do, Nora?" Fae asks. She smirked when I arrived without Eli like she somehow knew he wouldn't show. Luckily, no one mentions his absence either.

I nibble the edge of my sandwich to give me a moment to think of a response. "I live with my aunt. My stepmom was a total step-monster, so I jumped at the opportunity when my aunt asked. She's a lawyer."

"My mom is, too. I bet they know each other," the girl next to me says.

"Yeah, Alexandra's mom knows everyone." Cherry leans across the table. "She pulled some strings for me when I was caught trespassing at the Spadena house last year with E—" She snaps her mouth shut, and I know exactly who she was going to say. I guess I wasn't the first girl he took to the Witch's House.

I swallow my jealousy since I doubt these girls want Eli anymore and smile. "It's okay to say his name."

Cherry raises an eyebrow. "You just seem kind of protective over Mr. Cocky. Last year, he told me his publicist didn't want him to be seen with me because it would hurt his career." She rolls her eyes. "Just wait and see until Jean Moreau discovers you. I wasn't even seeing Eli like that. We were friends."

It's the first time I've heard any of them call him Eli instead of Elijah. I lean my elbows on the table. "That's pretty lame." I don't know what else to say. Eli never mentioned any of this, and I'm not sure he would willingly. I'd have to drag it out of him. The fact that I would sends a wave of doubt and anger through me. I have to talk to him. Now.

I push from my seat. "Hey, I think I'm going to catch y'all later."

Fae grabs my hand. "Oh, come on. I'm sure Cherry's wrong about Jean. You look and seem like the girl-next-door. People eat that up."

Except I'm not the girl next door. I have a lot of baggage I left behind that could be dug up and put on display. People will ask the same questions I did. What did I do that was bad enough to get cut out of my own dad's will? One call to Cecilia would have her weaving a ton of lies. She's so good at the role she plays that she could win an Oscar for the best portrayal of a victim.

I pull my hand away and shake my head. *Why does any of this matter?* "It's not that." Not entirely. "I just need to sort some things out."

Fae turns to look at me. "Good luck, Nora. I mean it. He's been trained to circle questions without actually giving answers."

And I thought that was my specialty. I just hope she's wrong.

I meet Eli near a small fountain in the quad. The weather's warm enough that not many students take up the open space, and no one sits close enough to Eli to eavesdrop on our conversation.

I plop down at the table next to him. "You're eating alone?"

He laces his fingers together. "No, I just came from the auditorium."

"Oh."

Silence falls between us. I'm having second thoughts about pushing him to answer my questions. None of this should matter. It's not like we're official or anything. We've hung out a few times, and he walks me to class.

He breaks the excruciating silence first. "You said you wanted to talk to me." He swipes the back of his hand across his glistening forehead as the hot sun beats down on us. "You know, those words are something no one wants to hear, right?"

I bump his shoulder. "Relax. It's not that big of a deal. It's just Cherry said—"

"Of course she did," he says, cutting me off. His lips tilt downward, and he refuses to meet my gaze even though I'm studying his face longer than I should be.

I rest my hand on his. "Can you let me finish?"

He straightens his shoulders. "Why? It's not like you'll believe me anyway."

My eyebrows jet up on my forehead. "Are you kidding me? You don't know what I'm going to say or what I believe." I get to my feet and cross my arms. "I like you, Eli. A lot. But if this is how it's going to be, then maybe I shouldn't."

I turn on my heels and rush away. Tears prickle at the corners of my eyes, but they don't fall. I won't let them. I can't.

Eli doesn't rush after me, and I don't expect him to.

I head toward my Spanish class even though the bell won't ring for another ten minutes. I wait outside the classroom, sitting against the wall, and someone plops down next to me.

"You okay? I followed you from the cafeteria." Alexandra tosses her braid over her shoulder.

I stare at my knees. "So, you heard everything?"

She shakes her head. "No, I turned around when I saw you meet Elijah. But you ran past me, so I figured things didn't go so well. I don't have the same feelings toward him as everyone else. He's my cousin."

"Why don't you hang out with him?" I ask. "He hasn't introduced me to any of his friends."

She lifts and drops her shoulders. "He's been spending time with you. I refuse to be the third wheel." She laughs. "And he does have friends. Lots of them. Just not many here."

I pout my lip. "That's kind of sad."

She flicks my shoulder. "Don't feel sorry for him. Eli's going to have the life most people only dream of. Nothing sad about that."

"I guess you're right. I had a small group of friends back in Austin, so I don't know what I was expecting when he told me about his upcoming movie."

"That he'd be the most popular boy in school?"

"Yeah."

She laughs. "This is LA, Nora. Nothing is ever as it seems."

Alexandra couldn't be more right about that.

Eli sent me a dozen apology texts and asked to meet after school, but I told him I had to work. It wasn't a lie, but it wasn't the whole truth, either. I don't really have a set schedule, and I could tell Aunt Jen I have a lot of homework, and she'd just tell me not to come in because school comes first.

I sit on the curb, waiting for my aunt, and press my phone to my ear. "I miss you, Taylor."

A rustling noise echoes through the phone. "I know! That's why I want to hear all about your week, but you have to let me call you tonight. I have a minute before I'm late for work."

I sigh. "Okay, girl. Talk to you later."

I frown, hanging up, and a shadow falls over me. I tilt my head toward the cerulean sky and meet Eli's dark eyes. He smirks down at me, his playful smile attempting to persuade me into hearing him out.

I lean my elbows on my knees and purposefully refrain

from saying anything first. Maybe I handled the situation wrong, or maybe he did. I can't even remember now, just that he pissed me off.

"Do I have to grovel at your feet to forgive me? Make a scene with a musical number? I know people, you know. I can make it happen." He nudges my shoulder when I don't respond. "Not into that kind of thing? Well, how about I take you somewhere? Anywhere. Just name it."

I twist my lips to the side, trying my best to fake my grudge. "The moon."

"The moon?"

"That's what I said."

I peek up at him. He rubs the five o'clock shadow forming on his chin. "Deal."

I lift an eyebrow. "Really?"

"Like I said, I know people."

I can't help the laugh that escapes my mouth. He kneels behind me, draping his arms over my shoulders, and hugs me from behind. His chin rests on the nape of my neck, the closeness of him sending tingles from my stomach to my chest.

I shift my head so my lips graze his cheek. "I'm sorry about earlier. I'm trying really hard to understand, but a lot of people give you the cold shoulder."

"I've made some mistakes that I have to live with," he says.

I lick my lips. "And I'm not going to judge you...unless you seriously hurt someone—like murder or something. If that's the case, you should probably lea—"

Pressing his index finger to my lips, he cuts me off. "Jeez, Nora. You have a wild imagination." He shifts so he's sitting next to me and then laces his fingers through mine.

I suck in my bottom lip. "It's why I like to write."

He tilts his head to the side like what I've just told him was more surprising than it should be. "That doesn't seem like your thing."

I shrug. "It's been months since I've done it. My inspiration died." *With Dad.* I don't finish my statement out loud, but it's true. I haven't even thought about it either.

Darkness lines his eyes as if my admission stirs sorrow in his heart. "I'm a firm believer that inspiration never dies, even after a person does. Their inspiration moves on to someone else. All lives inspire others."

I shake my head. "No, mine did die."

"Nora..."

"Out of everything, this is the thing that bothers you most? That I disagree with your philosophy?" I pull out my phone to look at the time. Aunt Jen should've been here by now. This conversation has taken a turn I didn't expect, and I need a way to cut it off.

"Actually yes. I'm going to prove you wrong."

"You have a better chance at taking me to the moon."

He snorts, the gesture ridiculously cute coming from him. "You just wait."

I bump my shoulder to his. "I am waiting." I check my phone again. "On you and my aunt."

He places his hand on my knee. "Oh, I guess I should've told you. I'm your ride."

I brush my hand over my head, pushing the stray strands from my face. "Eli! I have to get to work."

"Then we should probably go, huh?"

"Yeah." I find myself not wanting to go. I could call Aunt Jen and fib about having a ton of school work, but I like having the extra money that I've earned. It makes me feel less guilty about her taking care of me.

Eli tugs me to my feet and slides his hand around my back until his fingers rest on my side. The campus still buzzes with life. Students head to their after school activities, and I wave to a few girls who shared my lunch table in the cafeteria. I ignore all their curious gazes. I'm not going to let them bother me.

"Getting used to the attention yet?" Eli asks, guiding me to the student parking lot.

I shrug. "Yes and no. Either way, it doesn't matter."

He opens the passenger's side door for me. "If it makes a difference, I think you'd get it whether I was walking with you or not."

I roll my eyes. "You're just saying that."

His smirk disappears. "Hmm, something else I need to prove."

I shake my head and smile. "You're something else."

He wags his eyebrows. "I know."

chapter 8

 Star-Struck

ALEXANDRA SITS ON the edge of my bed while I brush my hair in front of my full length mirror. We have a lot more in common than I thought possible, and she doesn't give me the constant side-eye that Fae and Cherry do even though they act nice to me. It's Eli who they clearly won't ever forgive.

"You're so lucky you get to live with your aunt. Jen is so cool." Alexandra bounces on the mattress.

I spin to face her. "She is, isn't she?" I apply some grape-colored lipstick that matches my halter top dress. "I think I'm ready. You?"

She hops to her feet. "I'm always ready."

I head to the door before her and step into the hallway. The TV blares from the living room, and Jasper jumps on my leg before moving to Alexandra's. She pets him under the chin before scooping him into her arms.

Aunt Jen sits in front of the TV, her feet propped on the ottoman, while she watches some documentary about Lola St. Pierre, the iconic perfumer. When she notices us hovering behind her, she pauses her show and reluctantly eases from her comfortable position on the couch, where she spends half her time off just relaxing.

"Wow! You girls look great! Maybe I need to dress up a little more." Aunt Jen's nose scrunches as she beams at us.

"Are you kidding me? People will think you're one of the models," I say, and Alexandra giggles.

Aunt Jen swats my shoulder. "Oh, stop it. I'm not fooling anyone." Aunt Jen clearly hasn't seen herself in the mirror. Her designer dress, one by Drea Duchannes, hugs her in all the right places, and it looks like she sat in front of a stylist and makeup artist all morning.

"Except me," Alexandra says. "Just wait. Lele Rose will have you on that catwalk by the end of the show."

Aunt Jen's laughter sounds through the air. She swipes her clutch from the counter and motions us toward the kitchen to go to the garage door. "You can invite Alexandra over any time, Nora. She's good for my ego."

The ride to the L.R. fashion show flies by and before I know it, a man from valet opens my door, and I step out in front of The Reef in LA. I spot a gigantic wooden chair sculpture in the parking lot next to the building, and I snap a few pictures of Alexandra with it in the background.

Glittery golden carpet directs us where we're going, but it'd be kind of hard to miss the buzz in the air from this exclusive fashion show for some of the biggest stars in Hollywood. Lele Rose is a client of Aunt Jen's law firm, so we were lucky enough to score our names on the guest list.

We enter a bright white room with shiny tan floors and a runway dead center on a platform. When Aunt Jen mentioned it was exclusive, I didn't realize she meant under fifty people, and if fame was contagious, I'd definitely be a celebrity the moment the show was over. Taylor would have a heart attack if she were here. I pull my phone from my pocket to sneak a few pictures when a brooding man in a designer suit steps in front of me wagging his finger.

He points to a sign that reads, *No Cell Phones or Cameras.* "Sorry, you need to turn it off and put it away, or I'll have to confiscate it until after the show."

I pout my bottom lip but do as he says. I turn to Alexandra who whips her cell out the moment the security enforcer turns his back and snaps a few pictures of us with the celebrity crowd behind us.

Aunt Jen waves her hand. "Quick! One of me, too."

We laugh, heading to our seats in the back row out of sight from the few press cameras allowed. People take their seats, and soft music hums through the air as the show gets ready to start.

The natural lights flicker before they switch to neon purple, changing the color of the white walls in a split second. White bulbs blink on under the glass stage, and I bounce in my seat, the excitement in the air nearly intoxicating.

The music rises in volume, and a few figures rush from the shadows near the door to take their places in the front row.

My mouth drops open. "What is your cousin doing here?" I ask Alexandra.

Her eyes widen. "Oh, my God. Of course he's here. I mentioned what we had planned, and I bet his publicist pulled some strings."

"Does he even like fashion?" I lean closer to Alexandra as an older woman with a long, platinum wig, plump lips, and stick-thin arms, wearing a brightly patterned onesie steps onto the stage.

Alexandra laughs. "No, definitely not. He wears what he's told. He's here because he likes you."

Eli doesn't take his eyes off mine from across the room. It's distracting enough that I haven't paid attention to the show at all.

People applaud and start moving from their seats. The show ended already, and I had no idea. I had expected it to go on longer than twenty minutes. Aunt Jen and Alexandra stand from their seats, and I force my eyes away from Eli for a moment when a man strolls up to him and shakes his hand.

Aunt Jen excuses herself to talk to Lele Rose, who is mingling with her guests. Alexandra nudges my shoulder and grins when Eli weaves through the crowd in our direction, only stopping to greet people to be polite.

When he reaches us, Alexandra smacks his shoulder. "Elijah Rousseau, how dare you interrupt my date with your girl-friend." She flicks him on his other shoulder. "And how dare you show up to a fashion show without extending a front row ticket to me."

He laughs, tipping his head back. "You never mentioned you wanted to come to one, Alex. And you shouldn't have mentioned this if you didn't want me to show up."

His gaze turns to mine, sending heat crawling up my neck. He takes in every ounce of me. The corners of his lips pull up in his irresistible smirk, and I can't help but study his face. Scruff prickles his jaw, making him look older than usual, and he's wearing a designer suit. I've never seen him in anything other than jeans and a T-shirt, which he wears really well, but this is exactly how I imagined a movie star would look like up close. I can't believe he likes me.

"You look different," I say after a moment to fill the silence falling between the three of us. "The look suits you."

He grins. "I should be the one complimenting you." He reaches out and brushes my hair over my shoulder and out of the way of my dress. "Because you look amazing. Better than any of those models on that runway."

Alexandra cracks up next to me. "You're so smooth, Eli-jah."

I don't think I've ever seen him blush before, but I totally love it. I touch his collar. "Don't worry. I like it." I grab Alexandra's hand. "Since you're here, why don't you introduce us around? I'm sure Alexandra's dying to meet Hugo

Gutierrez." I point at the actor who's taken over every billboard in town. I don't admit it, but I want to meet him as well. There are enough stars in this place to shine brighter than the night sky.

Eli offers his arm to me, and I lace my fingers around his elbow. Leading the way, he guides me through the crowd with Alexandra glued to my other side. Her fingers, linked with mine, tremble with excitement. We meet each other's eyes with huge grins on our faces.

"Be cool," I whisper to her.

She bares her teeth but not in a smile. "I'm trying. You need to be cool so I can be cool."

We laugh, and Eli stops in his place. "Do you need a fan or something?"

Tears blur my eyes as laughter grabs hold of me and refuses to let go. Alexandra snorts and giggles because I'm laughing so hard, and then Eli rubs his hand over his face.

People start to stare, and Alexandra and I fan each other, trying to calm down. When our laughter finally eases, we meet each other's eyes and start busting up hysterically all over again.

"Oh, my God. I'm not introducing you two to anyone," Eli says.

I wave my hands near my eyes to stop the tears from messing up my makeup. "I can't stop."

Alexandra sniffles, clutching her stomach. "Please, Elijah, just give us a moment."

A figure blocks the vibrant light emanating from the stage,

and a guy puts his arm around Eli's shoulders. "I didn't know you were such a comedian, Rousseau," Hugo Gutierrez says.

My laughter disappears immediately, and I stare at the real-life version of Hollywood's biggest heartthrob. Alexandra freezes next to me, squeezing my hand, and I finally understand what being star-struck is like. I'm definitely star-struck. I don't think I could say anything coherently no matter how hard I try.

Eli shakes his head, eyeing his cousin. "Hey, Hugo. I thought I saw you. How's the show?"

Hugo meets my eyes for a split second, and I can feel my knees start to give out. He turns back to Eli. "Great, man. A dream, really. I look forward to working with you in a couple of weeks."

I raise my eyebrows. "You landed a role on *Creatures of Slaughter Creek*?" I'd never admit how religiously Taylor and I watched the show. It is one of our favorites.

Eli pulls me closer. "It's a small guest role." I think he's starting to notice the stars dancing in my eyes. *Pull yourself together, Nora...*

"With the opportunity to join the cast as a regular," Hugo mentions.

I bite my tongue to stop myself from letting loose my inner fan girl. Eli's celebrity status has been easy to ignore so far since I haven't seen him in anything, but I don't know how I'm going to handle him playing a role on my favorite show. It'll surely draw more attention to him, which means more attention will be on me if we spend any more time in public.

I realize I'm squeezing Eli's hand harder than I should, considering I don't remember taking it in the first place. I kiss his cheek. "You'll be amazing."

Alexandra clears her throat. "Are you ever going to introduce us, Elijah?"

It's then that I realize the whole conversation has focused on Eli. I guess that's something I'll appreciate.

He raises his eyebrows. "Yeah, sorry. Hugo, this is my cousin Alexandra, and my girlfriend, Nora."

Girlfriend? It's the second time being referred to as Eli's girlfriend, but we've never discussed that sort of thing. It was bound to happen with the way things are going, but the title makes our relationship sound so serious. We haven't even kissed yet.

"That'll break a lot of hearts, man," Hugo says, staring at me more closely now.

I let strands of hair fall in my face. "Not really. We're not going public with it or anything."

Hugo nods his head. "Good idea. Dating in the spotlight is hard."

Alexandra surprises me by running her fingers up Hugo's arm. "I'm sure you could manage."

He laughs. "You guys coming to the after party?"

I turn to Alexandra, her eyes wide with excitement. "We weren't invited."

Hugo raises his eyebrows. "Well, you are now."

The LA skyline sparkles in front of me. I stand against the half-wall, half-glass barrier that'll prevent anyone from falling off the roof of this twenty-story building. The view steals my breath away and might be prettier than the stars I can't see above us.

Music pulsates from giant speakers positioned around the rooftop, and partygoers dance on the small stage, hang out around tiny, round tables or in small clusters, or like me, stare at the amazing view of the city.

Eli strolls next to me and hands me a drink he picked up for me at the bar. "It's non-alcoholic," he murmurs. "Your aunt wouldn't take her eyes off me while I was ordering."

I giggle. Aunt Jen wasn't going to let us run off with Eli and Hugo no matter how much I pleaded with her, but she actually fits in better here than I do. I take a sip, tasting the salted rim and limey fake margarita drink. "Sorry about that. She's a lawyer, remember? I don't drink anyways."

He slides his arm around my waist. "Me neither. My mom would die of embarrassment for that kind of tabloid scandal."

"You should introduce us sometime." I haven't wanted to bring it up but the last thing I want is for his mom to hate me if she finds out about me from someone else.

He tilts his head to the side like I said the most ridiculous thing. "You actually want to meet my mom?"

I shrug. "Why not?"

"I guess I don't have a reason for you not to. I've met your aunt, and I'm sure I'll meet your parents if they come to visit."

My heart clenches at his comment. One of these days, I'm going to have to let him know about my past. Just not tonight. I never feel like it's the right time. "They won't ever come to visit," I say softly, my voice barely a whisper.

Laughter peels through the air, drawing our attention away at the perfect moment. Alexandra dances with Hugo, her smile taking up half her face, and then she waves us over when she notices us staring.

Eli offers out his hand. "Wanna dance?"

I lace my fingers through his. "I thought you'd never ask."

He leads me onto the dance floor and slides his hands over my hips to match my rhythm. I don't know many guys back in Texas who like to dance or can do so well, and I take in all Eli's perfect moves.

I lean closer to him. "You're a great dancer."

"You can thank our school for that."

I laugh. "Really?"

He nods and spins me. My dress twirls around my thighs, and I revel in all the fun and excitement rushing through the party.

I'm still in shock over my luck. I never imagined doing something like this in my wildest dreams.

Eli gazes into my eyes, and after a while, he pulls me from the dance floor, and we stand under white lights strung above us like glittering stars. I run my hands up his shoulders, locking my fingers behind his neck, and he leans closer.

My heart bangs against my ribcage. He closes the distance

between us, his hands traveling from my waist up my sides, until he cups my face in his hands. I meet his lips with mine, our kiss starting off soft and sweet before his hands move to my shoulders. He pulls me closer, deepening our kiss.

His lips taste of lime, and I brush my tongue with his, teasing him just enough to have him shifting me against the glass wall.

After a long moment, I smile into his lips and whisper, "We should probably stop."

His warm breath tickles my lips. "Yeah."

A camera flashes from behind us, and Eli spins me, hiding me from whoever had the nerve to try to capture our first kiss on camera. I consider rushing over to the jerk and screaming at him, but Eli blocks me from even seeing his face.

He motions toward a side door that'll take us back into the building. "Come on. Paparazzi can be relentless. Let's wait inside until he's escorted out. Someone must've invited him as a publicity stunt."

I blow strands of hair from my face. "Okay."

We rush inside before the man can snap another photo, and Eli kisses me again in the stairwell.

"This night has been one of the best in my life," I say, taking in how dark his eyes appear in the dim lighting. I could get lost in their depths.

"Mine, too," he says, running his fingers over my cheek.

I smirk. "Really?"

"Yeah," he says as he kisses me once more.

chapter 9

ALEXANDRA SAUNTERS TO my locker and slaps a magazine against my chest. The bell rings for our next class, but I don't move to go. Instead, I hold up the tabloid and peer over the cover.

"We're famous," Alexandra says, grinning at me like I should be ecstatic about the blurry picture of my back and Eli's side profile cut out from the much larger photo of Alexandra's back as she dances with Hugo Gutierrez.

I force my nerves to settle and laugh. "It says we're mystery girls."

"I know! Won't be long before someone pieces it together." She hooks her arm through mine and pulls me in the direction of my Chemistry class, which is across from hers. She had tried to switch teachers, but both our classes are maxed out.

I shove the tabloid in my bag. "I hope not. Don't tell anyone either, okay?"

She pouts. "Fine. I get it. I'll already be famous anyway when Elijah's movie comes out." She giggles and pulls away from me to head into her class.

I wave at her and enter my own before sitting at the black lab tables. Mrs. Hampton pulls out a TV and turns it on, making my life a whole lot easier today.

I zone out through the film on elements and end up spending almost the entire period texting with Eli under the table.

When the bell rings, Alexandra meets me outside the door so we can walk to lunch together. Eli slides up next to me halfway to the cafeteria and links his fingers with mine. He leans down, kissing my cheek, and I smile up at him.

"I'm going to eat with Alexandra today," I say and wait to see his reaction.

He nods. "Cool. I'll come with."

"You will?" Alexandra and I say at the same time. A second later, we laugh. The only other person I laugh this much with is Taylor. I bet they'd get along great. I hope I can introduce them eventually.

"I don't joke about such serious matters," he says, his voice low and even.

I stop laughing. "Eli..."

He cracks a smile. "I'm teasing, and I also promise this isn't going to be a daily thing. I can only handle so much glaring."

Alexandra punches her cousin's arm. "Good, 'cause I don't

know how much of you two I can handle."

We enter the cafeteria, and I ignore anyone who gawks at us. Eli pays for both mine and Alexandra's lunches even though I protest, and we head to the table in the back corner where Fae, Cherry, and a few other people usually sit.

Fae's eyebrows nearly shoot off her forehead when she sees Eli with us, but she doesn't comment. No one does. They all act like it's an ordinary day and chat among themselves. I slide in next to Fae, and Eli sits down next to me while Alexandra plops down across from us.

She slaps her palms down on the table. "You'll never guess who I met this weekend."

The others lean in, waiting to discover who Alexandra met. She leaves me out of it completely, and I don't mind one bit. Eli holds my hand under the table, and I stab at my chicken Caesar salad with a fork. The food here is immensely better than what my old high school had. The variety surprised me at first.

Alexandra draws out the anticipation to the point where I kick her foot under the table. I already know her answer, but waiting to see the others' reactions is making me impatient.

"Hugo Gutierrez!" She squeals, waving her hands over her face. If I didn't have the tabloid in my bag, I'm sure she'd toss it onto the table as proof. Instead, she pulls out her cell phone and waves a photo she took with Hugo, their faces squished together and colorful lights reflecting in their eyes.

Fae snatches the phone from her hand. "How'd you manage that?"

Alexandra wiggles her eyebrows up and down. "My charm."

She winks at me, and I kick her under the table again. I'm not responsible for any of it. Aunt Jen took us, and our laughter drew Hugo's attention. If anything, she's absolutely right about her charm.

The chatter picks up between everyone, and after we're finished eating, I lean into Eli and whisper that we should make a break for it. He jumps up without hesitation and pulls me from my seat.

I wave at the others and rush out of the cafeteria, clutching Eli's hand. He spins me around when we're outside, and I stand on my tiptoes to give him a soft kiss. He pulls me closer, and I'm tempted to get carried away in the middle of the courtyard, but the low rumble of voices coming from a few lower classmen draws me away from Eli.

He grins while linking his pinky finger with mine. "That was torture."

"Awkward, yeah, a little. But torture? You're being dramatic." I flick his shoulder with my free hand.

"Well, at least my next role will be a breeze. Loner teen dream walker falls for transfer student."

My mouth falls agape. "Are you kidding me?"

He holds his expression serious, his dark eyes gauging my reaction. After a second, he says, "Yeah, totally. I don't have a script yet, and if I did, I couldn't tell you anything."

I scrunch my nose. "You can't? Ugh." I hate admitting it, but I was looking forward to getting the inside scoop before anyone else.

He lowers his eyebrows. "You're a fan?"

A burst of warmth waves across my cheeks. There's no way I can lie or evade his question. The answer is written on my face in the form of red blotches.

He grasps my chin with his thumb and index finger. "Uh-oh. You are." His lips curl up in the corners.

I pout my bottom lip. "It's my weakness. Please, don't ever bring this up again. I swear I won't turn into some crazy fan girl."

His laughter echoes through the air. "Oh, I will. Every chance I get."

"Don't you dare or else I'll tell Taylor and give her your phone number. If you think I'm a fan, you just wait." I smile as the words escape my lips because I can just imagine Taylor's reaction to the news.

I hop back, yanking away from him, and slide my phone from my pocket. Beaming my brightest smile, I wave my phone out of his reach.

He glares, making me laugh harder. As much as he tries to look angry, his face holds a happiness I wish I could carry around in my bag for any time sadness sneaks up on me.

"You wouldn't." He swings his hand out and misses my phone.

I pretend to tap the screen. "Don't doubt me."

He charges me, scooping me off my feet, and spins me around. The world blurs, and I cling to him, burying my face in his neck. Tears prickle my eyes from laughing so hard, and I know my stomach muscles will be sore later tonight. But I don't care.

I haven't felt so carefree in months, and I love how it makes me feel. How Eli makes me feel.

The lunch bell rings, and he sets me back on my feet.

Bending down, Eli presses his warm lips to my cheek. "Meet me after school?"

I nod. "Sure, I'll let my aunt know I have too much homework."

He clasps my hand. "Perfect. We can study at my house."

"Really?"

"You did say you wanted to meet my mom."

Eli turns onto Alta Drive, a street in the Flats of Beverly Hills, and turns into a long driveway that takes us through a canopied porte cochere to a garage stationed behind the enormous red brick home. The lawn is perfectly manicured and globe-like hedges line a stone walkway.

He puts his Range Rover into park. "Did you know a lot of the roads here have designated trees lining the streets? The ones out front are jacarandas. The purple flowers are a pain in the ass when they bloom in the spring, and I can't park my car under them, or they drip sap or something on it."

I raise my eyebrows while nodding my head. "Cool."

"And Palm Drive doesn't have palm trees."

I giggle. "You seem nervous."

He swipes his hand over his eyes. "I'm introducing you to my mom."

"So." I hold my smile.

"So, what if my family scares you away? I really, really like you."

I reach over and take his hand. "It's going to be fine." I shift close and kiss him. "And I really, really like you, too, Eli."

I hop out of the Range Rover before he can rush to open my door. He meets me at the rear, steals my bag from my hands, and hoists it onto his shoulder. He looks silly wearing it, and it takes everything in me not to snap a picture.

We stroll down a path lined with rose bushes to a dark wood door with a glass window cutout. When we enter, I peer around the small foyer with a shoe and coat rack, a long table full of family photos, and a woman with hair the same brown as Eli's but with bright blue eyes.

"Oh, Nora, I'm so happy to meet you!" The woman's voice rings through the quiet air with excitement. "Eli talks about you all the time."

"Thanks for having me over, Mrs. Evans." I glance at Eli, wondering what he's told his mom about me.

"You're welcome." She grasps my hand in hers. "Call me Liza, okay? I hate that last name stuff."

I laugh. "Okay, Liza." I call most of my friends' parents by their last names, so calling Eli's mom by her first feels strange.

Eli motions me to follow him. "We'll be in my room."

"Are you staying for dinner, Nora? We'd love to have you," Liza says before we can make a break for it.

I nod. "I'd like that, thanks."

Eli tugs me away from his mom, and we pass through a spacious living room with dark leather couches positioned in an L-shape. A glass coffee table with a ceramic vase full of fresh roses sits in the middle, and the biggest flat screen I've ever seen in a house takes up an entire wall with shelves full of books, movies, and knick-knacks surrounding it. A poster-size family portrait with a few accent photos takes up another wall. Sheer curtained windows allow in natural lighting, and I spot the kitchen through an arched door-less cutout.

We reach a set of wooden stairs off a short hallway with a bathroom and an office, and Eli guides me up to his bedroom, which is the first door on the right that overlooks the front yard.

Eli's room isn't exactly what I expect from a teenage boy. His bed is neatly made, his gray comforter matching his gray curtains. I don't even make my bed most of the time. A desk with a laptop sits near a door to a walk-in closet, and a few shelves of awards and pictures hang above short bookcases with an impressive collection of books. A flat screen TV with a sound bar rests atop a tall dresser and expensive headphones sit on his nightstand.

"This is probably the cleanest bedroom I've ever seen that wasn't in a movie," I say. I shuffle to the end of his bed and sit on the corner, well aware that we're alone in his room with the door closed.

"Amy has worked for my parents for twenty years. No matter how often I tell her that I can handle cleaning my room, she comes in while I'm at school three days a week." He plops on the bed next to me, lying back with his hands behind his head.

I'll never get used to the idea of a housekeeper. Aunt Jen said she has someone come in occasionally for a deep clean, but she hasn't called anyone since I've arrived. It's not like we're slobs, though. The house is usually tidy, just not museum status like Eli's house.

"Oh." I don't really have anything to say. "Your mom seems nice," I say, changing the subject. "What did you tell her about me?"

He twists his lips to the side in thought. "Everything I like about you."

I shift on the bed to face him. "And what's that?"

"How real you are. How you make me laugh. How you don't take my shit." He grabs my arm and pulls me to lie next to him.

I cuddle against his side, resting my hand on his chest. His heartbeat speeds up when I run my fingers in a circle, and his breath blows strands of hair in my face. His voice cuts off, and I'm sure he's just as aware as I am about how close we are. My legs dangle off the bed, and I consider sitting back up, but his arms are so comforting and warm. I don't ever want to move.

Brushing his lips against my temple, Eli shifts until his face hovers over mine. One of his legs rests between mine, and he props himself on his elbows, gazing into my eyes. I stretch my neck up and graze my lips over his, just light enough to make him suck in a breath.

Meeting my light kiss eagerly, he sucks my bottom lip into his mouth while brushing his fingers through my hair. He lowers himself onto me, our hearts banging against each other through our shirts, and tingles wash over me, quickening my breathing to match Eli's.

He kisses me deeper, our tongues brushing softly against each other, and his hands move from my hair. They travel down my arms and to my sides where he rubs his fingers along the sliver of skin showing between my jeans and shirt. I let out a soft moan as his hand makes its way up my shirt, running along my stomach with feather-light intensity, yet it drives me crazy in a good way.

His mouth moves to my neck, and I arch my back, pressing my hips into him, and he moans in my ear. Things get heavy pretty quickly, and I know if I don't say something now, I'm not sure I ever will. But his mom's downstairs, and the last thing I want is for her to catch us up here doing something I'm pretty sure she'd be unhappy about.

"Eli..." My words fall silent as his lips trail down to my collarbone, and his fingers slide into my bra.

I stiffen and he freezes, his breath now panting. He lifts his gaze to meet mine.

I suck in a deep breath through my nose to calm my racing

heart. "We should stop."

He bobs his head. "You're right." He kisses me once more before flipping onto his back to lie next to me.

I pull my shirt back down and stare at the ceiling fan in the middle of the room. He links his thumb with my pinky, and we don't say anything for a long while as we try to pull ourselves away from the heat of the moment.

I squeeze my eyes shut, finding the words I know I need to tell him. "I like you a lot, Eli, and I love hanging out and being with you, but you should know I'm still a virgin, just in case things ever get to that point."

He reaches out and tucks strands of hair behind my ear. "I should probably tell you I'm not."

I sit up on an elbow to meet his gaze. "I figured that. Do any of them go to school with us?"

His eyes dart away, answering my question without saying a word. "It was only with my last girlfriend, but we haven't been together since the beginning of junior year."

I lean over and kiss him. "It's fine. You don't have to tell me anything. I don't think I really want to know."

He presses his lips into a thin line. "Well, I'll be honest with you if you do."

I think about it for a second but decide to drop it. I really, really don't want to know. I don't want to wonder and compare myself to his ex. She's a part of his past like everyone I left behind in Texas besides Taylor, who's the only one who has even talked to me since I hopped on a flight from Austin.

I get to my feet and grab my bag off the floor. "How about we do something else for a bit? I did tell my aunt that I'd be studying."

He laughs, getting to his feet. "Whatever you want, Nora."

I meet his smile with my own. "I like the sound of that."

chapter 10

Afraid of Attention

THE REST OF the week rolls by uneventfully, each day exactly the same as the next except Eli doesn't join me in the cafeteria for lunch at all. I ended up leaving the table fifteen minutes before the bell rang for class and split my time between Eli and Alexandra because she never wants to be the third wheel. I don't blame her.

In my last class of the day, Advanced Journalism, I sit next to Fae, scouring the internet for ideas to use for our TV Production class.

Fae points her stylus at the screen. She rarely ever uses an actual pen and paper. Mostly just her tablet to take notes. "We could do a feature on the casting call for that Hollywood Teen reality show."

I purse my lips. "I'm sure everyone knows about that already."

She taps her finger on a key. "You're right."

I point to a press release about a new fragrance from Eva Devereaux, who happens to be one of Aunt Jen's clients. "What about this? I might be able to get an interview or something. She's one of my aunt's clients."

Fae bounces in her seat. "Are you serious?"

I nod. "It wouldn't hurt to ask."

"This could be our big break!"

My eyebrows shoot up. I don't exactly want my big break in Entertainment News. I just want to pass the class. I don't mention it to Fae, though. I know she dreams about this kind of thing. It's one of the few things we talk about—celebrity news and gossip, school work, and occasionally Eli.

Fae closes the internet window and turns to me in her rolling chair. "A few of us were going to hit up The Grove after school. They have some makeup event going on, and Cherry signed us up for makeovers."

"That sounds fun." Aunt Jen has been promising to take me for weeks but hasn't had the chance because of work. It's like she never takes a day off, and when she does, she always gets a call from someone who needs her. If I didn't spend a few days a week at her office, I'm not sure I'd see her for more than a few minutes a day.

Fae smiles. "It will be. We'll grab some dinner after. Make a night of it." She shoves her tablet into her bag, getting ready to leave even though the bell won't ring for another ten minutes. "Oh, and no boys allowed, okay?"

I stop myself from frowning. "I doubt Eli would want to spend his Friday night watching people do makeup."

She shrugs. "I just heard he likes to show up uninvited."

"Oh." I don't say anything else. I can't really defend Eli since he did kind of show up at the fashion show just because he heard I was going to be there. I'm surprised Alexandra mentioned it to Fae, though, since she didn't mention us hanging out at the after-party with Hugo Gutierrez.

We sit in silence until the bell rings, and then I stroll next to Fae to where we meet Cherry, Alexandra, and a girl named Piper, who doesn't say much at lunch but spends most of her time glued to her phone.

Alexandra's smile widens when she sees me. She slides her arm into mine to saunter next to me. "I'm glad Fae decided to invite you. I would've, but she's the one who planned it."

"It's cool. I'm the new girl and all." I suck in my bottom lip as hurt grabs hold of me for a split second. I thought Fae and I got along pretty well in class. I don't like feeling that she doubts me or isn't sure she wants to be friends. I wish Alexandra hadn't said anything about it at all.

We reach Fae's car, a clean yet older Mercedes, and I squeeze in the back between Piper and Alexandra since my legs are the shortest. I send Aunt Jen a text message on the drive over that I'm hanging out with the girls, and she replies with a simple smiley face.

The Grove is a nightmare traffic wise, and I'm so thankful

I don't have to drive in it. After what feels like an eternity, we finally turn and pass the LA Farmers Market to find the parking structure.

Fae doesn't bother with public parking and pulls right into valet, and we all hop out. I shove my wallet and phone into the pocket of my jeans and keep pace with Alexandra as the others walk in front of us.

The Grove buzzes with life as late afternoon shoppers arrive to shop after work. The outdoor mall is more impressive than the one back in Austin. We walk through a wide path with a restaurant on each side and immediately notice a temporary stage set up with chairs and cameras. Under lighted canopies, makeup artists dressed in black stand in front of their beauty stations with tackle boxes and suitcases filled with cosmetics.

A woman in a neutral-colored, patterned dress hovers near the two steps that lead to the platform. She scribbles stuff on the clipboard she's holding, and when Fae approaches her, she offers a pleasant smile.

I tug Alexandra's arm. "I'll watch you from over there." I point at a bench in front of a towering sign that says, *The Grove.* The makeovers were scheduled last week, so I was already aware I wasn't getting one. I only came to watch.

Alexandra purses her lips before strutting to the woman and whispers something in her ear. The woman draws her gaze from her clipboard to glance at me, and then she waves me closer.

"I have an open chair with Chris if you want to join your

friends. You have to decide now because there's a wait list." The woman motions toward a young man with the most perfect cat-eye eyeliner I've ever seen.

I nod. "Yeah, I'd love to."

Alexandra squeals. "Perfect!"

A moment later, after I sign a waiver and attach Aunt Jen's business card so they can reach out to her for permission, we're rushed to our chairs. I shift in my seat, slightly away from the crew with the video camera.

"Don't be nervous, my lovely," Chris, the makeup artist, says as he removes the small amount of tinted moisturizer and mascara I put on this morning. "You have a great face for this."

I offer a closed lip smile. "Thanks. It's my first makeover."

"You'll look like a starlet after I'm through."

He talks as he brushes all sorts of stuff on my face. I've never worn so much makeup in my life, but somehow, it doesn't feel heavy or weird. I spend half the time in the chair with my eyes closed, and when he's finished, he doesn't let me look at myself.

A man with a camera comes and snaps a few photos, and then I'm ushered to where my friends wait for what I guess is the big reveal.

Alexandra's mouth drops open when she sees me. "Whoa, Nora. You look amazing!"

I grin. "So do you!"

Fae, Cherry, and Piper close the space between us, and they all have smiles on their lips as well. Fae looks ready for the red carpet. I almost don't recognize her because she never wears makeup, unlike Cherry and Piper who probably spend hours getting ready in the morning.

"Ladies and gentleman settle down." The woman who's organizing the makeovers saunters over with her eyes glued to her clipboard. "If I could have everyone stand near the curtain. We'd like to film everyone's reactions for our promo ad."

I turn to Alexandra. "We're going to be on TV?"

She smirks. "Duh. I thought Fae told you."

I shrug. If she did, I wasn't listening. I just assumed signing the waiver and whatnot was just a part of the deal in case something happened and the makeup artist spilled liquid eyeliner in my eyes. I can hear Aunt Jen talking about reading the fine print now. Oh, well. I'm not backing out.

I don't respond. Instead, I peer around and catch a crowd standing around the temporary stage. I've been so wrapped up in the excitement of the makeover that I totally forgot we were in the middle of a crowded mall on a Friday afternoon. Of course there are onlookers. It's strange having all these eyes staring at us, and I'm one of the people they're looking at. I'm not the mystery girl kissing Elijah Rousseau anymore. At least no one knows that.

I shift on my feet, standing between Alexandra and Fae, facing a tall black curtain. A few cameras flash, snapping pictures, and the curtain slowly opens for the unveiling.

I gawk at my reflection in the mirror. I don't even know who the girl standing in front of me is. I swear my nose is thinner, my cheeks are higher, and my lips look like I've had injections to make them fuller.

"Whoa," I say under my breath.

"Tell me about it," Fae says from next to me. "We're so hot. Not that we weren't before but damn. I need my own personal makeup artist."

After a good five minutes of staring at our reflections, the organizer shuffles us off stage to a behind the scenes area. I'm told to sit in an actor's chair in front of a cameraman, and the organizer sits across from me.

"Thank you for participating on Makeup Madness Teen Edition, Nora." The woman rests her hands in her lap. "How did you enjoy the experience?"

I concentrate on not licking my lips or tugging at my hair. I straighten my shoulders and smile. "Amazing. Chris is a talented artist."

"He is." The woman, who I learn goes by the name Chrissy, spouts off a couple more questions about what I liked best, how I felt about myself before and after, and if I'd do anything different. I respond with short, sweet answers until she says, "I have one more question for you. You're here with your friends, right?"

I nod. "Yeah. Fae, Alexandra, Cherry, and Piper. They talked me into coming."

She smiles like I've said the most interesting thing. "Stunning girls by the way." She looks directly into the camera. "Anyway, I happened to overhear one of your friends mention Elijah Rousseau. Do you know him?"

I offer a tight smile. "Yeah, he's Alexandra's cousin."

"How do you think he'd react if he saw you?"

"What?" I shift in the seat. "I don't know."

I don't like where this is heading. I don't know what she's overheard, but I don't like her taking advantage of the situation. She probably thinks this will help boost her career so she doesn't have to host some low-budget mall reality show.

"Are you two good friends?"

"What does that have to do with my makeover?" I glance between her and the camera. "Do you have any other non-personal questions?"

The woman offers her hand. "No, that's all. Thank you so much for participating." She slouches when the cameraman shuts off the camera.

"I don't want you to include that in the show," I say, getting to my feet.

"You signed a waiver, and we already have your guardian's approval." She gets to her feet and meets my gaze. "I just wish you'd realize the opportunity I gave you that you blew. You could've been famous."

I sneer, pushing past her and out of the small curtained area. Alexandra hovers outside with a frown on her face while Fae and Piper chat. Cherry smirks at me like she found the whole thing hilarious, which I know she could hear since the curtain doesn't exactly allow a lot of privacy.

I run my finger under my eyes and pray that the mascara

used was waterproof. "Well, that was fun." Sarcasm lines my words, and I stroll toward the first bench I see and plop down. I'm tempted to lose myself in the crowd and call Aunt Jen to pick me up, but I'm not going to let them think I'm being a baby. It was only a few stupid questions for a stupid TV show no one probably watches.

A few minutes later, Alexandra plops next to me. "Chrissy didn't care about us at all. All she did was ask about Elijah. I shouldn't have told her he was my cousin."

I frown. "Why did you?"

"To get you priority. I didn't say anything else, though. I swear."

I sigh. "It's okay. I was just surprised. I don't know why I'm afraid of the attention."

She drapes her arm over my shoulder. "You should enjoy it."

I take a breath. "I guess you're right. Just don't expect me to go looking for it."

We sit at a pizza place at the Farmers Market next to The Grove, definitely overly made up for our date with the large cheese pizza and garlic bread.

I pull out my phone while the others talk about how much fun they had, and I read a few messages from Eli.

Eli: Having fun?

Eli: Text me when you're done.

Eli: Unless you don't want to.

Eli: I hope you do.

I hide my smile before taking a bite of pizza, keeping my phone on my knee so it's not obvious I'm not listening to Cherry go on and on about how she thinks one of us will get discovered and she hopes it's all of us.

I text Eli back.

Me: Nope. Don't want to.

Me: JK. Can't resist.

Eli: Knew it. Still there?

Me: Eating pizza. Ruining my new perfect lips.

Eli: Mmm. Doubt that's possible.

Me: Haha.

Alexandra nudges me, and I realize the others are watching me smile at my lap. I quickly send one last message to Eli.

Me: I'll call you later.

I slide my phone back into my pocket. "Sorry about that. My best friend from home wanted to know all about it." I don't know why I lie, but I can't help it.

Cherry lifts an eyebrow. "With the way you were smiling, I thought it was Elijah for sure."

I roll my eyes. "It's not always about him, you know."

"Oh, I know," she responds.

Alexandra sets her glass of water down a little too hard and some of it splashes on the table. "Enough about my cousin. We get that you're still mad at him, Cherry, but you don't have to take it out on Nora. Or me for that matter."

Cherry purses her lips together. "You just wait and see.

He'll toss you aside like the rest of us. His fascination will run out, and he'll use his fame as an excuse."

Everyone goes silent at her words. She swore she was never with Eli, but I'm starting to realize that things go a lot deeper than him dropping her as a friend because it was supposedly bad for his reputation. I'm pretty sure she liked him. Who wouldn't?

Cherry pushes from the table and struts off. Fae and Piper get up and follow her, and I expect Alexandra to do the same, but instead she takes another slice of pizza from the pan and takes a bite.

She sets the pizza on her plate. "I swear. You'd think it was Cherry who used to date Elijah."

"She didn't?"

"God, no."

I'm surprised by how relieved I am to hear that. "Then why does she hate me?"

She laughs. "I don't think she does. She's just always like that. You'll get used to it."

I shake my head. "I highly doubt that."

Alexandra laughs. "True. I guess I haven't yet."

chapter 11

Biggest Fan

I BOUNCE IN my chair in TV Production, waiting for Fae to come into the room. Aunt Jen heard back from Eva Devereaux last night, and she agreed to a short interview about her fragrance. I've been freaking out since.

"Drink too much coffee this morning, Nora?" Anthony, my other teammate on the entertainment side of things pulls his chair next to mine.

I fiddle with a loose string on my shirt. "None, actually. Just waiting to tell Fae something."

"Tell me what?" Fae asks, plopping down in her seat beside me.

I slap my hands on my knees. "She agreed!" My voice squeals out over the quiet classroom.

Fae's eyebrows scrunch together as she tries to decipher

what I'm talking about. A second later, realization crosses her face, and she claps her hands. "Eva Devereaux agreed! Oh, my God! Yes!"

The other students gawk at our excitement, and Ms. Valentine saunters over from her desk and stands in front of us. She places her hands on her hips while raising one eyebrow and waits for us to calm down.

"We're filming in ten. I hope you can settle down before then," she says.

I bob my head. "Yes, ma'am."

Fae dances in her seat. "I don't think I can. Nora just got us an interview with a supermodel!" She takes a breath. "Eva Devereaux is going to let us interview her for the paper!"

Ms. Valentine tilts her head to the side. "It's been a while since we've included something special in one of our broadcasts. Want to see if she'd be willing to be featured on the show as well? You may do the interview, Nora, since you've put in the effort to schedule such a treat."

I open and close my mouth in surprise. "Oh, no, that's okay. Fae is much more prepared for something like that. She should do it."

Fae grins at me. "I'd be happy to."

Ms. Valentine shakes her head. "No, I'd like you to give it a shot. Fae does the entertainment feature every week. It's important for everyone to try their hand in front of the camera. Who knows? You could be great at it."

Fae's face falls, and I want to beg Ms. Valentine not to put me through the torture of having my first—well, first in class—interview in front of the camera with such a high-profile celebrity. That is, if Eva even agrees to it. Maybe she won't. I kind of hope she doesn't.

"Uh…" My voice trails off.

Ms. Valentine shakes her head. "It's settled, Nora. Please, don't argue."

I meet Eli outside his class to walk with him to the quad for lunch. I was going to sit with the others in the cafeteria, but I'm pretty sure Fae needs some space. She barely said two words to me since Ms. Valentine pushed the Eva interview on me, and I know she's upset even though none of this is my fault.

Eli kisses the top of my head. "Where's that beautiful smile you always greet me with? Something happen?"

I blow strands of my light brown hair from my face. "I'm being forced in front of the camera for an entertainment piece."

Eli slides his fingers in mine, pulling me to meander next to him through the crowded hallway. "Hey, that's a great opportunity. Not everyone gets camera time, you know."

I lick my dry lips before pulling lip balm from my bag. "Yeah, but Fae really wanted the feature."

He snorts. "She wants every feature, Nora."

"This one's different. It involves Eva Devereaux."

He bobs his head, smiling. "That is a big deal. I bet Fae is still crying in the bathroom."

I lightly slap his arm. "Knock it off. It isn't funny. I don't even want to do it."

He squeezes my fingers. "Okay, I'm sorry."

Our conversation tapers off, and we enter the front lawn to grab a bite to eat from one of the food carts. Eli pays, like always, and I sneak a few dollars into his backpack, like always. One of these days, he'll notice, but until then, I'll keep doing it.

When we have our food and settle down at a table near the fountain in the quad, I take a few bites of my sandwich before setting it down and resting my chin on the backs of my hands. I gaze at a few other students making their ways to their friends and wonder what Fae has told the others. I'm sure Alexandra will tell me if she says anything crazy.

Eli bumps his shoulder against mine. "What are you doing on Saturday?"

I draw my eyes up from my half-eaten sandwich to peer into his brown eyes. They crinkle in the corners as he smiles at me, and I lean forward and kiss him on the lips. I could really use a distraction right about now, and he's perfect for that.

I slowly pull away before he can deepen the kiss. "Hanging out with you, why?"

He chuckles. "I want to show you something."

I raise my eyebrows. "What?"

He pokes my nose. "Just wait and see."

Saturday couldn't come soon enough. While Fae's eyes water every time she sees me, she's officially talking to me again as long as neither of us brings up what I now like to call the stupid

interview with Eva, who agreed to the broadcast feature. It's set to happen in two weeks on a Friday after school so not as many students will be on the campus.

Taylor watches me twirl in front of the mirror from my computer screen. I model the third outfit I've put on this morning. The light cotton dress swirls breezily around my thighs, and the sweetheart neckline enhances my cleavage.

Taylor squeals. "That's the one! It's perfect." The video shakes as she shifts on her end of the camera. "God, I wish I could move in with your aunt, too. You're living my dream, Nora. Hollywood, celebrity boyfriend, televised makeovers, interviews with models, fashion shows. I want to be you."

I crinkle my nose. "It's not as glamorous as it sounds."

She brings the camera closer to her face and applies some lip balm. "Who cares? It's better than working at H.E.B while missing your best friend and spending Saturday at the movies with Chad Miller."

My mouth drops open. "Chad? You didn't tell me you were seeing Chad." Chad Miller is an All-American Texan boy who lives on a ranch with his parents, plays football, and drives the biggest truck I've ever seen.

She covers her face with her hands. "I know! I couldn't turn down those damn puppy dog eyes. He's sweet, though."

"As long as you're happy."

She grins. "I am."

My phone buzzes with a text message from Eli, saying he's ten minutes away. I quickly send a reply before turning back to

Taylor.

I press my palms on my desk and lean close to my screen. "Eli's almost here. I'll call you later."

She blows me a kiss. "Have fun! Send me pictures."

I blow her a kiss back and log off my computer. I retie my ponytail, add a spritz of the Eva Devereaux perfume sample Aunt Jen had given me last night, and put my phone and wallet into a small purse from my aunt's closet.

The doorbell rings five minutes later, and Eli engulfs me in a hug the moment I open the door to greet him. Jasper barks from behind me, and I wave to Aunt Jen before I shut the door. I stand on my tiptoes and kiss Eli for a minute on the porch, tasting the sweet mint flavor of his toothpaste, and then we head to his car parked on the street.

Eli starts his Range Rover and pulls from the curb. "Hungry or anything? We could stop at a drive-thru if you want."

"I just ate breakfast, but we could stop for you," I say.

He intertwines his fingers with mine. "Nope, I'm good."

He turns on the radio and drives us out of Beverly Hills toward Century City. I have no idea where he's taking me, and I'm anxious to find out.

"Are you ever going to tell me where we're going?" I ask. "Is it a long drive?"

Peeking at me in his peripheral vision, he says, "No and no." He glances in his side mirror before changing lanes.

I glare at him even though he doesn't see me. "Not even a hint?"

"Nope."

A few minutes later, Eli turns into the wide driveway of Hall Studios and stops the car in front of a guard house with a boom barrier that leads into the gated property. The guard gives him two passes after verifying his identity, and he parks in a parking space marked for guests.

I jump out of the car the moment he puts it in park. "This is where they film *Creatures of Slaughter Creek*, isn't it?" I can't stop my wide smile.

He laughs. "Yeah, but that's not why we're here."

My smile falters, but I catch myself. "Then why?"

"I have a promise to fulfill."

I try to recall any promises Eli's made but only one comes to mind, which is never to let fans get between us when we're out on dates. The paparazzi have also been added to that list since the after party. Other than that, I have no idea what kind of promise would have him bringing me to the studio he'll be filming at starting next week.

Eli doesn't let go of my hand, and we follow a cement path through a street where both cars and golf carts occasionally pass. Within each giant warehouse-like building lies what brings a lot of TV shows and movies to life. Several white trailers sit scattered throughout the property, and I wonder how many famous people rest or hang out in them while not on set.

We pass a twenty-story building with the Hall Studios logo at the top of it, and Eli informs me that's where a lot of the business side of things occurs. I've never put much thought into how things happened before I moved here, but now that I've gotten a small taste of it, I have a deep respect for the effort, time, and how many people it actually takes to produce some of my favorite shows. The actors are only a small part of it.

The deeper we get into the studio lot, the bigger it feels. It takes up at least a few blocks, and they have actual outdoor sets with stoplights, paved roads, houses, a few fake stores, and even a fake school, which I recognize from *Creatures of Slaughter Creek.*

I slide my phone from my pocket. "Please, please, please tell me I can take a picture."

Eli snatches my phone from me and holds it up. "Smile."

I bet I look absolutely ridiculous with how big my grin is, but this is so cool. I'm embarrassed by how excited something as little as a set makes me.

I take my phone from him. "Now, one of us."

I hold the phone out and squish my cheek against his, trying my best to get as much of the background as possible even though it cuts off our chins. Eli turns his head to face me and surprises me by grasping my chin so he can kiss me. I shift in his arms, sliding my hands around his neck while still holding my phone, and I kiss him harder. He squeezes my sides and presses into me. If we weren't in the middle of a fake street with the possibility of people showing up at any moment, I'd push him toward the green bench in front of the fake bus stop.

Apparently he has the same thought I do, except instead of refraining, he does move us toward the bench without ever letting go of me.

He tugs me down, and I swing my legs over his, half sitting in his lap, and I let his lips trail down my jaw to my neck.

It's then that I see someone I recognize staring at us.

I jerk away and cover my face with one of my hands, hiding the blush reddening my face. "Hugo's watching us."

Eli scrunches his brows before peering in the direction I'm looking at. He laughs like it's nothing to be mortified over and tugs me to my feet, nearly dragging me in the direction of his soon-to-be co-star.

Eli offers out his hand. "Hey, man. Thanks for hooking me up today. I wanted to show Nora before things start to go crazy, you know?"

Hugo smiles at me before turning back to Eli. "You're welcome. It's not a problem. We have to hurry, though. I have to be back on set in an hour."

"Yeah, okay. We're ready." Eli bumps my shoulder while smiling at me. "Right?"

I grin. "Totally."

Hugo laughs and starts strolling, motioning us to follow him. He waves at a few people who jog toward one of the buildings. One of the girls looks familiar, but I can't place her. I'm too nervous to ask. I don't want to seem like a crazy fan even though I'm dying to ask Hugo to take a picture with me to send to Taylor. She's going to lose her mind when she hears about this.

"So, Nora. Ever been on a set before?" Hugo asks, making

small talk.

I peer around, trying to keep my excited voice at bay. It tends to be ten times more high pitched and would probably cause him to wince.

"No, this is my first time. Unless you count being on a low budget makeover show, which I didn't even realize was happening until the stupid host cornered me to talk about Eli," I say.

"Chrissy York, right?" Hugo points toward the blue metal door of a warehouse marked with a giant three on the side.

My mouth falls open before I catch myself gaping. "How'd you know?"

"That woman is brutal. Try being cornered on a red carpet."

I laugh. "No thanks."

Hugo chuckles, swiping a keycard, and opens the door. Cool air wraps around us as we enter a hallway lined with doors. He leads the way, taking us farther into the building, and the hallway curves to lead us down another corridor.

"What's behind all the doors?" I ask, trying to read the labels, but I'm nearly running to keep pace with both Eli and Hugo and their long legs.

"Some offices, dressing rooms, wardrobes—you name it. We're going to the sets, though. Come on. Almost there."

When we reach another hallway that runs perpendicular to the one we're in, Hugo cuts right, and I notice a few of the doors have glowing signs that say *Filming in Progress* above them. I wonder what exactly is being filmed, and I've never been so tempted to peek into a door before.

"This is so amazing," I say to cut the silence between us. Eli has barely said two words since we've entered the building, and I wonder if he's letting it all sink in—that soon enough, he'll be here to work for who knows how long.

"I still can't believe I've been fortunate enough to get such an awesome job. Eli mentioned you're a fan of the show." Hugo stops in front of a door where the sign isn't lit.

I nod. "I'm kind of embarrassed by how big a fan I am. My best friend is going to die when I tell her."

Hugo nudges my shoulder in a playful way. "Hey, don't be embarrassed. I love my fans." If Taylor were here, I'd fan myself because Hugo freaking Gutierrez loves me—well, loves me as a fan.

I clench my teeth to keep from squealing. Eli watches me, smirking, and I suck in a slow breath before I start to nervously laugh again like at the fashion show. This time I don't have Alexandra to help take some of the attention away, and I'll just look crazy.

Eli slides his hand around my waist and into my jeans pocket to retrieve my phone. "Why don't I take a picture of you two so you can send it to Taylor?"

Hugo takes my hand, pulling me closer before draping his arm over my shoulder. "Sure. You can send me a copy, too, since you'll be famous because of Chrissy York."

My cheeks heat at his joke. "Oh, God. Don't remind me."

We smile for the picture, and I nearly melt to the ground

when he hugs me. I sneak a look at Eli, but his smile never falters, and I'm glad because if I were him, I might be a tad jealous. Hugo is just my celebrity crush, though. It's his fictional character that I love to watch. Eli, on the other hand, is my real-life crush, and that's ten times better.

Hugo's phone rings from his pocket, and he pulls it out and reads a text message. He turns to us. "Looks like things have been moved up. I have to go." He turns to Eli. "Go on in and stay as long as you like."

Eli and Hugo do a half hug thing. "Thanks. I'll call you in a few days so we can meet up to run lines before rehearsal."

Hugo nods. "Yeah, cool." He turns to me and hugs me once more. "Glad you two could stop by. Eli should bring you on set when he starts filming."

"I had planned on it," Eli says.

Hugo says goodbye and leaves us standing in the quiet corridor. Eli wraps his arms around me, pressing his chin into the nape of my neck. His warm breath tickles me, and I resist kissing him again.

"You're cute when you're flustered, you know," he says, meeting my eyes.

I wish my face would quit blushing already. People are going to start thinking I'm sunburned all the time.

I giggle nervously. "I'm so embarrassed. I don't know what came over me. I'm afraid I'll be a mess when I watch your episodes. Can you handle your girlfriend being your biggest fan? I can't promise I won't turn crazy."

His laugh echoes through the hallway. "I'll love every single second of it."

Eli breaks our embrace and places his hand on the door that I assume leads to one of the sets that Hugo mentioned. He raises his hand to cover my eyes and opens the door, but his fingers don't block my view completely.

I pull away from his hand and stare in front of me. "What is this?"

"I told you I'd figure it out."

I gawk at the enormous set in front of us that mimics what it'd look like if I were to step on the moon. Fake gray and white rocks create the moon landscape, and I step onto the set and feel how squishy the ground is under my feet, like someone lined it with rubber. I step down into a crater the size of a kiddie pool and twirl around to look at the green screen behind us where the stars and earth are digitally added.

"You brought me to the moon," I say, waving Eli to step down into the crater with me. "I almost don't believe it."

"I told you I knew people."

I laugh, kissing him, melting deeper into his arms. My lips linger on his as today sinks in. I can't believe all this is real. I almost feel like I'm dreaming, about to wake up at any moment, but then I pinch myself, feel my heart racing, feel the warmth of Eli's arms, the softness of his lips, the solidness of his body pressing against me, and I know this isn't a dream.

I pull away after a long moment. "This is the sweetest and cheesiest thing ever. You seriously amaze me."

He leans over and kisses my forehead. "Good, because I think that about you every second of the day."

"You do?"

He nods. "Always."

chapter 12

Steal the Spotlight

I SPEND THE next few days studying and preparing for my interview with Eva with Eli's help. When Friday rolls around, I spend half the morning feeling sick to my stomach. I force myself to eat the bagel Aunt Jen offers me.

"Stop stressing so much, Nora. Eva is a doll, and she knows this is your first time interviewing in front of a camera." Aunt Jen leans over her steamy cup of coffee.

I inhale a long breath through my nose and shove my notebook into my bag. I drape my plastic-covered dress and blazer over my arm and peek out the window even though I know Eli will knock on my door.

"I wish Ms. Valentine would just let Fae do it," I say. "It's basically put a strain on our friendship. Totally not worth it to me." I check the time on my cell phone. Eli should be here any second.

Aunt Jen taps her fingers on the counter. "I know you didn't ask for my advice, but I'm going to give it to you anyway. If Fae can't step back and be happy for you, then you shouldn't waste your time with her. Would Taylor quit talking to you over something like this? What about Alexandra? This is a great opportunity for you, Nora, and I'm sure Fae will get her own."

I hate admitting how right she is. I've always loved writing and journalism, two fields with almost impossible competition, and if I ever want to do anything with either after high school, I need to take advantage of what has been given to me.

Aunt Jen shouldn't have to look out for me forever, and it's not like I have my parents to fall back on if I fail at life. *You're not going to fail, Nora. You're going to do great things.* I push away the words my mom used to say to me. It's been so long since I've thought about her. It's better that I don't. Not today.

A knock sounds on our front door, and I swing it open without looking through the peephole. I block Jasper from running out to jump all over Eli's legs and wave at Aunt Jen, who will meet me at my school later with Eva and her team.

I shut the door and turn to Eli. "Any chance I can convince you to go over my interview with me a million times today?"

He laughs, strolling next to me on the way to his Range Rover. "Like we did yesterday and the day before yesterday?"

I crinkle my nose. "I'm afraid I'll mess things up."

He opens the door for me. "Over-thinking it might mess it

up. You know all your questions. You've practiced a dozen times in front of a camera. Come on, you're not a stranger to celebrities."

"It's different. This is serious business, Eli."

He rests his hands on the door frame above my head. "It's our high school news show, and it's only on the public access channel, not prime time."

I glare at him. "Sure feels like prime time. I don't know how you do it."

He doesn't answer me right away. Instead, he walks around the car and climbs behind the wheel. "It's because I like what I do," he finally says. "Hey, and you never know. You might like it, too."

"Doubt it." I slide on a pair of sunglasses when he turns the car around and we head toward the morning sun.

"I guess we'll just have to wait and see."

I kiss Eli in the hall outside of TV Production and make my way inside to find Fae and Anthony quietly chatting at their desks. Anthony greets me with his usual goofy, friendly smile, and I plop in the seat next to him.

Fae glances at me before her gaze darts toward the blank page of her opened notebook. I wonder if she'll hold a grudge against me forever or if her attitude will change once everything is over. It's hard to tell with her. One moment she's nice and then the next, not so much.

Ted Rowland, this week's director of our news broadcast,

strolls up to me. He clutches a clipboard against his chest and clears his throat before saying, "I'd like you to rehearse your interview on camera so we can watch it and make the adjustments we need."

My mouth dries. I already hate the idea enough as it is, but I was semi-okay, knowing that I wouldn't be surrounded by my peers while I interviewed Eva. The fact that I have to pretend like I am, while being filmed and critiqued, sends my stomach rolling. My hands tremble in my lap, and I suck in my top lip, trying to think of an excuse.

I come up with nothing. "Oh, okay." My voice cracks, causing Ted to raise an eyebrow. His skepticism in my ability doesn't help with my nerves.

Fae reaches out and touches my knee. "I'll pretend to be Eva if that helps, Nora."

I nod. "Yeah, th-that'll be great." I swallow, trying to moisten my tongue so I don't stammer on camera for everyone to laugh at later.

"Great! Give us ten." Ted waltzes away to gather the camera crew, and a few of the set designers arrange the broadcast area to mimic what you'd see on one of those fancy interview shows. A black backdrop, two director's chairs, a fake potted tree behind where I'll be sitting, and a round table with Eva's fragrances and skincare products completes the makeshift set.

Fae pulls a compact mirror from her bag and applies a layer of matte brown lipstick and blows herself a kiss. I follow her lead and use my cell phone's camera to check myself out. I look like ordinary old Nora. As long as nothing gross is on my face and my hair isn't a mess, I'm good for now. Alexandra volunteered to do my makeup later in the day before the actual interview.

I crack my knuckles and peer over my interview notes once more. I have the questions memorized, so I leave the papers on my chair and meander after Fae when she stands and crosses the room.

Sitting across from Fae, I cross my legs at my ankles. I meet her caramel eyes, and she smiles before tossing her shiny black hair over her shoulder. Fae rarely wears a lot of makeup, not like she needs it either, but today she's camera ready. I wonder if she's secretly hoping something happens to me so I can't do the interview. *Stop being paranoid.*

Ted clears his throat. I'm starting to wonder if he's getting sick with how many times I've heard him clear it in the last ten minutes. "Nora, is that how you plan on interviewing Ms. Devereaux?"

I twist my lips to the side and shift my gaze to look at my pants. With the way Ted's looking at me, I thought my fly was down or something.

"No, I have an outfit to change into later," I say.

He shakes his head. "That's not what I meant. You look like you're going to fall out of your chair with the way you're slouching."

Heat slithers up my neck and into my cheeks. I scoot farther back in the chair and straighten my shoulders, mirroring

Fae's perfect position. She smirks at me, and I'm tempted to snap at her to knock it off and stop hoping I fail.

I bite my tongue and say, "Sorry," to Ted instead. I'll mention something to Fae when all eyes aren't on us.

Ted taps his pen on his clipboard. "No problem. You ready?"

I nod. "Whenever you are."

He gives me a thumbs up and without warning, says, "This is rehearsal take one for the Eva Devereaux interview with Nora Novak in three, two, one. Action."

My heart races, and deafening silence fills the room. I force myself to smile and lift my gaze to the camera. "Hello, I'm Nora Novak, and today I'm here with supermodel Eva Devereaux to discuss her new fragrance line, Catwalk Paradise. Welcome, Eva. Thank you so much for being here."

Fae grins at the camera, her eyes crinkling in the corners. "Thank you so much for having me."

I miss a beat, forgetting everything I've prepared, and I clutch the armrests. *Think. Think. Think.*

"It's not every day you get this kind of opportunity. I'm just so happy you've enjoyed my fragrance enough to invite me to be a guest for your school's news show," Fae says. She keeps in character, but her words jab at me in such a way that my nerves melt into anger.

I clench my teeth and smile. "Of course. You're a true inspiration and a selfless person. I couldn't think of anyone else I'd rather interview today."

Fae fakes a smile, and we continue the interview as if tension isn't brimming between us. When Ted finally calls cut after I manage not to mess up anything else, Fae flies from her seat and out the classroom door. I race after her, anger making me clench my fingers into fists, and I push the door open with enough force that it hits the wall.

I grab Fae's shoulder. "What's wrong with you? You know I didn't purposely steal your spotlight. I told Ms. Valentine I didn't want to do the interview. Be mad at her, not me."

Tears spring from Fae's eyes. "Oh, come on, Nora. You're enjoying every minute of this!"

I frown. "What? I don't even know what you're talking about."

"You've made it your mission to take away everything I've worked so hard for. Did Elijah put you up to this? He always told me he'd get me back." Fae covers her face with her hands.

I step back, afraid she'll lash out at me. "Why would I want to hurt you? You're my friend. And why would Eli?" I'm more surprised that she thinks Eli is somehow involved in a situation purely in the hands of our TV Production teacher.

"Don't act stupid, Nora. I know you know."

I throw my hands up. "Know what?"

"About me and Elijah." She says it like it's obvious. Like I can read her mind.

"I don't know anything."

She glowers at me through wet eyelashes. "Whatever. I know you're lying."

I suck in a breath. "Why would I? Fae, you have to believe me. This is all in your head. You're my friend. Eli and I don't talk about the past. I didn't even know you had history like that."

She shakes her head. "Just forget it, okay? Good luck with the interview."

With those final words, Fae spins on her heels and dashes down the corridor, leaving all her belongings behind. I stand in the empty hall, holding myself, wondering what the hell just happened and if our friendship will ever recover from this, or if I even want it to.

I pull myself together and head back into the class, smiling at Anthony like nothing happened in the hallway. I pack up my stuff and leave the room. As much as I want to meet Eli outside his class to ask him what happened between him and Fae, I don't. I head to my next class and wait outside to avoid him, and then I hide in the nurse's office for our one class together. I can't afford any more drama today. I've had enough in my life to last me forever.

"A lot of people missed you at lunch," Alexandra says as she finishes applying my makeup. She's been excitedly chatting about Eva since she met me outside TV Production, so she hasn't really said much else.

I rub my sweaty palms on my dark gray dress. "I was rehearsing."

"Eli came looking for you."

I press my lips together. "I know. I was avoiding him...and Fae."

Alexandra sets her makeup brush down. "Okay, you need to spill. Fae wasn't at lunch either. Cherry said she went home sick."

I raise an eyebrow. "Not sick. Crazy. She lost her mind this morning over the interview. Accused me of trying to ruin her life and then swore I was conspiring with Eli against her."

Alexandra makes an O-shape with her lips. "Again? She did that to me too, after the two of them broke up."

"They were together?" I don't know why it surprises me but it does. They seem like they have nothing in common. Eli never mentioned it. Of course, I never asked, but still. I wouldn't have begged him to eat lunch with us ever. Knowing they have a past like that explains a lot. I wouldn't exactly want to hang around with Cesar Flores from back in Austin, and we were only together for like two weeks.

Alexandra snaps her lips shut. "You know what? Why don't we talk about something else? Eva should be here any minute, and you're going to rock this."

I blow air through my lips. "You better tell me everything later."

Her lips tilt downward. "Only after you talk to my cousin first, okay? I don't want to get in the middle. You're one of my best friends, Nora, and he's my family. You understand, right?"

Her words make me smile instead of frown because she pulled the best friend card. "Yeah, totally."

A knock sounds on the door, and Aunt Jen peeks her head in. "Mind if we come in?"

I hop to my feet and rush across the room with Alexandra on my heels. Ms. Valentine rises from her desk, and Ted and the productions team also get to their feet.

Aunt Jen struts in with Eva Devereaux at her side, while a man in a dress shirt waits in the hallway. I beam my brightest smile. Eva looks exactly like her picture—wavy, strawberry blond hair, blue-gray eyes, full lips, expressive eyebrows, and gorgeous.

"Welcome to Beverly Hills High, Ms. Devereaux," Ms. Valentine says, offering her hand like she shakes supermodel's hands every day.

Eva's eyes light up as she smiles. "Thank you for having me. My publicist thought it was such a cute idea to build hype among my younger fans. I'll be having a meet-and-greet at The Grove on launch day, so what better way than to get everyone as excited as me."

"We're all ecstatic, right, Nora?" Ms. Valentine asks.

I bob my head. "And Catwalk Paradise is so amazing. Thanks for sending me a bottle."

Eva slides her arm over my shoulders. "You bet."

When everyone settles, Eva takes her place across from me in front of the camera, and we go over the questions. She asks to change a few things to include her launch party and meet-and-greet.

My nerves calm as we talk, and when Ted calls action, it's

like Eva and I are two friends just hanging out.

"Can you tell me about the inspiration for Catwalk Paradise?" I ask after covering a few basic questions.

Eva cradles the beautiful blue and turquoise ombre glass bottle in her hands. "I wanted to capture the energy and bliss I feel strutting the runway. I've always dreamed about being a model and wearing the best clothes designers had to offer, and this scent perfectly embodies my life."

I smile at the dreaminess that crosses Eva's face. "And now everyone can channel their inner Eva Devereaux."

Eva laughs. "I love that!"

We finish the interview on the first take, and when the cameras shut off, I release a relieved breath. I half expected Fae to rush in at any moment to ruin everything, but everything runs as smoothly as I'd hoped.

When Eva stands, she reaches for her bag and pulls out an envelope. She hands it to me, and I open it to see a dozen or so VIP guest tickets to her meet-and-greet.

She kisses both my cheeks. "For your class and a few extra for any of your friends."

I beam a smile. "Thanks so much."

"Walk me out?"

Ms. Valentine and the rest of the production crew say their goodbyes, and Alexandra and Aunt Jen follow Eva and me out of the classroom with her security personnel greeting us with a stern face.

Eli stands nearby, waiting for me, and I kiss him on the

cheek. "Hey, walk with us?"

He nods without saying anything.

Eva offers him a small wave before turning to me. "Your aunt mentioned you were seeing Elijah Rousseau." She shifts her gaze to Eli. "You're a lucky guy."

He grins. "Don't I know it."

They chat like old friends, and Eva invites us to her launch party that'll take place after the meet-and-greet. Aunt Jen agrees since she'll be attending as well, and I can't help but think about how lucky I am to be walking these hallways with the coolest people in the universe.

Eli opens the exit door for us, and I step outside with him and freeze. Cameras flash through the darkening evening as paparazzi wait for Eva to appear. Word must've gotten out that she was here, but instead of the paparazzi snapping pictures of the supermodel who remains inside behind us, they focus on Eli and me.

I cover my face with my hands, and Eli pulls me back into the building. Alexandra rushes to the nearest classroom, probably to call security, and I turn and stare at my aunt and Eva with wide eyes.

"You okay, Nora?" Aunt Jen asks, glancing from my head to my toes like somehow the camera flashes managed to injure me.

I swallow and shake my head. "Yeah, I'm just surprised."

Ms. Valentine's heels snap against the shiny floor as she runs in our direction. "I'm so sorry, Ms. Devereaux. Security will be here shortly to escort you out the back."

Eva nods. "Don't fret. I'm used to the attention."

Ms Valentine nods. "We'll find out who leaked your appearance, and they'll be punished accordingly."

A pit forms in my stomach. I meet Fae's shining eyes as she leans against the wall just down the hall. She doesn't even have to say anything for me to know it was her and why she did it. It wasn't to draw attention to Eva. It was to draw attention to me and Eli. So far, we've managed to avoid the press, but not now. They have the perfect picture of me and Eli and just in time for his role on *Creatures of Slaughter Creek*.

I can feel it deep in my bones that things are about to change, and I'm not sure for the better.

chapter 13

Everyone's Someone

I REFUSED TO leave the house all weekend, and Aunt Jen didn't complain when I insisted I was sick come Monday morning.

"Why would Fae do this to me?" I ask Aunt Jen, who sits across from me on the couch.

Aunt Jen straightens her shoulders, her face turning serious. I know that expression anywhere. She's about to go into lawyer mode. "I think you should go to the school with your thoughts so they can investigate the situation. As of now, nothing will be printed or uploaded online. Those paps were trespassing at your school, and you and Eli are protected under privacy laws. They'd be asking for a lawsuit."

I blow my hair from my face. "At least that's something. If I go to the school, Fae will really think I'm ruining her life. I just hope this blows over."

Aunt Jen shifts on the couch, folding her legs under her. "I'm sure it will with Fae, but I want to talk to you about the other stuff. About Eli."

I turn to stare out the window. "Is it so wrong to want to avoid the spotlight?"

"No, but you have to take things into perspective. Eli's career is about to launch to levels most people only dream of at his age. You'll be in his spotlight by default. If that's something you're not okay with, then maybe you should slow down with Eli. Maybe take a break until you're ready for that kind of attention."

Just the thought of taking a break sends tears to my eyes. "Aunt Jen, I really, really like him. I don't want to change our relationship. I'm just scared."

She moves closer and covers my hand with hers. "Of what? You're one of the bravest people I know. Look at all that you've been through."

I rake my teeth over my bottom lip. "That's exactly what I'm afraid of. No one knows about my past—not even Eli."

Her brows crinkle together. "He doesn't know that your parents died?"

I shake my head. "It never felt like the right time to tell him, and I don't want to be the girl everyone pities."

"Oh, Nora. I understand your hesitation, but if you like Eli like you say, he deserves to know. He's not going to think any differently of you. If he does, then you don't need him." She squeezes my hand. "There is nothing to be ashamed of. You're a victim of bad circumstance, but you shouldn't let it define who you are."

I sigh. "You're right. I'll tell him." I stand up to head to my room. "Thanks, Aunt Jen."

She reaches out to grab my hand. "Wait. I'm not done. I want to talk about the seriousness of your relationship with Eli, too."

I squeeze my eyes shut, knowing exactly where this is heading. "Don't worry. We're not at that level yet. I'll be safe if we ever are. Promise."

She puffs air through her lips. "Thank God. I don't want to fail at this guardian stuff."

I laugh. "I couldn't have asked for anyone better."

The next two weeks at school fly by like nothing ever happened between Fae and me. We pretend she didn't have a nervous breakdown, and I pretend I don't suspect that she was the one who notified the paparazzi. It's almost ridiculous how fake we're being with each other, but I'm worried she'll turn the school against me, and I already have a limited number of friends as it is.

The final bell rings, and Eli meets me in the hallway outside my last class. I've been so worked up over finding the nerve to let him into my past that I haven't asked him about his previous relationship with Fae or anything else apart from his new role on *Creatures of Slaughter Creek,* which he hasn't really been able to tell me about but promises he will soon.

"I just got a call that filming has been pushed until tomorrow. Want to come over for dinner? My mom's been asking about you." He laces his fingers through mine.

I smile. "Sure. I'd love to."

Now that he'll be spending a few afternoons and evenings a week on set for the next few weeks, I have to take advantage of our time. I've taken his absence to throw myself back into my part-time job with Aunt Jen, where I spend most of my time doing homework between faxing, filing, and making copies. It's better than staying in my room alone when Alexandra can't hang out.

We head to his Range Rover, and I try to find the words I've been planning to tell him every day that always find a reason to stay locked in my heart.

I tap my fingers on my knee. "Can we stop by that little bakery near my house first?" Those aren't the words I expect to come out, but I swear, by the end of the night, Eli will know about my past.

He nods, turning onto Wilshire Boulevard to head toward Dayton Way. It's out of the way to his house, but it'll only take us a few extra minutes. Plus, I love their pastries and want to surprise Liza with something.

Street parking is non-existent when we arrive, so Eli parks in the Rite Aid underground parking, which will be easy enough to validate.

A few minutes later, we head toward the bakery, hand-in-hand, having to stroll to the end of the block to use the crosswalk. A small crowd gathers outside an Italian restaurant at the end of the block, and my heart sinks into my stomach. It's not an ordinary crowd but a few tourists with cameras, posing for some pictures with Hadley Tyler, a popular reality TV star on the show *Hadley's Hollywood*. Taylor would be so jealous. She loves that show.

"Wanna turn around?" Eli asks, wiggling his fingers in my death grip that cuts off circulation to his hand.

I shake my head, remembering Aunt Jen's pep-talk about learning to deal with this sort of thing if I want Eli to remain in my life. Plus, these people are here for Hadley, and I doubt they'll even know or recognize Eli next to a woman whose personality shines brighter than the sun.

We stay on the outside of the sidewalk, and Eli pops on his sunglasses that hang on the front of his shirt. I wish I had a pair with me, but I left them in the car on his dashboard. He pulls me closer, sliding his hand around my waist, clutching my side. I half bury my face in his chest.

No one notices us walk by, and when we pass the crowd, I release a breath.

"Isn't that Elijah Rousseau? Who's he with?" The voice comes from a girl sitting at a patio table.

Eli turns to look at the girl and offers her a quick wave. He told me he doesn't want to be one of the celebrities people are disappointed to meet when they get blown off.

"It is!" The girl next to her squeals, and they abandon an

older couple, probably their parents, at the table. "Elijah, can we please have a picture?"

Their voices rise through the air, and it's enough to draw the attention of the people surrounding Hadley, and a man with a professional camera snaps a picture of us before we have a chance to turn around.

Eli leans into me. "I don't want to make a scene, so go ahead to the bakery, and I'll meet you back at my car."

I nod. I don't mind him staying behind one bit as long as I can get out of here and not have any attention drawn to me. He kisses my cheek, and I glide away from him and don't look back, making my way to the bakery.

I take a breath, trying to calm my nerves. The lady behind the counter offers me a free French macaron because she claims that I look like I need one. I order a mixed sample basket with miniature cupcakes, cookies, and cheesecakes, and then push out the door.

I hear the snap of the camera before I see the man, the one with the professional equipment, standing next to the fake, white painted tree in the alcove of the bakery.

"Hey, sweetheart, you dating Elijah Rousseau?" the man asks.

My heart pounds in my ears, and I clutch the white paper bag to my chest without answering him.

He rushes ahead of me and then walks backwards so he's facing me, aiming his camera in my face. "Don't be shy. I heard he had a mystery girlfriend. What's your name?"

I keep my eyes trained on the ground. "Please, just leave me alone. You might miss an opportunity of getting a great shot of Hadley. I'm no one."

He laughs. "Everyone's someone with a good enough headline." He snaps another photo, and I glower at him.

A good enough headline? Is he for real? If he doesn't leave soon, my headline's going to read, *Mystery Girl Throws Bag of Pastries in Man's Face.*

I ignore him, covering my face. He takes another photo. I don't know how celebrities do it. Taylor and I used to love looking at pictures of celebrities doing ordinary things, like leaving the gym or pumping gas, but now I feel bad about it. This sucks.

A horn blares as Eli stops in the middle of the street, ignoring the honks echoing from behind him. "Come on, Nora!"

I dash toward the Range Rover without a second glance at the man with the camera, who captures every second of my departure. Eli hits the gas and rolls through the empty intersection, ignoring the stop sign.

I lean back in the seat, clutching my bag of desserts to my chest. I let out a breath. "You gave him my name."

Eli curses. "I'm sorry. I wasn't thinking."

I slouch in my seat. "I guess it was bound to happen at some point."

He reaches over and clasps my hand. "It shouldn't have gotten out from me, though. I'm sure it'll go public by tomorrow."

I bring his hand to my lips and kiss his knuckles. "Maybe we should make it less of a story."

His eyes sparkle. "Are you sure you're ready for that?"

"Better us than them."

"This is why I love you, you know." He smirks after he says the words, nearly melting me into a puddle on the floor.

"You do?"

He rubs his thumb under his chin, keeping his eyes on the road. "Yeah."

"Thanks." I blink, embarrassment washing over me. I can't believe I just thanked him when he admitted he loved me. Surprise left me feeling a little lost and stupid, and I'm pretty sure I ruined the moment.

He laughs, his smile never leaving his face. "You're welcome."

I rub my hands over my face, my shoulders shaking with nervous giggles. "I'm sorry, Eli. You really took me by surprise."

He watches me in his peripheral vision. "Don't be sorry, Nora. I love you, and you don't have to say it back. I just wanted you to know."

I nod without saying anything else.

I touch up my makeup in Eli's bathroom mirror and prepare to unveil myself to the world. All he's going to do is post a photo of us across all his fan pages with a short caption, and that'll be all for now. We both agreed not to read the comments either, but I'm sure Taylor will do that for me and give me an idea of everyone's reaction. I'm not into that kind of self torture. I've read plenty of the horrifying comments strangers leave for celebrities as if they aren't real people.

A tap sounds on the half-opened door, and I turn, expecting to see Eli. His mom hovers in the doorway instead. She greets me with a warm smile and leans on the doorframe.

"Eli was right about how beautiful you are," she says.

My cheeks tint with my oncoming blush. "Thanks, Liza."

"And you're polite."

I laugh. "My mom always told me to accept a compliment graciously."

"She sounds like a lovely woman."

I press my lips together, forcing my tears to stay away. "Yeah." I almost add on that my mom was lovely, in past-tense, but I don't. Eli should hear it from me first. I swear I'm going to tell him tonight. I have to.

I stroll toward Liza, and she moves out of the way so I can exit the bathroom. She touches my arm, and I stop in my tracks.

"Eli told me what you two are planning to do. You know you don't have to do it. We have a few friends who manage to keep their families out of the spotlight, not to mention our own family, and you shouldn't feel obligated to announce it to the world because the press might." Her sincerity wraps around me, and I almost reconsider.

I nod my head. "I know. It's just I'm tired of hiding. The press has less news to try to get if we share it ourselves."

"Okay, I understand. I just wanted you to know that there are always options, Nora."

She hugs me, and I let her, smelling the scent of her powdery floral perfume that reminds me of something my mom would've worn.

Eli knocks on the wall with his phone, drawing my attention away from Liza. "Ready?"

Liza pats her son's shoulder and leaves us without another word.

I pucker my lips to him. "Do I look okay?"

"More than okay, Nora." Eli strolls to me, wrapping his arms around my neck and kisses me softly on the lips. He slides his hands over my shoulders and down my back, pulling me into him until our hearts beat against each other's through the fabric of our shirts. He pulls away after a long moment. "God, you look hot."

I smile. "Save some of that for later."

"Always."

Eli guides me to his room, and he plops down onto his bed, waving me to come forward to sit next to him.

I place my hands on my hips. "Our first public picture is not going to be us on your bed."

His laughter echoes through the room. "Yeah, I guess you're right. Let's stand by the window."

I step in front of the window, allowing the sun to halo us in golden light. Eli holds out his phone and snaps a few pictures of us smiling, and then one of him kissing my cheek. The sun adds just enough mystery that if someone sees the picture, they probably wouldn't pick me out in a crowd, but it's enough that the paparazzi won't have a good headline come tomorrow.

I flip through the pictures. "Your choice."

He smirks, turning the phone away so I can't see, and a moment later, he says, "It's done. You're officially my girlfriend to the public."

"Goodbye, mystery girl," I say, hugging my arms over my chest, praying that this was the best thing to do.

Eli hugs me. "It'll be fine."

"I hope so."

"It will. I promise."

chapter 14

Can't Run from the Past

MY PHONE RINGS in the quiet of my bedroom. It's not even dawn yet, but I know who it is before I glance at Taylor's smiling face from my contacts. I accept her video call and grin into the phone with half-closed eyes.

"Oh, my God, Nora! Eli posted a picture of the two of you, and it's trending everywhere." Sun shines behind her as she sits on her bed, probably getting ready to go to school.

I yawn. "Did you forget you're two hours ahead of me? It's still dark."

"I couldn't wait! People are dying to know who you are. Like, if you created a public page, thousands of people would follow you. You're living every girl's dream. Lots of speculation about how you two met and if you're an up-and-coming star." Her words pour from her mouth so fast that I almost don't understand her.

I sigh and flop back on my pillow, holding the phone above me. "Let them think what they want. All I wanted was to beat the paparazzi to it."

She shakes her phone like it'll somehow shake me. "Don't you get it, Nora? You're famous now, which makes me famous by association. We need to discuss how I'm going to handle all the questions. People will know we're friends in no time."

I laugh. "Relax, Tay. You're over-thinking things. If someone reaches out to you, which I doubt they will, just tell them good things, okay? I know you couldn't handle not commenting at all."

She whistles through her teeth. "What about the Step-Monster?"

My blood cools, and shadows edge my vision. I haven't thought about Cecilia much at all since I stepped on the plane to come here. I haven't heard from her either. She's the type of person to milk something like this. God, I wish there was a way to make sure she never finds out, but she's a celebrity gossip junkie. Worse than anyone I know. Even Taylor.

I grimace. "Thanks for reminding me. I have to go. I need to call Eli."

"Call me later, okay?"

I blow her a kiss and disconnect. I was so wrapped up in everything last night that I made yet another excuse not to tell Eli about my past. But I'm going to stop procrastinating. I'll tell him now, even if it has to be over the phone at four-thirty in the morning.

I shoot him a text before calling.

Me: You awake? I need to tell you something.

Eli: Been awake for an hour. My publicist isn't happy.

Me: Why?

Eli: The photo.

Me: Oh.

Eli: Yeah.

I stare at my phone, trying to decide if now's the right time after all. *There will never be a right time for this...*

My phone buzzes in my hand.

Eli: Can I come over?

My heart races.

Me: Yeah. I'll make breakfast.

I turn the heat on low for the scrambled eggs and potatoes and pull the bacon from the oven. Eli knocks on the door a moment later, and I pad across the living room to answer it.

His eyes trail from my bare feet to take in my shorts and tank top, and then he stops at my lips. He sucks in his top lip, his eyes flickering with the same intensity he gives me when we're kissing, and he steps inside.

I wave my wooden spoon at him. "I'm making breakfast tacos."

He raises an eyebrow. "You know breakfast burritos are the thing here, right?"

I laugh. Breakfast tacos are a breakfast staple at most restaurants in Austin. "I'll roll yours then."

He follows me into the kitchen and rests his fingers on my hips, standing behind me, looking at the stove from over my shoulder. I hand him a square, blue plate from the cabinet and he helps himself.

"Want to eat in my room? Aunt Jen won't be up for at least another hour." I grab my own plate and motion him to the hallway.

It's in this moment that I realize he's never been in my room before. He peers around, taking in my plain bedding, neat desk, and messy, half-opened closet. I perch on the end of my bed, resting the plate on my knees, and he takes a seat at my desk.

"So, Taylor woke me up this morning. She's probably read every single comment left on the picture you posted." When Eli doesn't say anything, I take a bite of my taco. He'd usually make a joke or something, but instead, he just stares at his food. "She said people ate it up and they want to know more."

He scratches his stubbly chin. "I know."

"I thought you weren't going to read the reactions," I say, suddenly feeling a little uncomfortable.

He meets my gaze. "I didn't. I'm talking about my agent. He said I nearly gave Tatiana a heart attack."

"Who?"

"My publicist."

I frown. "Oh."

"Yeah. They want to meet you, learn more about you and

your family—figure out a strategy for the public." He finally takes a bite of his taco, and I'm wondering if it's so he doesn't have to see the confusion on my face.

"Why can't you just tell them?"

He sets his plate down. "Because as it turns out, I don't know anything. Why didn't you tell me?"

My heart slides into my stomach. I know exactly what he's referring to without him having to pry out the details. I was a day too late. I should've forced myself to tell him last night. I'm such an idiot.

"All it took was a quick search of your name, and my team knew more about you than I do," he continues.

"Why didn't you do that then?" I start building a wall around me, piece by piece, using the broken remnants of my past to do so. But I'm right. He could've popped my name into a search engine. Both of my parents' obituaries come up on the first page besides a few articles I wrote for my school paper back in Austin.

He smacks the palms of his hands on the desk, startling me. "Because you should've told me."

Tears burst from my eyes. "I couldn't! I can't even stand to think about them. I didn't want your pity, Eli. I just wanted to forget. It's not like you've exactly been honest with me, either."

He runs his fingers through his hair. "What are you talking about?"

I take a deep breath. "Fae. I'm talking about Fae and whatever the hell you did to her to make her hate you so much that she thinks you've convinced me to ruin her life for you."

He throws his hands up. "That's crazy! I haven't done anything to her. She's the one who broke up with me. She couldn't handle that I landed a dream role."

I cross my arms. "You could've told me."

"You didn't want to know about my past."

"She's my friend, Eli! Of course I'd want to know. I wouldn't have tortured you by asking you to sit with us. I'd have been more careful around her. You know she's the one who set up that paparazzi stunt at the school. Because she knew I didn't want to be in the spotlight."

We stare at each other for a long, quiet moment. I don't even know what to say next. This wasn't supposed to turn into us accusing each other of hiding things. This was supposed to be where I told him about my parents' deaths, where he'd hug me and tell me he understood. But it's not. We're both angry and hurt—all because of the team who controls his celebrity reputation. They shouldn't be controlling his life, though.

Angry tears burn red tracks on my cheeks, and I force myself to bring my gaze to meet Eli's. He watches me, his lips tilting downward, and then he rises to his feet, leaving his half-eaten breakfast on my desk.

He shoves his hands into his pockets. "This isn't how I wanted things to go this morning."

I rub my wet cheeks. "I'm sorry I didn't tell you about my parents sooner. I am. But you have to understand why. I didn't leave Austin on good terms with my stepmom. Actually, they were the worst possible terms. My dad left her everything, and she turned into a nightmare and wanted me out because I wasn't her problem anymore. It got so bad that she even hit me. It's why I came to Beverly Hills. To escape her."

Eli's furrowed brows soften, and he surprises me by sitting on the bed next to me. I fully prepared myself for him to run out of the house after breaking up with me. But he doesn't do any of those things.

Instead, he hugs me.

"I feel like such a jerk, Nora. I'm sitting here, letting people freak me out about my reputation, and I didn't for once think about how you might be feeling." He laces his fingers through mine. "I'm sorry for that. I'm also sorry about Fae. I had no idea."

I rest my head on his shoulder. "What's your publicist going to say?"

He shrugs his shoulders. "Who cares? There was a reason I didn't run you by them in the first place. The last time I did that, it turned me into a pariah at school. I don't want to lose you."

I shift on the bed and crawl into his lap, wrapping my legs around his hips. He slides his arms around my lower back and scoots further back onto my bed.

Spinning me around to lie on my bed, he bends forward and kisses me. I sink into him, letting his kiss push away my hurt feelings. His lips brush against my jaw before moving to my neck, where he kisses me all the way to my shoulder. His warm breath sends a shiver through me, and I clutch him tighter, my fingers caressing his lower back. I run my hands up his shirt before pulling it over his head.

I lean back a few inches and take in his sinewy muscles as they twitch and move under my touch. He leans in for another kiss, his hands tugging my tank top over my head before tossing it to the floor. Shifting, he pulls me closer so our bare chests touch, the heat of our skin together sending a wave of desire over me.

His hips press against mine, and he supports his weight on his elbows. I run my fingers up his sides, just wanting to feel the smoothness of his skin, memorize every curve of his muscles, every detail about him.

Another deep kiss leaves me breathless, and he pulls away, searching my face. "You don't even know how badly I want you right now."

I tilt my head up and kiss him again. "I think I do know."

He rolls off me, and I snuggle into his side. As much as I want to take things to the next level with Eli, I'm not sure now is the right time, and he agrees with me. Plus, I promised Aunt Jen I'd be safe, and I wasn't expecting Eli to even be in my room this morning.

He brushes my hair from my face and kisses my cheek. "I should go before your aunt wakes up."

I grab his hand. "Please, stay. I'll get ready real fast, and we can try breakfast again in the dining room."

He grins. "I'd like that."

I take a quick shower and change into a pair of jeans and a floral printed top and head back to my room where I find Eli sleeping on my bed. I don't wake him right away but just watch his chest rise and fall. He couldn't be more perfect in this moment.

My phone buzzes from where I left it on my desk, and I scoop it into my hands and glance at a text message from Taylor.

Taylor: Ding-dong, the witch just called.

My hands shake, and I take a deep breath. I never wanted to hear from that devil woman again.

Me: What did she say?

Taylor: Nothing. I didn't answer.

Me: Good. Don't. Ever.

Taylor: I won't. Just wanted to tell you. At school now. Let's talk later.

Me: Okay.

I drop my phone back on my desk with a bang, and Eli sits up, rubbing his eyes. I turn away from him, hiding tears threatening to escape, and clutch my hands to my chest to stop my whole body from shaking. I don't know why I'd expected anything less from Cecilia. I knew she'd eventually come calling, but I want nothing to do with her.

Comforting arms slide around me, spinning me on my feet. Eli tilts his head. "Everything okay?"

I shake my head. "My stepmom must've seen something about us. Maybe she's one of your fans. I wouldn't put it past her. She just called Taylor."

He crinkles his nose. "I'll take care of this."

I clutch onto his shirt. "No, I don't want you anywhere near her. I'll handle it."

He frowns. "You sure?"

I puff a breath of air through my lips. "I can't run from my past forever."

chapter 15

Make You a Star

A WEEK PASSES, and thankfully, nothing eventful happens. I limit my outings with Eli, keeping to school, home, and his house, and he doesn't complain. He's managed to get his team to back off and things settle as much as they can. For now at least.

Alexandra rushes up to me in the hallway after another long, boring day at Beverly Hills High. She hooks her arm through mine, pulling me along with her until we're out of the crowded hall and in front of the cement steps on the sprawling front lawn.

A few people wave at us, and I smile. More people have been talking to me in my classes, and with the airing of my interview with Eva, I think I've made a pretty good impression for a girl who hasn't grown up in this way of life.

"We need to go shopping. Right now. I looked in my closet last night for a dress to wear to Eva's launch party, and I have nothing. Nothing!" She pulls me along toward the street where her dad usually picks her up since he works on a New York schedule.

I laugh, pulling out my cell phone to text Aunt Jen. She always gives me extra time before showing up since I don't always need a ride to her office. "I doubt it, but I could use something. It's my first official appearance with Eli, you know."

She waves her hands. "Oh, I know. Guess who else is going to be there?"

I don't even have to guess since Eli told me Hugo asked about Alexandra again. "The captain of the football team at Slaughter Creek High?"

She lightly smacks my arm. "Not fair that Elijah told you first."

I grin while I roll my eyes. "Hugo's almost twenty-one, Alexandra. Think of the scandalous headline."

Her smile widens. "Oh, shut up! I turn eighteen in a month and a half. The press can kiss my ass."

"They just might try if they get word of your budding romance."

"Friendship, Nora. Friendship." She tilts her head back, her laughter echoing through the air. "My parents wouldn't ever let me leave the house if they thought my celebrity crush could turn into something. They're forcing me to stay out of the public eye. I'm non-existent like everyone else in our family."

I have a feeling that's not going to last long. Eli's mom told me that they stay out of the limelight, but I don't think Alexandra wants to stay out of it. If things were different, I'd probably still be hiding in the shadows. At least no one seems to care about Eli and me yet. Taylor says the internet is buzzing, but it hasn't spilled into my daily life, thankfully.

Alexandra's dad waves at us through the window, and she flings open the passenger's side door. I climb into the back of his Tesla, and a moment later, he pulls from the curb. I'll never get over how quiet this car is. I didn't even think it was running.

"Take us to Robertson, Dad. Nora has nothing to wear tomorrow, and I promised I'd help her." Alexandra glances at me in her visor mirror with a look that says her dad disagrees that she doesn't have anything for tomorrow.

Oscar, as he insisted I call him, shoots a glance at me as well. "Your aunt is chaperoning, right? I always worry about these events."

I nod even though his eyes focus back on the road. "Yes, sir. Eva Devereaux is my aunt's client, and this launch party event is a big deal. It's invite-only, and Eva said the paparazzi aren't welcome inside except for a few magazines that will be running some features."

He offers a closed lip smile. "Good. You girls don't need that sort of stress in your lives. You have plenty of time for that when you're adults."

I sink lower into the seat because I'm pretty sure he knows

about Eli posting our picture. He doesn't say anything, but his eyes speak a thousand words. If only he knew what the real stress in my life was.

When we reach Robertson Boulevard, Oscar pulls to the curb and puts the car in park. He pulls out his wallet and hands Alexandra a few bills, and I try not to gawk at the amount. Aunt Jen probably wouldn't think twice about giving me a few hundred for a dress for a special occasion, but tomorrow isn't prom or the winter formal, and there's no way I'd ask her.

Alexandra kisses her dad's cheek, and we both hop out. He leaves us in front of a row of boutiques, and Alexandra nearly drools in front of the window display.

She points to a sparkly half-romper, half-dress gown in the window. "Come on. I have to try that one on. I saw Penelope Pleasant wearing something similar at a charity gala."

I follow her into the store, where a woman in a deep purple dress that's perfect for fall with a fun, bright jacket over it greets us. Alexandra explains the occasion, points to both of us, and ten minutes later, we're standing in a private dressing room with wall-to-wall mirrors and the best lighting.

I slip out of my clothes and hold a turquoise mermaid tail gown in front of me. "Can I ask you something?"

Alexandra spins in the romper dress without zipping up the back. "That dress is amazing. This one, not so much on me."

I shake my head. "You're right. Try the ivory one." I slip my own gown halfway up and slide it off a moment later. "Hand me the midnight blue one."

Alexandra holds it against her first before handing it to me. "If you hate it, I want to try it on."

I smirk. "Okay. I hate it."

She passes me the ivory one instead of taking it for herself. "So, what did you want to ask me? I can tell it wasn't about the dress."

I step into the ivory dress and let Alexandra zip me up. I peer at my reflection and how perfect the material hugs my curves, accentuating my cleavage in the low-cut bodice. "I'm worried about tomorrow."

She lowers an eyebrow. "That's not a question."

I sigh. "Do you think I should show up with Eli? I know his team already considers me a thorn in their sides, and I'm wondering if showing up at such a big event together is a good idea."

She taps her finger to her chin. "Why wouldn't it be a good idea?"

"I don't know. People might hate me."

She wags her finger at me, swirling it around to outline the dress. "For everyone that hates you, just remember those of us who care about you love you a million times more. Plus, hate isn't going to change how amazing you look in that dress."

I smooth the light fabric with my fingers. "You think so?"

Her eyes widen. "I wish I'd have tried it on first."

Aunt Jen stands near the front window of Liza's living room, gazing at the setting sun. We spent the afternoon at Eva

Devereaux's meet-and-greet before coming over here for a late lunch and to get ready before the party.

Alexandra hands Eli her phone for the hundredth time. "This is the last one. Promise. It's not every day I get my hair and makeup done by professionals."

I peer at my reflection in the giant wall mirror hanging above the fireplace. Eli's publicist had sent a team of people over, because apparently she didn't think I was capable of handling things myself. I don't mind, though, but Eli did have to send his stylist to get coffee when she insisted I wear the dress she brought for me. I was too afraid to wear something I would be borrowing, plus, I really, really love the dress I picked out with Alexandra. The owner of the boutique said it was an original and even gave me a huge discount as long as I promised to mention her name if anyone asked.

I press my cheek to hers and Eli snaps the picture. "Okay, Alex. It's our turn."

Eli pulls me to him, sliding his arms around my waist. I watch him as he smiles at Alexandra. I steal her phone away, crop the photo down so it only shows the design on the bodice of my dress, and I text it to Eli to post the vague picture.

He winks at me before he posts it to his fan page. The doorbell rings and draws our attention away from each other. Liza answers the door, and a man in a black suit stands on the porch. He must be our driver—also arranged by Eli's team.

After packing ourselves into the limo, sitting in what feels like a year's worth of traffic, we arrive on Hollywood Boulevard at a club Eva picked especially for the event. A red carpet sprawls across the sidewalk where guests are dropped off out front. Both sides of the carpet are lined with gates and security guards, and flashes pop as people huddle to snap a coveted picture of the celebrities who've come to celebrate with Eva.

The never-ending line of cars finally dissipates, and our driver pulls to the curb in front of a stone building with intricate carvings on the front façade. If it wasn't so busy and overwhelming, I'd stop to take a picture to send to Taylor. Instead, I snap a picture of the crowd from the window.

As the driver holds the door open, people call out Eli's name, and then I hear the most shocking thing ever—they call out my name, too.

Eli clutches my hand, holding me tightly like I'll somehow float away amid the chaos. When we hit the red carpet, he stops in his tracks, and we turn to give the crowd an opportunity to get a few shots.

"Elijah! Elijah!" A man holding out a microphone calls out. "How does it feel to break a ton of hearts everywhere?"

Eli offers a smirk. "My fans understand."

"How'd you meet Elijah?" asks a woman with sleek blond hair standing next to him.

I squeeze his hand tighter. "The local farmers market. He liked my T-shirt."

The man barks a laugh. "I bet."

My cheeks warm, a blush threatening to turn my face into a giant tomato. Eli kisses my cheek and turns away from the crowd.

"Nora! One more question!" I glance over my shoulder at the woman. "I have a source who says you were cut out of your father's will. Care to comment?"

My heart nearly explodes from my chest, and I grip onto Eli to stop from crumbling to the floor as the world presses in on me.

Aunt Jen, who has been quietly hanging behind us with Alexandra steps forward, blocking everyone's view of me, and she points her finger at the woman. "How dare you."

I swallow, trying to find my voice. "Aunt Jen...please. It's okay. Let's go inside."

Eli guides me forward, studying my face in his peripheral vision, and Aunt Jen and Alexandra follow us into the club. The swelling murmur of the reaction-hungry crowd disappears as music and lights and fragrant air engulfs me, tugging me away from reality.

Eli pulls me into his arms and hugs me. He rests his chin on my shoulder and breathes his warm breath on my neck. "I'm sorry, Nora. I should've said something out there."

I take shallow breaths to calm my rattled nerves. "No, you did the right thing. No need to make a scene." I lean back to meet his eyes. "Let's try to have fun, okay? I'll be better prepared next time."

He cups my face, kissing me softly. "Okay."

After a moment, I turn to Aunt Jen. "Go have fun. We'll be fine."

She nods, switching her clutch purse between hands and heads in the direction of Eva, who is mingling with some A-list celebrities. Alexandra's eyes search through the crowd, and she lifts her finger to point in the direction Hugo stands, chatting with someone I don't recognize.

"Don't make me go alone," she says, hooking her arm through mine, stealing me away from Eli.

He trails behind, Alexandra strutting us through the crowd on the dance floor with purpose. Her magenta gown brushes against mine, and I admire how pretty the beaded hemline is as multi-colored lights reflect off it.

Hugo grins his award-winning smile, watching us approach, and pulls Alexandra into a bear hug, sweeping her off her feet. Her giggles tinkle over the music, and Hugo sets her down before turning to Eli and me. I let him kiss my cheek, and he half-hugs Eli. I still can't get over the fact that I've spent countless hours watching Hugo on TV, and here we are, acting like old friends.

"I saw that you finally took the plunge in stepping into the limelight," Hugo says, meeting my gaze.

I toss my hair over my shoulder to keep it from veiling my face. "Yeah, I was kind of forced into it by some weird circumstances, but whatever. Figured we'd take it into our own hands."

He chuckles. "You happy with how things are going? The excitement from the fans won't last long. Unless you do some crazy shit, you can go back to the fringes."

I eye Eli in the corner of my vision. His intense gaze begs for me to turn to him, but I remain facing Hugo. "It's been pretty uneventful until tonight. I'll be relieved when they stop snooping into my life. It just feels too personal."

"That's what people love. They want to know it all."

I jiggle the sapphire bracelet on my wrist. "Tell me about it."

He laughs, shaking his shoulders. "Be careful what you ask for because I could keep talking about this for a month straight."

I offer a smile. "How about we all dance instead?"

Hugo hooks his hand around Alexandra's waist. "You don't have to ask twice."

"Nora, my love, I'm so happy you came to celebrate." Eva slides her arm over my shoulder, air kissing my cheek.

I sit at the bar, sipping a glass of iced water and watching Eli, Hugo, and Alexandra dance in the middle of the crowd. I needed to sit down before I fell on my butt because my feet are about to fall off and I'm about to pass out from overheating. While I love my gown, I should've picked out something much cooler.

I clink my water glass to her champagne flute. "Thanks for inviting me. It's been amazing."

Twirling her glass, she sloshes alcohol across the bar. "You'll have to tell the world that."

I laugh, turning in my seat before she knocks her glass into my arm. "I'm sure the world knows, Eva."

She wobbles on her heels, and I wonder how many glasses of champagne she's downed in the last few hours. "Then tell the universe!" Her high-pitched voice cuts over the music, and she tilts her head back, laughing. I peer around to see if anyone notices. It's not until this moment I realize that they probably don't, because more than half the crowd looks drunk—and I know drunk. Cecilia favored drinking a margarita or ten with dinner, especially after Dad passed.

Eli must've been watching me from the dance floor, because a moment later, he runs his fingers over my bare shoulders. He leans over, smiling at me before smirking at Eva, who winks at him.

She downs the remaining champagne in her glass and plops it on the bar. The bartender hurries to refill it without her having to ask. "You can order whatever you want, you know. Tonight's about having fun."

I raise my eyebrows. "Oh, I am." I hold up my water glass. "Been having fun for a while."

She clinks her glass with mine, hitting it a little too hard, and some of her champagne spills onto my knee. I hop to my feet, grabbing the cloth the bartender tosses toward me, and I pat the liquid the best I can. Luckily, it's not wine, or else I'd have to figure out how to hide a stain on my way out. All I need is a picture of me leaving in a ruined dress and being deemed the next party girl in Hollywood.

Aunt Jen saunters up next to Eva. "Eva, you look hungry.

Come join us at the table. Lee Schwarz just arrived to say hello."

A man in a dark blue suit offers his hand out to the model. I've never seen him before, but Eva latches onto him like he's the only thing keeping her upright—which he probably is. He turns to the bartender and motions for him to cut her off.

The two walk away, leaving Aunt Jen alone with me and Eli. She blows strands of curly hair from her face. "The crowd is getting kind of wild, and I think you three should probably head out."

I frown. "What about you?"

She glances at the crowd of people behind her. "I can't pass up this opportunity to mingle. Lots of potential clients here." She turns to Eli. "You guys take the driver, and I'll figure out a way home."

Eli taps his fingers on my shoulders. "You sure? I can call for another car."

My aunt twists her lips. "That would be wonderful if you could. Less stress for me."

He nods. "Of course."

Aunt Jen hugs me, hands me some cash, and then slinks back into the crowd surrounding Eva. Eli tugs me toward Alexandra, who I'm sure will pout the moment we tell her my aunt suggested we leave. Sliding my arms through hers, I sway in rhythm with her for a moment on the dance floor.

I press my chin into her collarbone. "Don't hate me, but we have to leave."

She stops dancing, puckering her bottom lip. "Really? I'm

having so much fun."

I mimic her expression. "Eva spilled champagne on my dress, and Aunt Jen thinks things might get a little wild for us, and she knows how your parents are."

Alexandra turns to Hugo. "They're making me leave."

He grabs her hands and pulls her to him, spinning her around. "How about I walk you out?"

She smiles. "I'd like that."

The four of us head to the exit of the club where Eli asks the door greeter to call us a car so Aunt Jen can keep the limo. We step outside, the crowd no longer hanging around the door. The crisp fall air sends goosebumps over my arms, and I hug myself.

Eli slips his jacket off and hangs it over my shoulders. "It might be a while. Let's walk."

Hugo and Alexandra trail behind us, quietly talking without holding hands or anything. Eli holds me close, and my hand rests on his side in a half hug. Hollywood Boulevard dances with life. Tourists and club goers stroll the sidewalks in an eclectic group of different clothing styles—from casual to runway-perfect—and only a few people give us a second glance but don't bother us.

I read the gleaming pink and gold stars laid within black tiles on the sidewalk, trying my best to act like I'm not totally excited to see the Hollywood Walk of Fame in person again. It was one of those touristy things on my to-do list that I just haven't gotten around to. I haven't seen it in years, and I kind of wish Hugo and Alexandra weren't right behind us because Eli wouldn't mind if I stopped and took a picture. He'd pose with me.

I point my finger at the next star. The name *Jamie Christine* in all caps with a golden record emblem underneath it shines in the streetlight. I slow down to get a better look at it. When Eli notices I'm craning my neck, he halts in his tracks, causing Hugo to bump into my back. Hugo latches his fingers onto my shoulders, steadying me before I fall, and Alexandra laughs.

"Jamie was my mom's favorite singer. She'd have loved to see this," I say, unable to control my excitement. "You have to take a picture of me with it."

Eli pulls his cell from his pocket. "Sure."

Hugo spins me around and kneels next to it, waving Alexandra to join us. She crouches on my right on the inner side of the sidewalk with Hugo on my left, and I force myself to smile at Eli even though my heart starts aching, thinking about how I can't actually send Mom this picture. She creeps into my mind more and more these days, and I just wish it weren't always so painful.

"Hugo Gutierrez and Elijah Rousseau. Surprised to see you've left Eva's party so soon." A light bulb flashes, and I blink the spots from my eyes to see a bald man with a camera start to jaywalk across the busy street.

"Oh, my God! Hide me." Alexandra whispers from next to me. "My dad will kill us all if I end up online or in a tabloid with Hugo."

I shrug out of Eli's jacket and hand it to her so she can cover her head. I nudge her to move toward the enclave of a closed shop where the man can't see her from his position.

He raises his camera and snaps another picture but keeps his distance. "This must be Nora Novak. I see you've gotten to know some of Hollywood's most eligible bachelors." A cocky smile tugs at the corner of his lips, half hidden behind a graying mustache.

My cheeks redden, and I open my mouth to say something, but Eli shifts to stand in front of me, blocking the paparazzo from taking another photo. I clutch the back of his shirt and peek over his shoulder.

"Get your pictures and get out of here," Hugo says, standing up straighter.

The man snaps another one without hesitation. "So Nora, how did a girl like you end up on the arms of two guys like them?"

Tears prickle the edges of my eyes. He belittles me for no other reason than he can. Anger slithers around my heart, stealing away all the happiness and excitement I felt only moments before.

"What's that supposed to mean?" Eli asks. "Stop trying to bait my girlfriend."

The man snaps another picture. "You know what I mean, Rousseau. An orphan girl winds up with you. That's not a coincidence."

Eli steps forward clenching his fist. Hugo reaches out to

grab him, and the man takes another picture. Alexandra waves at me, motioning that we should make a run for it while the paparazzo is occupied with the boys.

But I can't move. Not yet.

"You need to head on your way." Hugo doesn't take his hand off Eli's arm. "You got your pictures. This is harassment. You think the cops are going to appreciate you harassing Nora?"

The man leers at me. "You lookin' for fame? Money? Come on, sweetheart. No one's going to judge you after your daddy left you penniless. I can make you a star."

My stomach churns as he reminds me of what I've pushed to the back of my mind for months. I shouldn't care so much about my dad's will, but I was shocked and heartbroken that he didn't want to take care of me—or that he trusted that an evil witch would. But what can I do about it now? Nothing. Move on and forget. Except I can't. Not with people like this man digging up memories I had buried.

"You monster!" I scream. My voice echoes through the air. "How dare you do this to me!"

He snaps a picture. "Don't blame me, sweetheart. I wouldn't be complaining if I were you. Not with these two begging for your atten—"

Eli moves forward first, and I grab the back of his shirt, but just as fast, Hugo rushes toward the man. My heel catches on a crack in the ground, and I fly forward, losing my balance. My shoulder hits the concrete first and then my head, and pain explodes behind my eyes.

Alexandra screams from beside me. Tears cloud my vision, and the hazy light from the orange streetlamp is the only thing I can see.

"Oh, God, Nora!" Alexandra kneels next to me, pulling my head into her lap, but I can't seem to get her into focus.

The ringing in my ears deafens me to the nightlife noise. I blink, trying to stay awake. Shifting the best I can to get off the ground, I see the man bolt away through my foggy vision.

"Nora? Nora? Look at me." Eli's voice wraps me in warmth. "You hit your head pretty hard. You can't go to sleep."

I try to respond, but the pain in my head only allows me to blink.

"Stay with me, Nora," he pleads.

But I can't.

The pain, both in my head and my heart, sits heavily on my soul, and I just want to escape it. The only way I can is if I succumb to the darkness of my own failing consciousness. I let it sweep me away into nothingness.

chapter 16

Not Cut Out for Hollywood

I STARE AT the sunbeam cutting across my bed through the crack in my curtains. I haven't left my room all week since Eva's party, though I can't remember all that happened. The doctors tell me amnesia is a side effect of the concussion I got from tripping over my own heels.

Aunt Jen pokes her head into my room, drawing my attention from the shadowy spots dancing in the sunlight. "Julian will be coming over in ten minutes, but I have to leave. I have a meeting I can't miss."

I ignore the ringing in my ears. At least the nausea subsided yesterday. "I don't need a babysitter."

The corners of her lips tilt downward toward her chin. "Nora, please. It's not for you. It's for my own peace of mind."

I sigh. "Fine, but he better bring food."

She laughs. "He promised ice cream, too."

I sigh again. "Fine."

She chuckles as she closes the door.

I reach for my phone next to me. It hasn't left my side since I feel like I'm missing out on what's happening in the outside world. Aunt Jen took my computer away and disabled the data on my phone to my utter surprise because she wanted me to heal without having to stress about everything else.

And no one will tell me anything—not Eli, not Alexandra, not even Taylor. It's like all the people I care about stand around me, protecting me from the world like I don't know how to protect myself.

I read my latest message from Eli.

Eli: What do you want for dinner?

Me: You.

I blush after I realize how bad that sounds.

Me: Pizza.

Eli: I'm coming now. School can get over it.

Me: Haha! Nooo. I need my school work.

Eli: Fine. No more teasing though.

Me: Oh, I'll tease all I want.

Eli: And I'll like it.

I smile at my phone, wishing that he really could come over this morning instead of Julian.

Me: Tell Alexandra I miss her for me.

Eli: What about me?

Me: I'll show you how much I miss you later.

Eli: I have to go before I can't stop myself from going to you.

Me: Muah!

I set my phone down. Jasper barks up a storm in the hallway, and I hear Julian let himself in. He talks to Jasper in an excited voice for a minute before knocking on my door.

"Come in," I call. I run my fingers through my hair and promise myself that I'll take a shower before Eli comes over. I'm just afraid the nausea will come rushing back the moment I do anything other than stare out my window.

Julian greets me with his biggest smile, though his eyes shine with a sadness I haven't ever seen in them. "How are you feeling? Your aunt said you just got your appetite back so I brought over one of everything off the menu at Panera Bread since I know you love them."

I smile and wave him into my room. "Yes, sir. Thanks so much. I'm starving."

"Oh, stop it with that sir crap. You know I hate it." He lifts a few bags by his feet and carries them over to my bed, setting them on the end by my feet. "I brought you a few other things, too."

He digs through one of the canvas bags and plops down a few candy bars, some nail polish in colors bright enough to blind me, a few movies, and a couple of magazines. He drops everything on my bed next to me. "Just some entertainment. I know Jen has you on lockdown."

I roll my eyes. "They think I'm made of glass."

"Which is clearly untrue. I know I saw some diamonds sparkling in your eyes last time I saw you."

I tilt my head back and laugh, the sudden movement sending a wave of dizziness through me. I blink a few times and smile at Julian. "You're ridiculous."

His eyes widen, and he waggles a finger at me. "Look! I see them again."

I brush strands of hair from my face, dropping my gaze to the stack of magazines on my lap. My heart freezes, sending another wave of dizziness through me but not because of the pounding in my head. I slowly flip the magazine open to a page with a headline in big, bold yellow letters.

Teenage Gold Digger? Underneath the title reads, *Orphan Nora Novak left with nothing moves in on Hollywood's newest heartthrobs.* Below the caption are a few pictures of me clinging to Eli and Hugo. I'm wearing the dress from Eva's launch party, but I have no idea when this was taken. I can't remember much of the party, or even the hospital.

Julian snatches the magazine away from me and throws it out of the room and into the hallway like it'll burst into flames. He scoops up the other magazines and tucks them under his arms before his saucer-sized eyes meet mine.

"I'm so sorry, Nora. I thought I avoided all the magazines with tabloid features." He looks on the verge of crying.

Tears slip from my own eyes. "My life is ruined. How could someone publish that? I don't understand."

Julian pulls me into a hug. "I'm so sorry. I'll call Jen."

I sniffle. "Don't. She doesn't need this. Just give me a minute, okay? This wasn't your fault. No one should've kept this from me."

He stands from my bed looking like a sad puppy. "I'll be right outside."

I cover my face with my hands and cry. It's all I can think to do.

Eli shows up at my bedroom door with his hands full of flowers, candy, and balloons. He adds them to the ever growing pile on my desk. He's brought something new every day even though I haven't even touched the sweets.

I haven't talked to him since this morning, and I'm not sure how I'm supposed to talk to him now. He turns to me with a smile in his eyes though his lips press together. It takes him less than a second to suspect something's wrong.

He rushes to my side and sits on the edge of the bed. "What's wrong? You don't look so good."

Tears prickle in my eyes. "Why didn't you tell me?"

He studies my face, realization pinching his eyebrows together. His mouth opens and shuts, and he combs his fingers through his hair. I shift my gaze away as silence lingers between us—silence so heavy that it suffocates me. All I can think about is rushing from the house into the cool twilight air. But I can't. I can't show my face in public. The tabloids make me out to be some sort of money-hungry lost girl with an agenda.

I rub my fingers under my eyes. "You should've told me.

You know, I love you so much, and I might have left some things out from my past, but this is my present. It's yours, too. You should've told me. I feel like an idiot. Because I didn't know, I couldn't defend myself. I haven't felt so much grief since my parents died."

His face falls, my words sinking in. It's the first time I've admitted to loving him, but the words cut deep into him, and I know what heartbreak looks like. My heart has been shattered so often that I'm afraid the pieces are too damaged to fit perfectly back together again. I've learned to live with it though, learned to move on and be happy, but in this moment, I'm not happy.

I'm not sure I can ever be with the way my life has taken a sudden turn. It's true that not everyone is cut out for Hollywood—for fame and recognition. I'm definitely not cut out for it. It'd be wrong for me to pretend I was as strong as all the rest. The true stars who deserve the fame.

Eli still doesn't say anything. He's never been one to be speechless, and I'm starting to think he's afraid to say anything at all.

My head pounds as another splitting headache threatens to send me back to my pillow. The pain in his face only intensifies mine, making me feel like the bad guy. But neither of us are. I'm aware of good intention when I see it. I'm sure my aunt had discussed it with everyone, and they all agreed to this, but good intent doesn't always have a good outcome. Like now.

I suck in a breath, my bottom lip quivering as I find the

words I need to say. "Eli—" My voice shakes, and I snap my lips shut.

He pulls me into a hug. "Don't. Don't say anything."

I sniffle into his shirt. "Eli, I have to."

He shakes his head before resting his chin on my shoulder. "No, you don't. I'm handling everything and by the time you're healed, everything will have blown over."

"Until something else blows it up again."

He brushes his lips against my forehead. "I'll fix this."

He tilts his head to kiss me, but I turn away. It's too easy to lose myself in his love and kisses. Feeling his arms around me, squeezing me tight enough to feel like things can't ever fall apart, isn't going to change things. It's not going to stop people from butting into my life and twisting it to make a great head-line.

I don't want the fame that leaves people questioning why I'm famous in the first place. What I crave is a life without complications, being able to do what I want without having to think twice about how it'll appear to those standing on the fringes. Something I can't have with Eli. I don't need love to conquer all. I need to be comfortable in my own skin standing on my own feet, instead of hiding in the shadows.

Hot tears drip onto my cheeks, burning trails down to my chin where they fall off and soak into Eli's cotton T-shirt. "I really, really wanted this to work, Eli. I thought it could work."

He cups my face in his hands. "It will." He swallows. "It is."

My heart hangs heavy in my chest, and my throat burns with the words I must force out of my mouth. "I think you should leave. I—I need some space."

He sucks in a quick breath through his teeth like I've physically hurt him. His gorgeous brown eyes plead with me, beg me to take back the words. As much as my heart wants me to, my mind refuses to face this new, scary world that's based on appearances and superficial personalities.

"Nora, pl—"

I pull away from him and lie down on my side, facing my wall. "I said I need space."

Without another word, he stands and leaves, quietly clicking the door closed behind him. Sobs convulse my chest, shaking my body, and I bury my face into my tear-drenched pillow.

My head throbs and my heart hurts so much, I feel like I'll die at any minute.

Nora, this is your life, and you get to choose how to live it. No one else. You. But you have to make sure you're happy. If it doesn't make you happy, let it go. My mom's voice whispers in my memory as I imagine her sitting on my bed with me back in Austin, rubbing my back like she used to when the world felt so wrong.

"He's the best thing to have happened to me in a long time, Mom," I whisper, flipping over to glance at the ceiling. "But this life—his world—makes me unhappy. How do you choose if something completes you and tears you apart?"

The question hangs unanswered in the air. Because Mom

isn't here to answer it, and I doubt she would anyway. Like she used to tell me, "It's my life," but how on earth am I supposed to make the right decision when they're all wrong?

I ignore my buzzing phone for the millionth time and stare at the wall in my room. My depressing thoughts consume me, refusing to allow me to do anything except replay every miserable thing that's happened in my life over and over again.

A knock sounds on my door, and I ignore it. Aunt Jen should be home by now, but I'm not in the mood to talk to her.

The door creaks open behind me. "We need to talk, Nora."

I don't turn to face her. "Tomorrow. It's been an awful day."

"Julian told me what happened, and I've received a million voicemails from Eli, blaming me for making a mess of things." The bed shifts as she sits down. "Bold kid, but I still like him, and he's right about where the fault lies. I was trying my best to protect you."

I jerk upright to meet her eyes, digging my nails into my palms. "Protect me? Really? After everything, you think I need it now?"

Her gaze drops to her hands, and she grimaces. "Yes, I do. You've been through so much."

I glower through my tears. "That's my point. Where were you when I needed protection from my real life monsters? You left me with that monster of a woman even though you knew I needed you."

She pushes her hair from her face. "I didn't know it'd get that bad. She waited almost two months to even start probate for your father. She told me he had never finished his will, so I assumed you'd get your share of things. It's not like I can practice law in Texas. I hired a great lawyer for you, but then she pulled out a will from years ago at the last second. Contesting would've just racked up debt with no assured outcome. Cecilia promised to care for you. She told me she loved you like a daughter. I didn't know."

I smack my hands on the bed. "Don't say her name! I don't want to remember anything!"

Aunt Jen wraps her arms around me, pulling me to her. "If I could go back and change things, I would. I'd do everything differently. I'd have made the time to visit before Gil died. He left us so suddenly, and deep down, I know he wouldn't have wanted this. He'd have thrown that devil woman out on the street."

I sniffle through my tears, and Aunt Jen doesn't hold back as we cry with each other. She pats my back, rubbing circles just like Mom used to, and after what feels like forever, the tears finally dry, we're both left with red, puffy faces.

"I'm sorry for keeping the tabloids from you, Nora. You shouldn't blame anyone but me." She reaches for my phone on my nightstand. "You should give Eli a call."

I shake my head. "I can't, Aunt Jen. I wasn't lying about wanting to forget, and with Eli, I don't think the world will ever let me."

She hugs me. "Either way, I'm here for you. I'll always be here for you, Nora."

And I believe her.

chapter 17

Smarter than the Headlines

"IT'S NICE TO have you back, Nora," Ms. Valentine says as I enter the TV Production room. I took an extra few days off, even though I've been feeling much better physically, but I just didn't think I could make it through the day without crying.

I smile and nod, my heart not really into being here. "Thanks. I'm feeling a lot better."

"I'm sorry you found yourself in that awful situation to begin with. If you ever need to talk, my door's always open." Ms. Valentine waits for me to respond, but all I can do is nod.

Alexandra let me know that the whole school knows about the incident, but that she made sure they knew the truth about what happened and how I was trying to hide her from the paparazzi while dealing with the scumbag.

It doesn't make me feel any better though. The rest of the

world is probably eating the whole thing up.

I turn to head to my desk and stop in my tracks when I see Fae chatting with Anthony. Like she can suddenly feel my stare, she shifts in her seat and meets my gaze. I expect a smile to cross her lips, but all she does is lift her hand to wave.

I spin to face Ms. Valentine again. "Actually, Ms. Valentine. I was wondering if I could be moved out of Entertainment. I'm no longer interested in any of that stuff."

She purses her lips. "I'm sorry, Nora, but field shifts don't happen until the end of the semester. I'd like you to continue to work on the Entertainment segment. Why don't you use your new dislike of it to bring something fresh to the table? Have you thought about maybe doing a piece on tabloid embellishments? Rumors, maybe?"

My forehead crinkles. "What? Are you asking for a segment about me?"

She shakes her head, her long hair smacking her cheeks. "No, but I think you've learned some important lessons that would benefit your peers."

I sigh. "I'll think about it."

"Good. Please, do."

I can't avoid Fae forever so I adjust my bag on my shoulder and cross the room, taking a seat on the other side of Anthony. He offers me a small smile and hands me a few ideas he and Fae have been working on for the next couple of broadcasts.

"Seriously?" I ask, dropping the paper on top of the keyboard. "I'm on the list? Haven't I been through enough?"

Anthony grimaces. "It was Fae's idea."

Fae shoots him a look lethal enough to kill him. "Exactly, Nora. It's why you should do it."

I smack my hand on the table. "Like I'm going to listen to anything you say. You're the one who started this whole mess in the first place when you tipped off the paparazzi to Eva's interview."

Fae's mouth falls open, and Anthony excuses himself to use the bathroom even though I'm sure he just wants to avoid the line of fire. Fae studies me for a second, the surprise peaking her eyebrows.

I straighten my shoulders. "Don't worry. I'm not telling anyone."

"Why?" The color drains from her face.

I shrug. "Honestly, I don't know. You had no right to act this way. I didn't even do anything wrong except date your ex-boyfriend, but it wasn't like I knew. You don't even like him, anyway."

She shifts in her seat, lowering her voice. "I've been so stupid. I'm sorry. It's just that when I saw you with Eli, I kind of went a little insane. It didn't help that Cherry put all these thoughts in my head, like how it should've been me with Eli and how it should've been me who got to interview Eva."

"I wanted you to do the interview. You don't even know how much I wanted you to do it, and I would've given it to you if Ms. Valentine would've let me. The last thing I wanted was to mess up our friendship." I expected this conversation to head in a totally different direction, but this isn't a movie. Fae's not the type to start a fight. She's a student ambassador, the Entertainment News Anchor, and popular throughout the whole school and not in a mean girls sort of way. She's popular because people like her.

Fae frowns. "Which I did all on my own."

I twist my lips to the side because she's right. It'll take a lot to earn back my trust. "Yeah, you did."

She winces. "And I'm sorry. I want to make things right."

Closing my eyes for a minute, I think about all the things she could possibly do to make it up to me, but someone shouldn't have to buy back my friendship based on a good deed. It takes a whole lot of other stuff too, like not letting jealousy get the best of them and standing up for me when the world tries to push me down. *You should stand up for yourself...*

I push Mom's voice away. I might regret the sudden, all-consuming decision I'm about to make, but I don't know what else to do to fix things on my own. The last thing I want is for the world to think of me as some girl on a mission to rise from rags to riches through hooking up with celebrities. I don't want Eli to have to shield me and have his team clean up situations. Like with announcing our relationship, there's a better way to clear my name—to show people who I really am—and it's not through the tabloids.

The TV Production room buzzes with life as the class preps for tomorrow's broadcast filming. I suck in a breath, forcing my mouth to spill the words. "It's going to take time to forget what you put me through, but—" I wave the paper with the Entertainment segment ideas. "I think you're on to something. I want an interview."

She bounces on the balls of her feet. "Shouldn't you talk about this with Elijah? His team might have something to say about it. It's his reputation too, you know."

My heart aches hearing his name. "It's more than reputations. This is my life. And Eli, well, we're taking a break."

Her eyes bug out of her head. "What?"

I blink oncoming tears from my eyes. "Yeah. I don't want to talk about it, though. This is about me and fixing the things the tabloids ruined. People need to know the truth."

She links her fingers together, leaning closer. "This could be even bigger than the Eva story."

I crinkle my nose. I hope not. "That's why I want you to be the one to interview me."

"After everything?"

I nod. "Yeah, so you better make sure everything's perfect. I'm putting my faith in you."

"You won't regret it."

I hope not.

Eli doesn't show for our third period Economics class to my relief, and I don't see him at lunch either. Alexandra swore she had no idea of his whereabouts, but she also begged me to reconsider things between us.

We stand in the hallway after the final bell rings. She pulls some books from her locker and shoves them into her messenger bag. "I don't want to be in the middle of things, but I will if it means you won't be moping around campus."

I nudge her with the back of my hand. "I'm not moping. I still don't feel perfect—" I poke my head. "Concussions do that, you know."

She rolls her eyes. "So do broken hearts."

I clench my jaw. "I'm fine."

"You're not."

"Please, Alex. Just stop."

She throws her hands up. "Okay, okay. But I still think you're making a mistake."

So does my heart. As quickly as the thought comes, I force it to the darkest part of my mind where I keep everything else I don't want to think about locked away.

My book bag slips off my shoulder and catches on my folded arms. I dangle it in my hand. "Mistake or not, I need to figure things out." I glance around the now almost empty hallway. "I'll call you later, okay?"

She hoists her bag over her shoulder. "You better."

She heads toward the student lot, and I rush away the moment her back faces me. I can't wait to get home and go back to hiding. Today has been pretty miserable with the pitying looks and noticeable absence of Eli. Aunt Jen promised to pick me up on time for once, which makes it less excruciating since I won't have to hang outside alone to wait.

I fly down the stairs in front of the school and head toward the street. To my dismay, Aunt Jen's Lexus isn't waiting in her usual place. Keeping my head bowed, I stroll to the sidewalk. As I start to sit at the curb, a horn honks, and my soul nearly jumps from my skin. I half expect to see Eli instead of Aunt Jen pulling to the curb, but instead, Hugo surprises me.

He reaches over and pushes open the door of his shiny, black Porsche. The two seater is tiny inside, and the engine purrs over the rest of the slow moving traffic. My brain warns me not to do it, to stay frozen in my spot, but my feet start walking toward him anyway. After climbing into the car, one much lower than Eli's and Aunt Jen's, I buckle up. Hugo steers away from the curb, leaving behind a few gaping classmates.

My book bag hits the door when we turn onto Wilshire, heading toward interstate 405. He hits the throttle a little too aggressively, and my back presses into the seat. I clutch my hands in my lap even though I'm dying to brace myself.

After he doesn't say anything, I break down and ask, "What are we doing?"

"Going for a drive."

My nostrils flare, annoyance coursing through my veins. "I kind of got that. But why?"

He switches lanes, accelerating to make it through a yellow light instead of slowing down. "I'm your friend, aren't I? Can't we hang out?"

I narrow my eyes. "Yeah, but—"

He raises his hand. "Uh-uh. No arguing. You might hurt my feelings."

I slouch in the seat. "You're crazy. The press is going to ruin me if they spot us together. Why do you think I told Eli I needed space?"

He changes lanes and enters the freeway, picking up more speed. "See, now that's crazy talk."

Crossing my arms while turning my gaze out the side window, I watch him drive out of Beverly Hills to some unknown location. I send a quick text to Aunt Jen, telling her Hugo's decided we need to hang out, and she replies that she hopes I'm not angry and to be safe and text her if I need anything.

After forty minutes in traffic, Hugo opens the windows and crisp, salty sea air wafts into the car. I spot the Pacific Ocean ahead, the deep bluish-green water sprawling out forever. Traffic slows us down even more the closer we get to the beach, and eventually Hugo pulls into a paved lot near the beach and the Santa Monica Pier.

He parks his Porsche and kills the rumbling engine. I don't move to unbuckle my seatbelt until he does, and after a moment of silence, he shifts in his seat to stare at me. "Have you ever been here?"

I shake my head. "I've only seen pictures."

He motions for me to get out. "Well then, come on." He pops his hood, which actually turns out to be a cargo area, and hands me a hooded sweatshirt. He puts on a baseball cap and sunglasses, and when we're both sort of incognito, we head toward the massive wooden pier full of life, energy, and an enormous crowd of people.

We walk side-by-side, swinging our arms. "A lot of people don't get why I like this place, but the excitement takes over everyone to the point where no one really recognizes me. I'm just a nobody in the crowd."

I smirk. "You'll never be a nobody."

His shoulders shake as he tosses his head back, laughter escaping his mouth louder than I expected. My eyes bulge, and I wait for people to look in our direction, but no one does. The anonymity feels like life did before Eli.

He swings his arm around my shoulders and gives me a half hug. "No wonder Eli loves you. You sure know how to flatter someone."

My smile fades into a grimace, and I hug my arms over my chest. "So, why are we here, really? You've gone out of your way to hang out with someone you don't really know. Shouldn't you be trying to sweep Alexandra off her feet?"

Hugo watches me in his peripheral vision. "Alex and I have an understanding, and this," he waves his finger to me before swirling it in front of his chest, "this isn't about Alex. This isn't even about me. It's about you. I felt awful for how things went down. I don't think it'd have gone so far if I'd have just let it go, but my mom would be ashamed if I let someone talk to my friend like that."

Wind whips my hair in front of my face. "It wasn't your fault."

The intensity of his stare forces me to peek at him. His hazel eyes crinkle in the corners as we step from under the shade of a building and into the fiery glow of the setting sun. His deeply tanned skin soaks up the rays, making him look like a bronze statue, and I admire how he still manages to look like a star even without the glitz and glam of a tuxedo.

He doesn't say anything, strolling alongside me on the wooden pier toward a small amusement park. Most of the crowd faces the water to the right, lining the railing with their cell phones aimed to get the perfect picture. As the silence draws out between us, I start to relax, finally able to process what's going on.

And then I see him.

Haloed in the flaming sunset, Eli stands in between two dolphin-shaped shrubs under a huge purple octopus holding a glowing yellow sign that reads *Pacific Park*. It competes with the fiery sky and setting sun, but will soon win when twilight grabs hold of the evening.

He rocks on his heels, hidden behind his aviator sunglasses, and tucks his hands into the front pockets of his hoodie. A girl with long, blond hair, holding a bag of popcorn in one hand and a giant soft drink in the other rushes toward him from a cart with a rainbow umbrella. She stops a foot away, adjusting the popcorn in the crook of her arm and smiles in our direction.

I freeze in place. "We should go. You shouldn't have tricked me like this. I told Eli I needed space." I wave my hand in the direction of the girl. "And I'm not exactly in a good mood to deal with your fans."

Locking his fingers on my arm, Hugo pulls me forward.

"I'm sorry I didn't tell you, but would you have come otherwise?"

I drag my feet. "No."

"See. You'd miss the surprise." He points in Eli's direction again. "While that girl might be a fan of ours, she's your biggest fan."

A familiar voice squeals through the air, drawing my attention up to Eli and the girl. She hands her stuff to Eli and runs right for me, arms wide. It takes me a moment to realize that the girl isn't some random fan. It's Taylor.

I can't believe it.

"Oh, my God!" I yell. "What the hell are you doing here? How? When?" The words fly from my lips. "Why didn't you tell me?"

She latches onto me in the biggest hug, and we dance as we embrace each other for the first time in months. Her blond hair tangles with mine, and we laugh hysterically when we pull away.

Tears line her dark eyes. "Because I thought you could use the best surprise of your life, and that boy over there, who's madly in love with you by the way, bought me a plane ticket."

I lean in and whisper, "You still should've called. I told you that we're taking a break."

She shifts to look at me. "I still would've accepted. Come on, look around. I'm in Cali-freaking-fornia. I get to spend Thanksgiving with my best friend, and I'll totally be famous when I go home."

I roll my eyes. "It's not all it's cracked up to be."

She grasps my shoulders and shakes me. "How many times do I have to tell you that people are smarter than the headlines?"

"Even if people don't care, it still hurts me."

She hugs me again. "Why don't we drop all this fame talk? I came here to spend the best time with you. Let's enjoy it. If you want Eli to leave, tell me, and I'll send him away. Same goes for..." Her voice trails off as she draws her gaze to Hugo who stands next to Eli. She sighs and whispers, "The same goes for that sexy, hot, amazing man."

I smirk. "I'm fine if you want them to stay."

A smile couldn't shine any brighter. "Thank God!" She turns away from me. "Ready?"

Eli holds my gaze and nods without saying anything. Taylor hooks her arm with mine and pulls me toward the boys. The twinkle of all the lights from the amusement park sets the atmosphere aglow, and both Eli and Hugo remove their sunglasses. I try to remain calm as I start to worry about them attracting attention.

"Let's go on the Ferris wheel. It's the perfect time before it gets too dark," Hugo says, leading the way into the park and toward the ticket stand near the entrance of the Ferris wheel and a huge dragon swing ride. A rollercoaster car zooms overhead, clicking on the tracks, and a few people scream. The scent of burgers and fries wafts through the air from fast food places with brightly painted store fronts.

Hugo purchases the tickets and hands one to each of us. Taylor grabs Hugo's hand and rushes ahead toward the yellow-and-red bucketed Ferris wheel, now swirling with bright lights that dance along the frame. I can't even catch up before they get on, leaving me with Eli. Taylor waves as the attendant shuts the door to their bucket, and Hugo shrugs. I glare, knowing Taylor planned this all along. The buckets are large enough to fit us all, and I'd have much preferred to sit next to her. I've missed her. *And I hate that I've missed Eli, too.*

Eli nudges me forward when the employee waves us over to get in the round, red, enclosed bucket that could very well sit three people on each side of the door. He hasn't said a single word since I arrived, and I'm not sure he's going to say anything at all—which will make this the longest Ferris wheel ride of my life.

I hold onto the seat, sitting across from Eli, and stare off into the darkening horizon as we ascend. The Ferris wheel immediately takes us to the top and doesn't descend. It's the longest wait ever in the entire universe, and even then some, as we hang high above the pier.

"Wow," I say, taking in the view around me. The Pacific Coast is unlike any beach I've been to in Texas. "This is amazing."

"Isn't it?" Eli's voice rises barely over a whisper.

I turn my gaze away from the endless, now bluish-black water, to meet his eyes. "Eli," I say, leaning forward in the space between us, "Thanks for flying Taylor here. It means the world to me, but I want you to know that I still need time. Just because everyone wants us together, doesn't mean that's what's best for me. I'm still figuring things out."

He fidgets with the drawstrings of his hoodie. "What about me? It kills me that you won't even try to get through this together."

I run my fingers through my hair, pushing it from my face. "Are you sure you even want this? I'm bad for your reputation."

He clenches his fingers into fists and waves them in front of him. "Who cares about my damn reputation? This is about us."

I lean back as the bucket starts to descend, but it stops only a short distance from where we were. "I do. This is your life. You might regret being with me one day. What if I turn out to be the girl who ruins things for you?"

My hands tremble in my lap. Eli ignores the instructions to stay put and switches sides of the bucket to sit next to me. His hand cups my knee, rubbing small circles, and I breathe in his delicious scent. I can't help inching closer to him, feeling his leg against mine.

He gently pinches my chin between his thumb and index finger. "The only thing I'll regret is if I don't fight to keep you in my life."

Any sort of reply sticks in my throat. All I can do is lose myself in the depths of his dark eyes and wonder if I can gather the strength it takes to make this work. I really, really want it to work. But how can it if I can't handle stupid tabloids. *You can...*

I open and close my mouth, gathering my thoughts. "I—I don't know. Loving you is hard. Shouldn't it be easy?"

He tucks my hair behind my ear. "No. Love should just be worth it."

With those words, he pulls me close and kisses me, sliding his arms around my shoulders in a warm embrace. I sink into him, finding my tongue caressing his, feeling how much I've missed him. How starved I've been without him. The intensity of my desire for him overwhelms me, and all I can think about is getting away from here, hiding from the world, enjoying just him and me together without anything else.

The Ferris wheel jerks to a halt, and someone clears their throat. I reluctantly break away from Eli to meet Taylor's smiling face as she waggles her eyebrows up and down.

Eli twines his fingers with mine and pulls me from the ride. "Come on. Let me show you how life should be with me."

I ignore all my good senses and let him drag me away into the crowd full of life and laughter and the happiness I deserve.

chapter 18

The Past is the Past

"OH, MY GOD. Oh, my God. Oh. My. God." Taylor grips my arm, dragging me behind Eli as he guides us down a plain hallway in Warehouse Three of Hall Studios.

Alexandra squeals from my other side. "This is so exciting!"

Eli peers at me over his shoulder, his eyes begging me to calm my friends down, but all I can do is beam a huge smile because my excitement can't even be tamed.

Alexandra joined Taylor and me for a sleepover, and we watched the entire first season of *Creatures of Slaughter Creek* until five in the morning, and then barely slept before Eli picked us up just before noon with iced coffee and a box of doughnuts, which we devoured before we even got out of the Beverly Hills city limits.

When we reach a door with an unlit *Filming in Progress*

sign above it, Eli slides a keycard and takes us onto the crowded set of a fake school hallway with dark blue lockers, gleaming tile floors, fake school posters, and the works to bring the set alive. Right next to the hallway is a classroom with fifteen desks with various books and folders, a whiteboard, fake windows, and posters hanging from the walls.

I never knew how much I wanted to see *Creatures of Slaughter Creek*—well, the set of *Creatures of Slaughter Creek*—in real life until this very moment when I see the cast, including Hugo, getting ready to film a scene.

A woman in a gray uniform greets us, holding a clipboard, and she grins at Eli. "Who are these lovely ladies, Elijah?"

He kisses my cheek. "This is Nora, my girlfriend that I told you about, Maggie." He motions to my friends. "Also, my cousin Alexandra Evans and a good friend Taylor Mills. They should be on the roster for extras."

She searches over her clipboard and points at a page with her pen. "Yup, here they are. They'll need to sign NDAs and hurry to wardrobe."

The woman, Maggie, motions for us to follow her over to a table where she has a few clipboards stacked, and we each take a minute to fill out the Non-Disclosure Agreements. She pats Eli on the back when we're through, and he waves for us to follow him to a curtained room in the corner of the giant, partitioned room.

A team of three people motions us in, and Eli pulls me in for a hug before turning to leave to prepare for his day.

A bald man in jeans and a T-shirt looks me up and down before doing the same to Taylor and Alexandra. He sticks out two fingers, one pointing at me and the other Alexandra. "Where have I seen you two?"

I open my mouth to rattle off a dozen possibilities—from Eli's social media accounts to my interview with Eva to the tabloids—when a woman with tight curls framing her face swirls a makeup brush in our direction and says, "Chrissy York's show! The Makeup Madness one."

I cringe. The show aired during the week I stayed home from school, but I could only handle watching the first ten minutes of it. I was upset enough about the Launch Party Incident to want to see what kind of brutal things she had to say after I ran out in the middle of my concluding interview.

The man raises his bushy eyebrows. "Oh, yeah. That woman is something else. You two were lovely, though."

I puff air through my lips, relaxing. The stylists, Ken, who's the bald man, Dallas, the woman with tight curls, and Theresa, a woman with a faux hawk and full tattoo sleeves, get to work prepping us for a scene in the school hallway where Hugo and his on-screen girlfriend are supposed to get in some fight.

After an hour of preparations—including hair, makeup, and wardrobe—we're ready to join the cast for their rehearsal along with the other extras. Eli expects a full eight-hour day, but none of us complain. I'd stay for a week if it meant I get to see part of my favorite show before everyone else.

I spot Eli chatting with Hugo in the middle of the school hallway set, and he waves for us to come over. He introduces us to so many people, cast and crew alike, that I have a hard time remembering names, and after a few minutes of basic instructions, I find my mark near locker number thirteen.

Both Alexandra and Taylor settle at the tail end of the set where they'll be walking down the hall. All I have to do is turn to watch the oncoming fight with an expression of satisfaction. Hopefully my face cooperates and isn't completely stupid. After all the mess with the relentless paparazzi, all I need is to get made fun of for failing as an extra.

I consider backing out when Hugo and his on-screen girlfriend, Bria Falcon, laugh as they head to their marks only feet away from me. He winks, giving me a thumbs up, and my hands tremble. I turn and stare into my locker with a bunch of useless stuff I've never actually used at school. Doubt clouds my thoughts. I'm not made to be part of this life. I'm not made for the spotlight. *Shut up. This is the chance of a lifetime.*

I shake the nagging thought away. If I let uncertainty control me, I'll be miserable. I've let enough things control me over the last few months—not anymore, though. I'll be eighteen in four months, and it's time I do things the way I want. And I want the world to see me how I see myself and not for my past. It won't define me.

"You what?" A feminine voice rings through the air as Bria recites her lines. Even from the few minutes of meeting her, I know she's vastly different than Celeste, the confident, sassy witch she portrays on *Creatures of Slaughter Creek*. She was totally down-to-earth and soft-spoken. She even told me that I could call her if I needed help managing things. Not sure how much she knows about me, but it was sweet nonetheless. "I broke coven rules to perform that spell for you, Lorenzo."

"Shh! Keep your voice down," Hugo says.

I swivel on my heels to glance at the two actors right on cue. I cross my arms, smirking, and lean back on the locker like I have a front seat to the greatest show on earth, which I technically do. It takes everything in me to keep my heart from racing or my mouth from squealing.

Bria pulls a gleaming silver wand from her purse and points it at Hugo's chest. "No. I'm done with you."

Hugo raises his hands up. "Celeste, no!" He launches himself backward, falling onto a thick mat on the floor behind him, and I catch sight of Taylor and Alexandra as they rush down the hall, faking terror.

Bria points her wand at Hugo on the floor. Rolling her eyes back into her head, she chants something I can't quite make out.

"Stop!" My heart skips a beat when a familiar voice sounds through the set. Eli stands in a doorway a few feet away to my right. Dressed head to toe in black, he presses his palms against the door frame. His makeup makes him pale, and the contrast of his black contacts makes him look scary.

A few extras hover around, and I follow their lead and take a step closer to Bria. She straightens her shoulders, swirling her wand at Eli as he strides closer. Jealousy slithers through me at the seductive look she gives him, and I remind myself that she's acting. Bria's character, Celeste, is a force on the show to be reckoned with—and I love how fierce she is. If only I could summon that into real life.

Bria cranes her neck to peer over her shoulder to look at me and the two other girls who have joined me. I grin at her like I was instructed to do, and the blonde next to me props her elbow on my shoulder. I'm pretty sure Eli had something to do with the unnamed character I'm playing, and I hope I'm making him proud.

Sauntering to Eli, Bria grips the front of his shirt as he stands in front of Hugo, who remains in his position on the floor. She leans close enough to kiss him but doesn't. Instead, she whispers, "Careful, dreamwalker. I know your little secret. Are you willing to risk exposure for a liar?"

Eli bares his teeth.

"Get out of here, Dmitri. This isn't your fight," Hugo says, his deep voice rippling through the air in a very Lorenzo Ruiz fashion.

Eli raises his hands to Bria. "It is now."

The director calls cut, and I release the breath I've been holding to make sure my expression remained even. I relax my shoulders, stepping back to lean against the locker. Taylor bounds up to me and hugs me, bouncing on her feet.

"This is amazing. I'm going to be famous," she says, laughing.

Strong hands slide around my waist, and Eli rests his chin on my shoulder. "Having fun?"

"Yes!" Taylor answers for me.

I peer around and notice Alexandra talking to Hugo, touching his arm. She smiles at me, and I let everything sink in. "This is the best day ever. Thank you."

He kisses my cheek. "I told you the good would outweigh the bad."

"And it's not even over yet," Taylor says, shaking my arm.

I beam a smile. I just hope it stays this way. I don't think I'll ever be able to shake the feeling that no matter what, something bad will always happen. Maybe because it always does.

Eli wasn't lying when he said we'd be on set all day. By the time we wrap up, my feet kill me from the heels the stylist forced me to wear—shoes I'd never wear to school. After we change back into our regular clothes and Eli removes his Dreamwalker makeup, we head out to end the day with dinner.

We sit at a round, white-clothed table near the floor-to-ceiling window in Palm Bonita, a swanky restaurant owned by famous chef Edmund Rivera. A server in a black uniform with a bow-tie greets us with a smile and takes our order.

People mosey down the sidewalk, but with the mirrored window, all they can see are their own reflections. It's one of the reasons we've picked this place to eat. Staring out the window a minute longer, I shift my gaze to Eli, who watches me with a smirk playing on his lips. He grasps my hand under the table, and we quietly listen as Hugo waves his arms, telling Alexandra and Taylor about a misadventure on the red carpet at the Academy Awards that left him sockless. He claims to have started a suit without socks fashion trend that lasted the rest of the season.

I laugh even though I wasn't paying attention and only caught the last bit. A few people sitting at the surrounding tables listen in, nearly all of them captivated by Hugo and his star presence. I don't blame them. He's hard to ignore.

Eli leans close, drawing my attention away from the others as Taylor talks about Austin and her favorite things to do. I never doubted my best friend could fit in, but it's like she was made for this place.

"You okay?" Eli whispers.

I nod. "Yeah. I'm better than okay." I turn and plant my lips on his stubbly cheek.

"Y'all should fly out sometime. I can show you what Texas is all about," Taylor says, drawing my attention back to the conversation. "It might take some convincing to get Nora back, but I bet if you mention the Salt Lick and Barton Springs, we could have a killer summer."

Heat flushes my cheeks. "Tay, really?"

She shrugs. "What?"

The conversation quiets when the server brings out our plates. I stare at my lobster salad as the others immediately start digging in. I savor a bite of the tangy dressing, glad for the interruption.

Eli shoots me an occasional glance. My fork clinks against my plate, and I feel the heavy weight of the silent questions I know everyone is thinking. I've hidden my past for so long that it almost doesn't even feel like my past anymore.

I swallow the bite I'm chewing and take a sip of water. "Go on. I can feel the heat of your burning questions. Ask away."

Alexandra opens and shuts her mouth but doesn't say anything right away. Taylor stares at her plate without looking at me, and Hugo leans his elbows on the table. Eli's hand slides to my knee.

I set my fork down. "Really. It's okay. I've had a rough go at things losing my mom, and then when Dad died and left Cecilia everything—well, you can imagine how that went. Don't feel sorry for me though. I have Aunt Jen. Look at the life she's given me. Look at yourselves. You accepted me into your lives and for that I'm thankful."

Hugo's head tilts to the side. "Whoa, Nora. Who's this Cecilia lady?"

"My stepmom."

"And she shoved you out the door?"

I clench my fingers, hate and anger washing over me. "Not exactly. But she wasn't exactly easy to live with."

Taylor slaps the table. "That's an understatement!"

I hold up my finger as people start to stare. "Nothing to be done now. The past is the past and there's only one direction to head in as my mom would say."

Eli hugs my shoulders. "That's right, Nora. You're better

off anyway."

He's absolutely right. Maybe this was a gift in disguise. If things were different, I might not have moved to Beverly Hills with my aunt and would've never met any of my new friends or got to experience a sliver of what being famous is like. It has its downside, but the fun and excitement outweighs the rest. I know that now. I'm stronger for it.

A flicker of movement catches my eye outside the glass window, and I notice a few people grouped together, loitering on the sidewalk. The cameras hung around their necks send a chill down my back.

"Damn," Eli says, his eyes following what I'm staring at.

Hugo shakes his head. "It was bound to happen. I'm sure the people at the table two down think they're stealthy at taking their selfies with us in the background."

"What do we do?" Alexandra asks, leaning with her hand slightly covering her face.

"We eat," Taylor says like it's no big deal. "I'm not wasting my thirty dollar pasta."

I laugh. I can't help it. "She's right. It's not like your parents are going to be upset, Alexandra. They gave you permission to be here."

Eli smiles. "You're really okay with this?"

I rest my head on his shoulder. "I have to be."

We finish our meal, and Eli and Hugo split the tab. Before we head out the door, I excuse myself to the restroom. Taylor and Alexandra follow me despite my protests. Taylor fixes her makeup in the mirror and hands me my matte brown lipstick from my bag. Might as well look good if I'm going to have my picture taken.

Alexandra smiles at me in the mirror. "I bet they'd let us out the back if you want to avoid the paparazzi or the boys can go first, since they're the ones the media is really after."

Taylor pouts her lip. "I'll do whatever you want."

I wring my hands together. "This is so stupid. Why am I letting them scare me like this? It's not like I have anything left to hide."

Taylor bumps me with her hip. "That's right, babe."

I suck in a deep breath. "Let's get this over with."

When we step from the bathroom, the sidewalk in front of the restaurant has turned into a mad house. Security guards hold people away from the valet drop off, and Hugo and Eli stand near the door, both of them crossing their arms over their chests.

"Holy crap," I say, stopping next to Eli.

Hugo grins. "We have a huge fan base. People already love Eli though only press pictures have been released."

"We need to go before we cause any problems," Alexandra says, peering over the restaurant, all eyes falling on us. The maître d' hovers at his podium, waiting to help us with anything he can.

"Sirs, we can escort you out the back," he says when we don't move.

Eli and Hugo look at each other for a minute. Finally, Hugo shakes his head. "No thanks. We'll greet a few of our fans before we go. Sorry for the hassle." He hands the man a card. "Contact my team if you need anything."

He shakes his head. "We always appreciate good press."

With saying that, he opens the door for us. Alexandra dashes to the Range Rover, sliding into the backseat. Taylor follows her, but Eli doesn't let go of my hand. He smiles at a few people snapping his picture and signs a few random items. Hugo does the same, thanking a row of girls for enjoying the show.

"How ya feeling, Nora?" a man asks, holding up a camera to snap a picture.

I fake a smile. "Great. All healed up now."

"Mind answering a question? I swear not all of us are crazy." He drops his camera an inch.

Eli starts to pull me toward the car.

I resist. "Not tonight, but you can submit a question to my Friendconn page. I'm holding an interview after Thanksgiving."

Eli furrows his brows. I haven't told him about the piece I'm working on with Fae and Anthony. I've actually kept Fae out of all our conversations because I know his feelings about her after the way she treated me.

"Aw, come on. Give me an exclusive," the man says, bringing his camera up again to get a picture of Eli studying me. "I'll make it worth your while."

I bare my teeth in a wider smile. "Sorry. I promised that to someone else."

I tug Eli toward the car, and Hugo slides in back with the

girls. I get in the front seat, and Eli honks at a few people in the way before taking off.

When he reaches the corner of Wilshire, he stops at a red light. Shifting in his seat to meet my gaze he says, "What was that about?"

I don't answer him right away.

He pinches the bridge of his nose. "When were you going to tell me?"

I shift to look at the others for help, but they sit quietly like they're afraid to even breathe. My heart races, and I motion forward as the light changes to green. Eli doesn't drive, though. I don't think he will even with the horns starting to sound out behind us in a cacophonous melody.

I lean against the window. "It slipped my mind. Can you just drive?"

He hits the gas after a moment and turns to head toward LA where Hugo's penthouse apartment is. I sink lower into the seat. I bet the others are considering jumping out at the next stoplight. I might even join them to avoid the sudden anger lacing Eli's words.

He races through a yellow light, and all I can think about is if he'd slowed down and stopped instead of running it, I could've made my escape.

"I need to talk this over with my publicist," he finally says after loosening his grip on the steering wheel.

I rest my chin on my fisted hand. "It's not going to change anything. It's a school project."

"Then you can back out," he says.

I flick my stare to Alexandra and Taylor before turning back to the road. Taylor's saucer eyes speak a thousand unsaid words as she reads my now frustrated mind.

"No." I rub my lips together. "Do I need to remind you that your team isn't my team? I don't need anyone's approval. I want to do this. I want to take control of the situation and clear the air. I refuse to pretend that those horrifying headlines never existed."

His shoulders lower when he realizes he's not going to win. "Then I want to do it with you."

My mouth gapes open in surprise. "You really don't have to."

He laces his fingers through mine. "We're in this together."

I close my eyes for a minute. I decide to drop the conversation since the others are in the car. The last thing I want to tell him is that Fae, his ex-girlfriend, is the one interviewing me. I'm sure that'll go over well.

I clear my throat. "It'll be great."

"Yeah." With his words, I'm pretty sure he doesn't believe it.

I don't blame him. I'm not sure I believe it either.

chapter 19

If This Was a Movie

THE SCENTS OF Thanksgiving—roasted turkey, buttery mashed potatoes, the sweet, spicy scent of pumpkin pie—waft up the stairs and into Eli's room, lingering from the feast we shared with his family and a few of his parents' close friends.

I sit next to Taylor on the window seat, looking through the photos on her phone with her. She's taken more pictures in days than I have in months. Eli's parents invited me, Taylor, and Aunt Jen to join them for Thanksgiving dinner when Eli mentioned we were going to be eating at a restaurant since Aunt Jen doesn't really cook, and we don't have any other family to celebrate with.

Eli enters his room, holding up two wine glasses for us to take. "It's a tradition in the Evans' house to have a special occasion glass of wine after dinner."

Taylor claps her hands. "Can I have an invite to Christmas, too?"

He chuckles, handing me the deep red liquid. I sniff the rich scent and sip a tiny amount. It tastes exactly how it smells but burns going down my throat. I set the glass on the window ledge.

"My parents had a similar tradition," I say, "except it was with mimosas, and Dad always bought non-alcoholic champagne for me." My eyes prickle in the corners, thinking about how Dad's not here, cooking the turkey while watching football. I would make the mashed potatoes while Mom made pumpkin pie from scratch. It's one of the few times I've actually thought of him before Cecilia came into our lives.

Eli drapes his arms over my shoulders, pressing his hips into the side of my crossed legs. He bends down and brushes his lips against the top of my head. My scalp tickles as he sucks in a breath of my mint-scented conditioner.

"Beer's big in my house," Taylor says, breaking the sudden silence. "Oh, and football. I'm actually surprised it's not on downstairs. I didn't even see a TV in your living room, and I'm starting to think you live in a museum."

He chuckles, showing off his heart-melting smile. "That's because you haven't been to the game room."

She waggles her eyebrows. "I guess I need to go find it."

Taylor, never the one for subtlety, lightly punches my arm and excuses herself to explore the rest of Eli's house to find the entertainment room. She smiles, turning the lock on the door and slamming it shut behind her. Eli takes her spot on the seat next to me.

Lifting my discarded wine glass, he takes a long sip, finishing half the wine. I peer out the window, trying my best not to get caught watching him straight on. He bumps his knee into mine, fidgeting, and I wait for him to tell me what I already know is on his mind. It's been a few days since we've seen each other, and it's the first time we've been alone all week to talk about it.

He holds the glass with his knees. "Are we ever going to talk about our conversation in the car?"

I swallow, wishing I could steal the wine back from him even though I don't really want to drink it. I was hoping we could avoid it until after the interview actually happened. I was hoping to figure out a way to do it without him.

Sucking in my bottom lip, I lean closer. "And here I thought you were going to take this opportunity to kiss me."

He hums under his breath in consideration. "You're trying to distract me."

My mouth lingers an inch away from his, the scent of wine swirling between us. "Is it working?"

Without answering, he cups my face and brushes his lips against mine. His hands travel down my neck and over my shoulders, playing with my long hair. I tease him with the tip of my tongue, flicking it into his eager mouth.

He pulls me onto him, and the wine glass drops from his knees and spills across the wood floor. I pull back, surprise in my eyes, but instead of getting up to clean it, he guides me toward his bed, leaving the mess.

His fingers trail up my dress, squeezing my thighs, and he lifts me off my feet and sets me on the edge of his bed. I fall back and his weight presses into me, our hearts racing, beating against each other. My head swims with love and lust and everything good in between. As his fingers trail up my leg, lifting my dress to my waist, I shiver.

"I love you," he breathes through kisses, his fingers gliding along the bare skin of my back.

I shimmy up to the head of his bed. His spicy cologne lingers on his pillows, engulfing me in a wave of desire, and I stare into his brown eyes. We don't move. We just stare at each other, both breathing heavily. All I can think about is how I'm in bed with him and how much I love him.

He rests his elbows next to my ears. "No one will bother us."

I smile. "What are you saying?"

"Do you want to...?"

Tingles rush through me, a million thoughts crossing my mind. I never expected my first time to happen on Thanksgiving with someone like Eli. But I knew from the first time he told me he loved me that it would be with Eli regardless.

I nod my head, kissing him. "Yeah," is all I can manage to say into his lips.

I thought I'd want to plan things out, have the moment be absolutely perfect, but nothing in my life has ever been planned with certainty, and I don't want a moment like this, a moment I want, to pass.

With gentle fingers, he slides my dress over my head, dropping it to the floor. His gaze travels from my eyes to the rest of me, lingering on my favorite, dark gray push-up bra I'm so glad I wore.

As he slides his own shirt over his head, he whispers, "You're so beautiful, Nora." He trails his fingers up my sides, gently exploring my bare skin with a feather light softness.

My breathing quickens until it matches his, the anticipation and longing squeezing my chest in the best way possible. I trace my fingers along his chest and around his neck before pulling him down on top of me.

"I'm so lucky." He kisses my lips before moving to my neck.

"I love you," I whisper into his ear. The weight of my words hangs heavy in the air. It's the second time I've ever said them, the first being when I told him I needed space. But I couldn't stay away.

He shifts to peer into my eyes, happiness and desire crossing his face. I've never wanted him so badly with everything inside me. He responds to me with another kiss so deep and passionate that he doesn't even have to say anything back. His love for me fills me up with everything he is and everything we are together. Everything I never knew I wanted.

A moment later, the heat of his skin presses against mine, and I allow him into my world completely.

"That was some Thanksgiving," Taylor whispers from next to me. I swear she's smiled more than I have since I found her yelling at the TV in the game room with Alexandra and the rest Eli's family like she was one of them.

"Totally," Alexandra says from my other side.

"Shut up," I whisper back, elbowing them both.

We grin at each other.

I never thought Thanksgiving would be a holiday I'd enjoy ever again, but I have so much to be thankful for. I glance between my two best friends, my boyfriend, the best aunt in the entire world, and Eli's family who've taken me in as one of their own. This is the best moment of my life since the worst moment of my life.

"Dinner was lovely, Liza. Thank you," Aunt Jen says, gathering her purse and coat from its place on the hook near the door.

I hold onto the giant tote bag with enough leftovers to feed us for a week—including a whole pumpkin pie. "We had the best time," I add, smiling at Eli.

He hugs me from behind and kisses my temple without saying anything.

"Any time. I just love having you all over." Liza pulls me away from Eli and hugs me. "Oh, and good luck with your interview this week. Oscar mentioned that Alex said you were letting Fae interview you. It's nice that you've forgiven her. Not many people would've. It really shows what a beautiful person you are."

I cringe at her words and shoot Alexandra a look dark enough that her eyes widen and she steps back. As much as I want to be furious with her for telling her dad, I can't. I know I should've told Eli, but I didn't want to.

A string of curse words flood through my mind, my perfect day getting washed away into my never-ending sea of secrets. I hold my face as expressionless as possible even though my heart threatens to explode at any second.

"Thank you, Liza. Everyone deserves a second...or third chance," I say, breaking my lips apart to force a smile.

After saying goodbye, Eli walks us out to the Lexus. While Aunt Jen and Taylor get in the car, I hover in front of Eli. His arms stay folded against his chest, and I hate how I'm starting to regret giving myself to him.

"Eli," I whisper, "You have to see where I'm coming from."

"No, you need to understand. Do you not get how bad it feels when I discover I'm the last one to find things out? Especially after..." His voice trails off, nearly cracking my brave façade.

Tears blur my vision, but I blink them away. "I'm sorry."

"You know how I feel about Fae. Did you even think about that?"

I sigh through my teeth. "Of course I did, but I'm trying to be the better person. I feel awful for not telling you right away, but I was going to. I swear."

"Like you were going to tell me about your parents?"

I jerk my head up to meet his gaze. "You're not being fair. It's not like you've been an open book."

"That's different."

I raise my hands up. "How?" I catch sight of Aunt Jen and Taylor watching us through the window. "You know what? I'm not doing this here. I'm not going to have you make me feel bad for things you've done yourself."

His brows pucker as my words sink in. "I don't want to end today like this."

I open the car door. "Okay, then I should probably leave."

He reaches out and takes my hand. "Nora, wait."

I give him a small peck on the cheek. "Goodbye, Eli. I'll call you later."

Sinking into the front seat of the Lexus, I clench and un-clench my shaking fingers. Eli closes the door with a quick goodbye to Aunt Jen, and he turns his back and heads to the house, glancing over his shoulder once before going inside.

Aunt Jen starts the car. "You okay?"

I sniffle. "I've messed up."

Taylor rests her hands on my shoulders from the backseat. "He'll get over it."

The pain in my heart sends more tears dripping down my cheeks. "I'm not so sure."

"Y'all are totally meant for each other. I know for a fact he will. I see how he looks at you, Nora. He's even told me him-self. You'll be okay." Taylor squeezes my shoulders. "But until then, maybe we should stop for ice cream."

I rest my head on the cool window. "I'd rather just go home."

"I can lie and say I missed my flight. I don't have to leave," Taylor says, stuffing the ten extra shirts Aunt Jen bought her from our favorite boutique on Robertson Boulevard into her suitcase.

"I wish," I say.

We've spent the weekend together, doing as many touristy things as possible, but now we must go to the airport so she can make her evening flight. I haven't spoken to Eli more than once a day since Thanksgiving, and two of those days were only a few text messages. Looks like our roles have been reversed, and he's the one in need of space. Being on the other end sucks.

With a final pat, Taylor zips up her suitcase and sets it on the floor. She plops on my bed and rests her feet on her luggage. "I hate the idea of going home without you. Video chats aren't as good as the real thing."

"Me, too." I sit next to her. "Maybe I'll suck it up and visit you next. I have a longer break at Christmas."

She pouts her bottom lip. "Then Jen will be alone. How about spring break?"

I nod. "Deal."

A tap on the door draws our attention away from each other. Aunt Jen peeks in from the hallway, and Jasper sneaks in through the crack, rushing to me and springing up and down on my shins. I scoop him up and cradle him in my arms before letting him run in circles on my bed.

"Would you mind if someone else took you girls to the airport?" she asks, studying my face.

"Uh, I guess not," I say, raising my brows. I turn my gaze to Taylor, who beams me a smile.

Aunt Jen winks. "Good, because he's waiting in the living room."

I lightly smack Taylor's arm when Aunt Jen closes the door. The smile on her face proves she was behind this, and I know exactly who's here. Facing Eli has me sitting on the edge of my bed now, bouncing my legs, because I know I have to face our problems head on the moment I say goodbye to my best friend. This is almost unfair. What if he breaks up with me? Taylor will be on a plane and unable to comfort me for three hours.

"What were you thinking?" I ask, burning her a fake glare.

She twists her mouth to the side for a moment before saying, "I can't stand when my friends fight. You might be pretending that nothing's wrong, but I know you better. I asked Eli to take me to the airport so I could see him one last time—and make sure you don't turn into a ghost on him."

I tuck my hair behind my ears. "I don't think I could do that even if I tried," I say, forcing a laugh.

Taylor doesn't even smile. "Just be honest. I already told him that, too. I haven't seen you this happy in months. I'm afraid you'll unintentionally sabotage it."

I grimace. "Why would I do that?"

"The step-monster had you doubting your existence. That's

not something easy to get over."

"Okay, Dr. Tay."

She rolls her eyes. "Hey, I might be one day. I'm taking psychology this year and rockin' it."

Throwing my arms around her, I hug her tightly, refusing to let her go even when she tries to pull away. She giggles, squeezing me back, and it takes a shout from Aunt Jen about being late to break us apart.

When we enter the living room, Eli greets Taylor with a huge smile, but I get something that stings like a cold shoulder. He half hugs me, then drops his arm to his side instead of holding onto me like he usually does. The awkward moment passes quickly when he takes Taylor's suitcase and heads out to his car, loading it into the cargo space.

Aunt Jen waves from the front door, and I turn my legs in my seat, pressing them into the door as I pretend to not be in the car with the boy who I hurt enough to make him possibly not love me anymore. If this was a movie, I'd find a magic redo button I could press and try again without Eli remembering. At this point, he could forgive me, but I know he won't forget how I have a problem with keeping things from him.

Traffic sucks as he drives down interstate 405 to LAX, and I talk to Taylor about how much I'll miss her. Eli pulls into a parking structure, and we walk Taylor inside the terminal she's flying out of. My heart hammers in my chest as a few people notice Eli, and he even waves to a few fans.

Taylor takes both our hands in front of security. She turns

from me to Eli and then back to me. "I don't know the extent of what's going on between you, but I know you'll get through it." She lets go and hugs Eli first, whispering something in his ear. He nods, pulling away, and strolls back to give me a moment alone with Taylor.

"What did you say to him?" I ask as I hug her.

"That I'd fly back here and murder him if he does anything to break your heart," she says, smiling.

Tears spring from my eyes while I laugh. She always helps ease the sadness. I just wish she could stay, and that we'd never have to be so far away.

After a long while, I pull away and meet her eyes. "Text me when you get on the plane and call me the moment you land, okay? I want a full update about school Monday night because I'm pretty sure you'll be famous."

She grins. "My friend requests on Friendconn have tripled. I might need my own fan page."

"Do it. You're much better at this stuff than I am."

"Oh, be quiet. You're the one who was made for this. You might not see it, but I bet one day soon, you'll be famous by your own doing. People love you."

We rock back and forth, hugging one more time before she heads into the security check line. Eli stands next to me, and we watch Taylor make it through and disappear to her terminal. After a minute, Eli gently takes my hand, surprising me.

Without a word, he guides me from the airport and back to the car where we sit in the parking structure in silence for a few minutes. His eyes stare at the wall as he gathers his thoughts, and I mentally prepare myself for the worst.

After a long moment, I finally say, "I messed up, and I'm sorry. Hurting you was never my intention, but I'm just—I'm not good at this sort of thing. Please, Eli, I don't think I can handle your distance for much longer."

He rubs his chin without meeting my eyes. "It kills me too, you know. Everything about this situation kills me. I'm trying really hard to understand where you're coming from, and I want you to be able to tell me anything. I kind of hate myself that you think you can't. That's what bothers me the most."

Finding the right words to say proves difficult, and the silence presses against me. I can't exactly pull the "it's me not you" response to why I keep things from him because it's partly him, too.

My shoulders droop as I arch forward to rest my elbows on my knees. "Please, don't hate yourself." My bottom lip trembles. "It's not that I feel I can't tell you everything, it's just—it's just I know how Fae drives you crazy."

"And you're giving the person who accused you of trying to destroy her a big opportunity when she doesn't deserve it." He grips the steering wheel even though he hasn't started the engine. "What if it's a set up?"

"It's not. She really does feel guilty about the whole thing." At least I hope she isn't setting me up. She was so genuine about the entire ordeal.

He sighs. "I might regret this, but I'd still like to participate, too."

I shake my head. "I'm sorry, but no. The segment isn't about you. It's about me and the effects rumors can have on a person's life. It's to show how the media twists the truth to fit their agenda and make great headlines."

He slumps in the seat. "Can I be there to support you?"

I lean over in my seat and hug him. "Of course you can. And I promise, no more secrets. But you have to promise me the same."

His lips meet mine for a gentle kiss. I melt against him, the weight of his arms reassuring me that my life is going to be fine. That our lives together will be fine. After a long while, we finally break apart.

He starts the engine and peeks at me a few times, smiling. "You're beautiful, you know. I wish I could change how things went down after Thanksgiving. I feel like I ruined it."

I hold up my hand. I don't want to even remember how I felt after I gave myself to him. "There's a lot I wish I could change, but you know, I don't regret it."

"It was one of the best moments in my life."

I smirk. "Mine, too."

My nerves relax, and he reverses from the parking spot and navigates back to the freeway. Century City looms in the distance, glowing in the darkness.

"You don't have to take me home if you don't want to," I say as he exits the freeway onto Wilshire.

"You're okay with going out?"

I nod. "I'm not going to hide anymore." Anything the headlines say will just fuel my motivation. "I'm going to face the world with a smile and give them something good to talk about." It's time that I take a stand. I want people to know they can't trust anything they read unless it comes from me directly. And that's what I'll do from now on.

He brings my hand to his lips. "We'll face this madness together."

chapter 20

Sometimes Villains Win

TO MY SURPRISE, the same team who made me up for Eva's launch party showed up two hours before my interview with Fae, courtesy of Eli. Instead of dressing up for the occasion, I remain in my black skinny jeans and gray sweater. My neutral makeup brings out the golden specks in my eyes, and I run my fingers over my curled hair.

Fae reads over her cue cards a dozen times. They contain over a hundred questions I chose at random from the thousands submitted to my Friendconn fan page. They're a mixture of questions for me about my life and about Eli, entertaining enough to hopefully not bore the world to tears, though that might be a good idea so they lose interest.

The night after dropping Taylor off at the airport, Eli pur-posely took me to Giovanni's, a popular restaurant celebrities go to for paparazzi attention, so we could get word out about my interview with Fae. We smiled together for a few pictures, Eli took some pictures with fans, and when people started asking questions, I told them to ask on my fan page.

"Everything is set," Ted says, coming over to me. "We're going to make history in this class by streaming it live online, so don't mess up, okay?"

As if I weren't nervous enough. Narrowing my eyes, I glare at Ted. "Thanks for your faith in me." Sarcasm drips in my voice.

He throws his hands up. "Sorry, Nora. I'm the nervous one. Questions will be coming in on your fan page, and Fae will screen and pick a few from her tablet. That okay?"

I suck in a nervous breath. "Yeah, I guess." I turn to Fae. "Nothing too intimate, okay?"

She rolls her eyes. "Fine, but that makes good TV."

The last thing I need is to become overwhelmed or speechless. Stumbling over my words would make me look stupid, and I'm not sure I could recover from something like that.

Eli hugs me from behind as I head to my chair in the setup identical to the way we had it with Eva. I turn around, standing up on my tiptoes to kiss Eli. Somehow, his presence manages to settle my nerves to the point where I don't think I'll pass out the moment the camera starts rolling.

"You're going to do great. I'll be standing over there if you decide you need me to step in," he says, whispering in my ear.

I spin in his arms and throw my arms around his neck.

"Thanks."

He leaves me to stand next to Alexandra. Taking my place across from Fae, I cross my legs at my ankles and rest my hands in my lap. I straighten my shoulders to stop myself from slouching. Ted directs us to get started, and Fae takes a deep breath before smiling at the camera.

"Hello, I'm Fae Yzarra with Beverly Hills High School, bringing you an exclusive interview with our very own Nora Novak, who also happens to be dating up-and-coming actor Elijah Rousseau. After a few weeks with what I can only describe as bad luck with the tabloids, Nora's decided to set some things straight and bring awareness to the ever rising problem with media portrayal and distorted headlines." Fae turns to me and offers her hand. "Thank you so much for joining me today. Why don't we start with a little about yourself before we get to the fan-submitted questions."

I nod while smiling. "Thanks, Fae. Most people who follow Elijah Rousseau know that I moved from Austin, Texas to Beverly Hills. My aunt asked me to live with her after my dad passed away late last spring. It was a bittersweet move for me, since I left all my friends in Austin, but my aunt is the only family I have left."

Fae puckers her bottom lip to show just enough sympathy. "I'm sorry to hear about your parents, Nora. The tabloids sure twisted that story."

Bobbing my head, I say, "And basically every story they come out with. When I came to Beverly Hills, I might not have had a lot, but my aunt has taken over as my guardian. I'm not in need and looking for some rich celebrity to save me. I don't need to be taken care of. I actually didn't even know Eli was an actor. It took a misunderstanding with some fans for me to figure it out." I laugh nervously, recalling how I abandoned him at the Beverly Canon Gardens.

Fae looks at the camera. "I can vouch for Nora if you don't believe her."

Fae asks a couple more questions about my life, and I give Taylor a shout out because she'd kill me if I didn't, and then we move on to the fan questions.

"I have a list of questions submitted by fans, and I thought it'd be fun to go over a few," Fae says. She looks at the camera again. "Also, for those of you at home, we have an on-going live chat we'll select a few questions from as well." Turning back to me, she reads from her cue cards on top of her tablet. "Courtney W. wants to know how your life has changed since publicly announcing your relationship with Elijah."

I smile at Eli near the door. "Honestly, it's been a rollercoaster ride. We decided to announce it over his social media to beat the tabloids. But with that, people starting digging for things that'd make a good headline. I turned into a teenage gold digger overnight after Eva Devereaux's launch party, when a man harassed me while I tried to keep a close friend out of sight. I got a concussion and that disgraceful title all because I was seen with two male celebrities. I'm just glad people are smart enough to know how things get embellished."

"Don't we know that," Fae responds. "The media can be brutal."

"Definitely."

Fae glances at her cue cards and asks a few more questions about what I like about California, what it was like being an extra for *Creatures of Slaughter Creek*, and other random things like my favorite flower.

"We'll now take a few questions from the live chat." Fae moves her cards and glances at the screen on her tablet. "Jamie H. wants to know how she can score a celebrity boyfriend. She says you're living her dream."

A blush flourishes up my neck. "Hang out somewhere with a funny T-shirt."

Fae raises her eyebrows. "Don N. asked, 'Will you go to winter formal with me?'"

I laugh. "Sorry, Don, but I can give your message to Bria Falcon."

Fae scrolls through the screen. "A whole bunch of people now have messages to pass on to Bria." She runs her finger over the screen some more. "Oh, here's one. Cecilia N. asked, 'Why do you think...'" Her voice trails off. "Never mind. That's not a good one."

My forehead creases. I reach out my hand and grab Fae's arm. "Wait, what did it say?"

Fae sets the tablet on her knees and pushes her hair behind her ears. She shifts nervously in her seat. "Really, Nora. You don't want to answer it."

Ted motions for us to move on by winding his hand in a circle.

Sweat prickles on the back of my neck. I shift my gaze to Eli. He leans with his back against the wall, arms folded across his chest, and just watches me with serious eyes.

Fae clears her throat. "Cecilia wants to know why you think your father left you out of his will when he died."

A jagged breath escapes from my lips. I don't even have to look at Fae's screen to know it's actually my step-monster Cecilia asking the question and not a coincidence from someone with the same name. She's dumb enough to use her real profile.

I take a moment to collect my thoughts.

Fae touches my knee. "You don't have to answer that vile question." She turns to the camera. "Who asks something like that, anyway?"

Her outrage surprises me. I thought she'd gladly put me in an embarrassing spot on purpose just to watch me fail.

I lick my lips. "Someone who wants to hurt me." I sit higher in my seat. "And to answer the question, I don't know. I loved my dad, and he loved me. We had a great relationship. It was surprising to discover, but all I can think of is that he thought the person he left his assets to would care for me. He might have expected us to remain as a family. Who knows? It is what it is though." As the words spill from my mouth, I almost believe them. Almost. Except that would mean my dad was blinded by Cecilia, and I know he was smarter than that. I'll never make sense of the situation. It's just something I have to live with.

Fae offers an apologetic smile while she bobs her head. "Death and money do crazy things to people. I'm sorry you went through that, Nora."

"Me, too."

Not allowing a minute of silence, Fae continues. "We have time for a few more questions."

I raise my hand to stop her. I don't want to answer anything else. "Actually, I have a surprise for those who've tuned in. Elijah is here and will be taking a few questions himself."

Ted's eyes widen as he sends the students in charge of sound to quickly hook a microphone to Eli's shirt. A girl rushes to add another chair to the mix, and a moment later, Eli's sitting next to me across from Fae.

She welcomes him, her voice only shaking for a second as she adjusts to the impromptu change. Eli smiles, talks about his upcoming appearance on *Creatures of Slaughter Creek* and his movie coming out in late winter before things settle.

Fae picks a question and meets Eli's stare dead-on. "Fans want to know how you got into acting."

Eli smirks at me. "My agent saw me perform in a play at school. Everything happened so quickly after that."

Fae scrolls through the screen of her tablet. She puffs a breath of air through her lips, jetting her finger across the screen. After a moment, she brings her eyes to mine. "I'm sorry, Nora. It seems that Cecilia doesn't want anyone else to ask questions."

I peek at Eli in my peripheral vision. "What is she saying?"

Eli grabs the tablet from Fae's hands, and I read a long list of "Nora is a liar," and "Nora, tell the truth," over and over again. It's so much so that every other person on the chat feed starts to mimic and repeat the same thing.

Tears prickle in the corner of my eyes. I don't know why Cecilia hates me so much that she's trying to ruin my life. There's no escaping her. Silence falls between all of us, and Ted makes all sorts of hand gestures at Fae, who doesn't take her eyes off me.

My throat burns when I clear it and look straight into the camera. "This is enough, Cecilia. I get it. You hate me. You'd rather see me fall off the face of the earth, but it doesn't change how I think my dad saw things play out in his head before he died."

Eli shows me the screen again. "She wants to take this off camera."

I raise my brows. "No. She called me out on our live stream. This stays on live." I turn back to the camera. "For those of you who haven't pieced things together, Cecilia was my stepmom, and the person my dad left everything to. She'd love to be famous, so go ahead. Make her famous."

With that, Fae pulls her flustered self together and thanks us for joining her. She thanks the viewers, and Ted wraps everything up.

When the cameras turn off, I remain in my seat and stare blankly at the floor. I knew Cecilia was a monster, but I didn't think she'd go to this extent to make my life miserable.

Tears drip on my cheeks, and Eli hugs me. "We'll get this sorted out. I'm going to talk to my lawyer and see what can be done about her. Maybe a restraining order is needed."

I melt into his arms, burying my face into his chest. "Thanks. I need to talk to Aunt Jen, too. I'm sure she'll be on this the moment she finds out."

"I'll see about hiring a permanent body guard, too," he adds.

I smile through my tears. "That's a little extreme. You're the one who should need the body guard."

He rubs his hand over my back. "I'll do everything in my power to keep you safe."

If only he could also protect my heart, too.

I pace my living room. Remnants of my train-wreck of an interview with Fae still linger in my mind. People ate up the drama, and it's been viewed more times than I can wrap my head around. Sorting through the mess of questions and screen capturing everything that Cecilia did online falls onto Eli. I can't even look at the screen without seeing red.

Setting his smart phone down, he motions for me to sit on the couch with him. "I'm saving some of the good stuff for you, too. Some people still have burning questions. Maybe you can answer a few more and show them the girl I know—how sincere and friendly and beautiful you are."

I plop down next to him and kiss him. "I'm sorry you have

to deal with this."

"Don't apologize, Nora. You wouldn't even be in this situation if it weren't for me," he says.

"You mean, if it weren't for my dad." The words come out sharper than I expected. "I'm just tired of reliving those months after over and over again. Cecilia used to threaten me daily, telling me, 'You just wait. You're going to regret that attitude.' She blew up at me when I only read a poem at my dad's memorial, like I somehow owed everyone my memories. Those are the only things I have left. They're mine. They're meaningless to everyone else." I sniffle into my hands.

Slinging his arms around me, he hugs me tighter. "She sounds insane."

"She is. She plays the victim so well that she has everyone convinced that I never loved my dad. Can you believe that?"

His mouth opens and closes. "Whoa. People don't seriously believe her, right?"

I rub my cheeks. "Like I said, she could win an Academy Award."

"The more you tell me about her, the more unbelievable it is that your dad would ever leave her anything. Something doesn't sound or feel right. And now she's attacking you from states away? This has to stop." He rubs his arms up and down my sides. "I'm gonna figure out how."

I suck in a long breath. "It's really okay, Eli. I don't want you in the middle of this craziness. You saw how she was. Do you really want the devil after you? I'll never forget how she made my dad cry one night because he wanted her to act like family, and she was being unreasonable. The only reason he didn't kick her out was because he was too sick to even deal. God, I hate her so much."

Eli falls silent, pondering whatever thoughts are going through his mind. I'm embarrassed sharing that terrible story with him, but I can't help it. I'm tired of hiding what happened. I'm tired of constantly having to defend myself.

After a long moment, he shifts to look at me. "Then let me help you figure out how to get her to stop. You don't have to do it alone."

"Let me discuss it with Aunt Jen. She hasn't even seen any of this yet."

"Okay, but I want to be here when you do."

I nod. "Why don't you show me all the good stuff while we wait then?"

Twenty minutes later, Aunt Jen flies into the house, her hair mussed and her eyes a little wild. She drops her briefcase in the hall, kicks off her heels, and plops down on the loveseat to the side of us. She tucks her bare feet under her before leaning on the armrest.

"You're not going to believe who called me today," she says.

"Cecilia?" I ask.

Her brows scrunch. "How did you know?"

I shrug. "She ruined my interview."

Aunt Jen thrusts her arms up. "Are you kidding me? That

woman has some nerve. She requested to speak to you, but I told her no."

I squeeze my eyes shut, rubbing my temple. I can't believe what I'm about to do, but this has gone on long enough. "I think I should talk to her."

She shakes her head so hard strands of hair fall from her bun. "Absolutely not. After everything she's done to you, she doesn't deserve to ever have contact with you again. We're going to get this all settled in the courts. She might want to talk to you as some twisted plan to get you to do or say something stupid."

I stare at my hands for a long moment. Aunt Jen has a point. The last thing I want is to be set up, but I know I have to face Cecilia once and for all. She thinks she can get away with intimidating me, but she can't. I'm not going to let her anymore. She's not my guardian—she's not anything to me anymore. She's nothing. Someone who is nothing to me can't have this kind of power over me. It ends here.

"I need to do this, Aunt Jen. I'll do it whether or not you want me to, but I'd love for you to support my decision and stay right here by my side as I call her." I swipe my phone from the coffee table and clutch it in my fingers. "I want to do it now."

Tears line Aunt Jen's eyes. "Okay, Nora. I'm here for you."

"Thanks."

I cradle my phone in my hand, staring at the digital keypad. I know Cecilia's number by heart. It's one digit off from what Dad's number was. My shaking hands stop me from dialing right away, and I consider not calling her after all. What if I can't find the words to shut her down? What if she hits one of my weak spots, and I lose it? The what-ifs pile high in my mind, nearly breaking the strength I've gathered to make the call.

After another long, quiet moment, I flick my gaze to Eli, and he gives me a quick nod. His hand rests on my knee, and I gather my nerve and tap Cecilia's phone number before putting my cell on speaker phone.

The long, drawn out rings echo through the quiet room, and just when I think it'll go to voicemail, Cecilia says, "This is Ceci."

I clear my throat. "Cecilia, it's Nora."

She doesn't respond right away. "Oh, hi, Nora! This is a nice surprise." Her nasally voice sounds sharp through the line. "How's everything going?"

My tongue sticks to the roof of my mouth as I try to determine what her angle is. She's acting like nothing happened between us—like we're old friends who haven't spoken in a while.

My breath sounds ragged when I inhale. "Let's skip the pleasantries. I'm calling because I need you to leave me alone. I don't know why you're trying to weasel your way back into my life, but I want you to stop. You've lost your chance at reconciling anything with me."

She snorts in the line. "Oh, Nora. You have such a wild

imagination."

I glare at my knees. "Stop playing games, Cecilia. You ruined my interview today."

She scoffs. "Are you kidding me? I made it a lot more entertaining, hon."

Anger washes over me in intense, hot waves. "You're insane and you need to stop. This is your only warning."

Her breath crackles in through the line. "What are you going to do?"

"I'll take legal action against you."

"Ha!" Her nasally voice hurts my ear. "Go ahead. The truth is already out there. Everyone knows that your dad didn't think you were worthy of anything. That's why he left you with nothing."

Aunt Jen flies up, attempting to snatch the phone from my hand. Eli waves his phone at her, showing that he's been recording the conversation.

My heart breaks all over again at the words it has taken me a long time to not believe. I still have trouble not believing them to be true. Dad had his reasons, but I can't think of any of them being good.

"Shut up," I finally say. "Dad wouldn't have wanted this. He loved me—and for some reason unbeknownst to me, he loved you, too. He wouldn't want you to treat me this way."

"You brought this on yourself, Nora. I warned you. I told you you'd regret the way you treated me."

"Treated you? You treated both me and Dad like dirt.

Someone had to stand up for him. What kind of person makes a cancer patient cry?" My voice rings through the air as I start to shout into the phone. I can't take it.

"You little bitch! You're going to regret that! I swear to God you will. You think I ruined your life before, you just wait. I know people. I can make things happen. I have made things happen." Cecilia's anger is so intense, I can feel it through the line.

"What's that supposed to mean?"

"I'm done talking to you. The next time you call, you better be begging for forgiveness."

"I haven't done anything wr—" The call drops before I have a chance to finish my sentence.

Eli wraps his arms around me, and Aunt Jen rubs my shoulder. Sobs burst from my throat, and all I can think about is how I poked the devil. Knowing Cecilia, she won't let this go. She'll figure out a way to make my life even more miserable. She won't stop. She never does.

"She's so in-insane," I stammer through tears. "What am I-I gonna d-do?"

Aunt Jen lifts my chin so I meet her eyes. "I want you to take a deep breath and relax. This isn't on you to figure out. I just want you to show her that she can't get to you. Then, I'm going to hire someone to investigate this entire situation. The things she said, well, they make me curious."

Eli hands me a few tissues. "I can help with that."

She nods. "That woman is not going to get away with

this."

I try to smile, but I can't. Cecilia has already gotten away with this. She's already won. Unlike the movies, sometimes the villains come out on top in the end.

chapter 21

Hello World

CUTTING CECILIA FROM my life has taken a team of people. After a week of finding her presence everywhere on the internet, commenting on every post, every picture, every article, and even everything of Eli's, Aunt Jen decided to hire someone to block and delete her from everything we could. Evelyn, the college student only a few years older than me, has been a lifesaver. She's tackled everything involving Cecilia with such finesse and professionalism. I wish Aunt Jen had hired her sooner. She even replies to Cecilia's comments on different websites, which makes Cecilia look crazy.

"Whoa, she started a blog," Evelyn says from my computer desk. "If only she'd put that kind of dedication to good use."

I pad across the room and peer at the computer screen from over her shoulder. "Today has been another awful day," I read out loud. "I miss Gil more than ever. He'd know what to do with his daughter. Her attitude is unbearable even though she's miles away. She blames me for how things are between us, but it was her fault. She thought she could do whatever she wanted since her dad was no longer around."

I cover my eyes with my hands and groan. "What should I do? She's spinning lies and twisting things."

Evelyn spins in the chair to face me. "Not much I can do since it's her blog, and she doesn't mention your name, but how about we start our own blog? Everything she writes, we can write the truth. People might eat it up."

I sigh. I'm living in an unrehearsed reality show that people love to follow. I hate the idea of writing a blog to contradict everything Cecilia says, giving people more drama to read, but I think Evelyn might be onto something. Clearly, ignoring her hasn't made her stop. It's time to fight fire with fire.

I lift my chin, motioning for her to get up. "I guess I'll give it a shot." Evelyn moves to sit on the edge of my bed, and I open up a blank document to write out my thoughts. It's been a while since I've written something personal. I have a lot of bad things to say, but I'm not going to stoop to her level. She might win the masses over with gossip, but they only pay any attention to her because she's a wreck. Everyone but her knows it.

The keys click as I begin to type.

Hello World,
I wanted to thank everyone who has been kind to me

over the last few weeks. Thank you for standing up for me, taking interest in me, reaching out to me, and making my life such a dream I never imagined was possible.

Y'all know I'm new to Beverly Hills and the industry. I'm only famous by association because of my love, Elijah Rousseau, and if it weren't for him, I wouldn't be receiving any attention at all. Life in front of a camera definitely isn't something I expected to happen, but I am thankful it has, because it's helped me cope with the turmoil of my past. It's helped me embrace my future.

As you know, I've lost both of my parents, and it was the hardest thing to ever endure. First my mother to an accidental fall and then my father to cancer. Both hurt equally, but losing my father devastated me because of what he left behind for me to deal with. You might think less of him for putting me in this situation, because what kind of father puts his child into a position that if it weren't for the help of family, they'd be nothing and have nothing? I used to question who my dad really was, too, but as it turned out, he always thought the best of people. He truly believed that his love for others rubbed off, and that others loved just as all-encompassing as he did. But the past is the past, and I'm sure if he could do something about it now, he would.

If you follow the drama of my life, I'm sure you've come across certain unpleasant people who criticize and shame me for purely existing, and I want you to know that while having hatred thrown at me is hurtful, I know in the end it can't really hurt me. I feel pity more than anything for those people—the ones who make it their mission in life to bring others down. Those who need to stand higher than everyone around them to feel good about themselves. Those who twist stories and live off the attention. You should feel sorry for those people, too. Because while they might look happy, they're not. And they might never be.

I'm taking the time to write this blog because I want those who follow me to know everything I've learned from the last few months. I want y'all to take it to heart and learn from my mistakes. I want you to know that I'm a real person with real problems. I want you to know that I do see you and hear you and think about you. I promise to be as transparent as possible. Feel free to reach out to me to ask about rumors or hearsay and never believe anything unless you hear it from me directly. I know you get it. We've all been gossiped about at one point in our lives. We are alike in a lot of ways.

Thanks for reading this, and please, don't egg on those who wish to see me down. I love y'all and wish only the best for you.

Love,
Nora Novak

The chair squeaks as I spin around to face Evelyn, who plays with her phone. My smile couldn't be any brighter now that I've got that off my chest. Even if no one reads it, I still feel better for putting the words out in the universe.

Evelyn stands at my desk and gazes over my blog. "Wow,

Nora. This is good. I mean it. It's really good. Not what I expected you to write."

I shrug. "I considered dragging Cecilia through the dirt, but she can do that herself."

She offers me a smile. "You were meant for the spotlight, you know."

I don't know how true her words are, but I'm going to try my best to get used to the lights and magic. I'm going to figure out how to make this my new normal. Not even Cecilia or my past can stop me.

Cool wind lifts up my hair, sending a chill over me. I snuggle up to Eli as we stroll through Beverly Canon Gardens in the direction of Rodeo Drive, walking instead of driving because I want to experience the magical feeling of the holiday season in Beverly Hills.

Christmas decorations shine from every light pole and store front, and strings of lights sparkle overhead. Magic hums through the air. The world is a glittering, California winter wonderland full of palm trees and city lights.

Eli rubs his hand up and down my arm when he feels me shiver. "Here, take my hoodie." White Christmas lights reflect in his dark eyes, and I lose myself in them.

"You'll freeze then. I'll be fine. Just hold me tighter."

He shrugs from his hoodie anyway, now wearing just a long-sleeved cotton shirt, and slides it over my head. I breathe in the scent of his cologne, the warm spices washing over me. It reminds me of every hug we've shared, and I can't help the smile crossing my face.

Eli laces his fingers through mine and tucks our hands into the front pocket of the hoodie. We stroll toward Wilshire to reach Rodeo Drive, and it's easy enough to lose ourselves on the crowded streets. It's as if all of Beverly Hills chose tonight to shop, and I peer around the festive streets in awe. I've never seen anything like it.

The palm trees on the center median of the road sparkle with red lights swirling up the trees like candy canes. White lights glitter from the smaller trees, and big, fake presents rest on the ground. Garland is strung over everything, and banners with holiday words such as joy, love, family, and giving hang from the light poles. A fountain trickles near a set of steps that leads up to stores and a giant Christmas tree with a bright star on top and hundreds of ornaments hanging from it.

The breathtaking sight is enough to take my mind off things. My blog post got more views than I ever dreamed of—and for the most part, it's been positively received according to Evelyn, who has been monitoring every comment as it comes in.

"Smile," Eli says, holding up his phone.

He snaps a photo before I have a chance to pose and stares at it for a moment before clicking a few buttons.

"What are you doing?" I ask, placing my hands on my hips.

"I want the world to see you as I do," he says.

How can I be annoyed with him after an answer like that?

When his smile widens, I stroll closer and drape my arms over his shoulders before linking my fingers together behind his neck. Gazing into his dark eyes, I stand on my tiptoes. I lean closer until our lips are only inches apart. "You know I love you, right?"

He grins before kissing me. After a long moment, he pulls away. My smile widens as the blinking lights dance around us. If it weren't for the hum of the shoppers and street traffic, I'd think we were in a world of our own.

A bright flash draws my attention away from Eli. I meet the eyes of a girl my age. She clutches a camera in her hands and stands frozen just a few feet away like she's considering running. It's how I felt the first time I met Hugo, and I can't help laughing into my hand.

I wave her over. "Would you like a picture with Elijah? I don't mind taking it." Over the last few weeks, I've decided not to run from Eli's fans. These are the same people who've supported me when my reputation was in shambles. If they talk about me online now, I want only good things to be said. I don't want to mess up their experience if they're brave enough to say hello.

Her eyes widen, and she looks over her shoulder as if I'm not talking to her. "I, uh, sure," she says after a moment. "I'm a huge fan."

She hands me her camera, and I snap a picture of her with Eli in front of the fountain. When I hand the camera back to her, she smiles at the little screen displaying the photo. "Can I have one with you too, Nora?"

My mouth falls agape. No fan has ever asked for a picture with me. It's weird. "Of course," I finally say when I realize I haven't responded.

The girl smiles and presses her cheek against mine when I put an arm around her. Eli takes a few of them, and I have him take one with his phone as well.

"What's your name?" I ask as she tucks her camera into her jacket pocket.

"I'm Melissa," she says. "And thanks for the pictures. You've made my day. I loved your blog by the way. I know how it feels to have bad things said about you."

Eli pulls me close again. "She's great, isn't she?"

The girl nods and then turns around when someone calls out her name. She waves once more and rushes off to a crowd of smiling people. I can hear her excited voice as she relays what happened.

Eli tugs my hand, drawing my attention back to him. "That was really nice of you."

I shrug. "I want to be known for my kindness and not for the things Cecilia says."

He kisses my temple. "You already are."

Movement from behind Eli catches my eye, and I notice a few people with cameras striding in our direction.

I squeeze his hand. "We shall see. Here comes trouble now."

He groans. "Come on, if we head inside somewhere, they

won't follow."

He tugs me along, and I ignore the voices ringing through the air, calling Eli's name. Before we reach the nearest store, a familiar voice echoes through the air, saying my name, and I freeze. The nasally sound sends anger and hurt through me, and I spin on my heels to face the woman who I wish would just disappear.

But she isn't among the crowd of paparazzi. I don't see her anywhere.

"Come on, Nora," Eli says, clamping his fingers on my shoulder.

"Nora, wait," a man says. "I have someone who wants to talk to you."

My mouth dries as I recognize the man. It's not the first time he's harassed me. He's the one who cornered me outside the bakery, promising me fame.

A scowl crosses my face, and the man next to him snaps a photo. It's enough to calm me down and remember that anything I do will be twisted and put on display for the world to see. I lower my shoulders and force my mouth to smile.

"You'll have better ratings if you focus on Eli. Have you seen him in *Creatures of Slaughter Creek* yet? He's amazing. It's one of my favorite shows, and I'm not just saying that."

Eli pulls me back a little, but I don't relent and stand firm in place.

"That's the only thing she's being truthful about," a feminine voice says from within the crowd.

My brows scrunch. "I don't understand."

The man holds up a tablet that I didn't notice before. The screen glows brightly, and my heart hurts as it clenches. It's one thing to hear Cecilia's voice over the phone—it's another to see her in a video call. Her naturally angry face greets me with a fake smile.

Eli slides in front of me, blocking me from glaring at the paparazzi and Cecilia. Who in the world thinks to do this? What do they get out of it? This is the vilest thing I've ever experienced.

"You better turn around and leave or you'll be hearing from my lawyer," Eli says. "Cecilia is not to contact Nora again."

"Hey, I didn't contact Nora. I contacted Hank. There's a difference." Cecilia's nasally voice rings out.

The other paparazzi continue to snap a few photos. Others from the growing crowd bring out their cell phones to grab a video.

I peek over Eli's shoulder. "Why are you doing this? I have done nothing wrong. I don't deserve this."

The crowd presses around us, onlookers more invested than they should be in what's happening. We couldn't easily escape if we wanted to. Dread slides down my back, the world closing in around me. The cool air warms as bodies block the breeze.

"You're right. You don't deserve this attention. You don't deserve the life you have. Remember your father, Nora? He died. I know you didn't love him as much as I did, and it shows with how you act. It's like you wanted him to die so you could move to Beverly Hills. He'd have never allowed this."

Surprise catches me off guard, her accusations stirring the rage in my soul threatening to come out. I'd love to give her a piece of my mind, but it's exactly what she wants. And now I know why she's been so terrible. She's jealous of me. She always has been. She was never the only girl in Dad's life, and she hates me for it.

A tear spills on my cheek. "Dad died of cancer. How can you even say that I wanted him to die? I'd accept having to deal with you for the rest of my life if it meant Dad was still alive."

"What's wrong with you?" Another voice says, coming from the crowd behind the paparazzi. "Don't talk to Nora like that."

More tears pour on my cheeks as the fan from earlier and her friends push through and get in front of the man, blocking his view of me.

"This is enough. You all got your pictures, now leave Nora and Elijah alone," a masculine voice says from behind me. "Come on, you two. You don't have to defend yourselves. There's nothing to defend."

I glance over my shoulder, my mouth dropping open when I see Alexandra's dad, Oscar, holding a few bags just behind us. Eli turns to his uncle and drags me with him. The paparazzi try to push past the people standing between us and them, but they can't unless they run into the busy street.

"You can't run from me forever, Nora!" Cecilia screams. "Don't think I won't fly out there."

I spin to face the paparazzo holding the tablet with her video chat on it. "Then fly out here. You won't accomplish anything. You'll just prove to the world how crazy you really are. I'm done with you. You can try to bring me down all you want, but you can't."

"Your dad would be so disappointed in the way you're treating me. You know how much he loved me. He did leave me everything, remember?" she calls out.

"Like you'll ever let me forget. I'm sure it wasn't his intention. I'm sure he wanted you to take care of me, Ceci." I haven't used her nickname in forever. "You thought I was out to try to take everything, which wasn't the case. You were my stepmom. It's not like it's the law that you *have* to keep everything, either. Like the model boat—my dad and grandma made it together. Why do you even want it? Oh, and I'd have loved to get some of my mom's stuff—like her wedding ring. That means nothing to you, but you hid it away so I couldn't have it."

Her lack of response shows I hit a nerve by airing my grievances publicly. Maybe I have finally showed her reason.

The crowd goes utterly silent. If it weren't for the cars crawling by, gawking out the window, I'd have thought I'd gone deaf.

"You poor thing," a woman says from next to me.

Without saying another word, I trail behind Eli through the parting crowd. Oscar motions for us to follow him to where he's parked on the street. A few people snap pictures of our departure, and I wave at Melissa, the girl who stood up for me.

Leaning back in the seat, I take a breath, letting my heartbeat slow. Eli slides his arm around me, pulling me closer. I release a shaking breath, tears threatening to consume me, leaving me processing all the good and bad. I don't look forward to the buzz I'm sure will be all over the internet tomorrow.

"You were really brave, Nora," Eli whispers into my hair.

I close my eyes. "I'm not really brave. I'm just tired of her lies and accusations."

"I think the whole world will be soon enough."

It's all I can hope for.

chapter 22

MUSIC HUMS INTO my ears. I blast my headphones, trying to finish my final paper for my English class before the semester's over. School has taken a backseat the last few weeks, and it's taken a lot of extra work to keep my GPA up. I've never gotten a C in my life, and I'm not starting now.

My phone lights up on my desk, drawing my gaze away from my monitor. I peer at Taylor's smiling picture. I hit the accept call button without removing my earbuds, since I'm listening to music on my phone.

I tap a few keys without typing anything. "What's up, Tay? Sorry I forgot to call you back. I'm swamped with homework. Next time text."

"No way. I needed to hear your voice. Did you see the links I emailed you?" She huffs air into the line. "I guess not," she says before I have a chance to answer, "because if you had, you'd have called me back immediately."

I minimize my essay and pull up my email. Dozens of notification emails and fan letters forwarded from Evelyn crowd my inbox, and I have to search for the one from Taylor. After a minute, I spot her untitled email and click it open. The link takes me to one of the most popular tabloid sites, and an image of Eli and me from Rodeo Drive pops up under the headline, *Elijah Rousseau, Prince Charming? Nora Novak, Modern Cinderella, Faces off with Wicked Stepmother.*

I cover my mouth with my hand. "Oh, boy. Who writes this stuff?"

"Shhh! Just read it. It's great."

Cecilia Armstrong Rogers Novak, 38, verbally harassed Elijah Rousseau and his girlfriend, Nora Novak, via video call on Rodeo Drive. Reps of Elijah Rousseau confirm that Cecilia leaked untruthful rumors to try to harness the rising star's reputation. What can only be described as family drama fit for the movies, a confrontation between Nora and Cecilia shines the spotlight on the truth behind the alleged story that Nora was using Elijah to gain fame after being cut out of her deceased father's will. Upon further investigation, an anonymous source has revealed that Gil Novak might not have actually left his assets to Cecilia. We contacted Cecilia about the situation but have been unable to reach her. Rousseau's reps could not comment on the legal matters.

My hands shake, and I inhale and exhale long breaths. I'm not sure who contacted the tabloid or if it's even true, but that would mean that Cecilia committed fraud.

"Taylor, this is crazy. Think it's real?" I ask.

"If it is, this would answer a lot of questions."

I push from my desk. "Thanks for looking out for me. Can I call you back later? I have to find Aunt Jen."

"You better."

I blow a kiss into the phone and hang up before I rush from my bedroom. Aunt Jen's voice echoes from the living room as she talks on her cell phone in the kitchen with her usual cup of coffee.

Her eyes meet mine, and they shine with an expression I've never seen on Aunt Jen before. A line puckers between her eyebrows. She starts to pace, lowering her voice a notch when she realizes I'm not leaving.

"You sure about everything? And she's willing to make a deal? Yes, of course. We can fly out in a few days." She eyes me when I raise my eyebrows. "I'd like to set things in motion as soon as possible. Thanks for all your help. I'll have my assistant email everything you need and set up the meetings. Great. Have a good day." She hangs up the phone and sets it on the counter.

"You're traveling?" I ask, leaning my elbows on the bar.

"You, too. We're going to Austin," she says.

I suck in a ragged breath. "Does this involve the anonymous source that says Cecilia committed fraud?"

She frowns. "How'd you know?"

"It's online."

Her lips make an O-shape. "Well, this should be interesting."

"What does it all mean?"

She strolls around to hug me. "It means you're going to get what is rightfully yours and karma has finally come to drag Cecilia down."

Eli rubs his hands up and down my arms. The crisp air of the Austin-Bergstrom International Airport wraps around us the moment we step through the automatic doors. I zip my coat all the way up and watch cars zip by the loading zone.

Winter break couldn't have come at a better time. School's out until January, and Eli's show doesn't resume filming until February. Also, as his movie launch closes in on him, things might get hectic quickly. Who knows when we'll have this kind of time together? If only I didn't have to face the demons from my past.

Aunt Jen and Julian bustle through the automatic doors, rolling suitcases twice the size of mine and Eli's. Aunt Jen groans when cold wind whips her hair and looks up at the dark, cloudy sky. A loud rumble hums through the air, and I smirk when the three of them jump. Beverly Hills doesn't get storms like Austin, and it's almost comforting to be welcomed by something so familiar.

"Our ride will be here in five. She's running late." Julian removes his scarf and wraps it around Aunt Jen's neck.

She pushes her dark hair from her face. "I don't miss this." Just as the words escape her mouth, rain starts pouring from the sky. She steps closer to the glass window behind us. "Yeah, definitely don't miss this. Of course it would rain the moment I return."

I laugh. "I told you there was a chance of rain."

"I forgot that a chance of rain here means it will definitely rain."

Eli snuggles against me from behind. A woman driving a black SUV pulls to a stop in the loading area and hops out with an umbrella big enough for three and opens the cargo area before heading our way.

"I almost didn't recognize you, Jen," the red-haired woman says as she air kisses Aunt Jen's cheeks. She shakes Julian's hands. "It's nice to finally meet you in person, Julian."

Aunt Jen turns to me and Eli. "Stacia, this is my niece, Nora, and her boyfriend Eli."

Stacia greets me with a warm smile. "I feel like I know both of you already. I'm glad we could finally settle this all, and you two can get back to worrying about someone catching you making a weird face instead of some criminal trying to ruin you. This whole situation still makes me sick."

I clear my throat as my mouth has trouble working. "Tell me about it. I can't thank you enough."

She reaches out and touches my shoulder. "You're lucky so many people care about you. That monster would've gotten away with it otherwise."

"This is all so surreal," I say.

"Like being part of a movie," Eli says.

Stacia purses her lips. "Maybe you should write the script."

After a moment, Julian and Eli help load the bags into the back of the SUV, and we all climb in, slightly damp from the rain that stopped the moment we shut the doors. Stacia and Aunt Jen discuss the action plan in the front on the way to the hotel, the same one my father managed. Sadness washes over me, remembering all the times I came here after my mom died.

I wish Aunt Jen had chosen somewhere else, but she trusted the staff to protect and keep our stay a secret. The last thing we need is unwanted guests and attention.

I don't move when everyone exits the SUV, and Eli stays at my side. "I'm not ready to go inside yet. Want to go grab something to eat instead?" I ask.

He nods. "I can call a cab."

"Why don't y'all just take my car?" Stacia says through the half-opened door. "I'll be here a while. You two shouldn't have to be bored on your visit. You should make the most of it."

Aunt Jen nods. "That sounds like a great idea."

Twenty minutes later, I direct Eli into the parking lot of my parents' favorite place to eat. Taylor waves at us from the front entrance of Trudy's, a Tex-Mex restaurant. She rushes to the car and flings her arms around me as I step out.

"I'm so happy you're here, Nora. What did I tell you about karma? I knew she'd come around to take the devil woman down." Taylor links her arm with mine and pulls me toward Eli, who's waiting at the rear of the SUV. She then grabs his arm, so we're on both sides of her. "Will she get jail time?

Please, tell me she'll end up where she belongs."

I shrug. "I honestly have no idea. Aunt Jen's handling everything as my legal guardian. I technically didn't even have to come, but she wants to keep me in the loop."

"God, this is fan-freaking-tastic," she says, smiling.

The hostess opens the door for us, her eyes widening as she sees Eli. It's hard not to be recognized these days when his movie trailer plays during what feels like every commercial break and pops up in every ad online.

Taylor pulls us past her with a quick wave and points to a booth in the corner. Chad Miller, Taylor's new boyfriend, sits on the side facing us. I haven't seen him since my dad's funeral, and he looks different than I remember him with his trimmed blond beard and lack of his usual baseball cap.

He slides from the booth when we approach and pulls me into an unexpected hug. He shakes Eli's hand next before turning to Taylor to kiss her cheek and let her slide into the booth before he sits down. Eli slides in the opposite side and laces his fingers through mine under the table.

In the middle of the thick, wooden table lies a giant bowl of chips and queso, and I immediately swipe up a chip and dip it. "This feels so normal."

Chad waggles his eyebrows at me. "You're all sorts of famous around here, ya know. Everyone wants to see you and meet Elijah. You've made Tay the most popular girl in school."

My cheeks burn with embarrassment. I sort of feel bad for not keeping in contact with anyone apart from Taylor. "Taylor did that all herself."

She grins at me while rubbing her hand up Chad's arm. "Yeah, babe. I told you I'm responsible for these two lovebirds, too."

Eli laughs next to me. "Nora might've not given me a chance if Taylor hadn't initiated a conversation with me."

I lightly tap his arm. "She was lucky to be states away, or I'd have killed her."

After we order our food from an extra friendly server, our conversation shifts to storytelling. I start to notice the people around us falling silent when Eli shares some funny stories from the filming of *Creatures of Slaughter Creek* and all the pranks he and Hugo play on his cast mates. Taylor and Chad laugh out loud, and I smile and hug Eli's arm. I never thought it would be nice to return to Austin, and I couldn't have asked for a better start to our trip.

"Well, what a pleasant surprise." The familiar voice sends dread up my spine. "I didn't expect to see you here, Nora."

My voice sticks in my throat. I shift my gaze to meet Cecilia's bemused eyes. I don't open my mouth to say anything. Maybe if we ignore her and pretend she didn't just ruin my entire evening, she'll leave us alone. I should've known better than to pick a place where there was even a slight possibility of running into her, but I wanted to bring Eli to a place that held so many good memories for me.

After a moment of utter silence from the table, I force words out of my mouth. "You should probably leave us alone."

"Can't the woman who helped raise you at least say hi? I'm trying to be nice."

Eli squeezes my fingers under the table before saying, "So now you want to be nice? It's a little late for that. Do what Nora asked and leave us alone before I have someone call the authorities."

She scowls, and I think if we weren't in public, she might've reached out and smacked Eli across the face. Cecilia stiffens, squaring her shoulders, and says, "Y'all are crazy treating me this way. You think you're too good being famous and all."

I shake my head while I press my index finger to my lips. The best thing to do is not engage with her. She feeds on attention.

Cecilia rolls her eyes when she realizes we're not going to respond to her remarks and plops down at the wooden table right next to us even though the server hasn't even had a chance to clear the table of empty plates from the previous patrons.

She leans on her elbows, playing with her phone, and I feel like she might be recording us. Taylor raises her eyebrows, looking between me and Eli, and then she waves for our server to bring us to-go boxes and our check since we've barely started eating.

Anger rolls through my heart that she still has any sort of power over me. I shouldn't have to leave because she's here, but I don't want any more conflict. She's well aware of our legal situation, but she's always had this air of self-entitlement, thinking that the laws don't apply to her.

After paying for the check, we head to the front. Eli and Taylor flank my sides with Chad leading the way. Voices mumble from behind us, and I can hear a server suggest that Cecilia stay a while and offer her a drink on the house.

She throws around F-bombs like it's the only word she knows, making a scene, and we don't even make it out from under the covered entrance before she's screaming at me to face her.

"Nora! We need to talk. Stop shutting me out. I know I've made some mistakes, and I feel really bad. I just can't help how angry I am at your dad." Her voice echoes through the air.

I spin on my feet, pulling myself from Eli and Taylor. "Are you kidding me, Cecilia?" I stride closer. "Do you hear yourself? You're treating me this way because you're mad at my dad?"

She clenches her hands at her sides. "Before he died, when he knew the cancer was going to take him, all he ever did was think about you. Not once did he think about me." Deep wrinkles crease her forehead. "I've spent the last few years doing everything for him, and he just goes and dies."

I close my eyes and suck in a breath through my nose. "You say it like he had a choice."

"He could've thought things through!"

Eli grabs my elbow. "Come on, Nora. She's trying to get under your skin."

I shake away from him, still facing Cecilia. "I don't even know what to say to you. If you would've just been there for me, treated me how Dad wanted you to treat me, things could've been so different. What you did was so mind-blowing and messed up. I have no words to even describe how I feel."

She shakes her finger at me. "Don't act like this is all my fault. I had to protect myself."

"Protect yourself? What the hell do you think would've happened if you'd just been honest? I'm not some awful person. You were my family. My dad loved you."

"Then why did he leave me with nothing?" She covers her hand over her mouth as the words escape.

My eyes widen even though I know that she committed fraud. It's just shocking to hear her admit it out loud. I step forward and touch her shoulder. I hate how much pity I feel for Cecilia. She made me feel this way when she blindsided me with what I now know was a forged will—one so well-done, it passed through court.

"He didn't leave you with nothing, Ceci. He left you with me. I wouldn't have kicked you out and left you in the cold."

Her eyes soften for a split second before anger narrows them. "Liar. All you've done is try to turn your dad against me."

"You're insane!" I can't stop my voice from rising. "You need some serious help. I'll even help you pay for it."

I don't have time to react as she raises her hand and slaps me across the face hard enough to jerk my head to the side. Pain explodes in my cheek, and the world blurs, tears bursting from my eyes. Cecilia's screams ring out louder than anyone's, and she locks her fingers in my hair to pull me down.

Commotion breaks out, and strong hands catch me, ripping me from Cecilia. Eli pulls me away, and Chad and one of the servers restrain Cecilia as Taylor yells in her phone. My heart races with anger and shock, and my entire body trembles. I replay everything in my head over and over again.

Eli sits me in the front seat of the SUV. He leaves me for a few minutes to return inside and then comes back with a towel. "Here." He hands me a tissue while pressing the damp towel to my head. "You're bleeding."

I sniffle, catching sight of the scratches on my temple, receding into my scalp in the rearview mirror. "Take me back to the hotel, please. I don't want to stay."

He slides his arms around me while still standing protectively outside my open door. "The police are on their way. Cecilia's not getting off so easily."

"She'll claim we set her up," I say.

He shakes his head. "Not gonna happen. Someone recorded it on video, and there were plenty of witnesses."

"Sorry you had to see that," I murmur.

He touches my chin. "Don't be. I just wish I could've protected you. It happened so fast."

Red and blue lights draw our attention to the covered entrance of Trudy's where I see Cecilia still being restrained by Chad and a server. Fear prickles over my arms, sending goosebumps over my skin, and two police officers step from their vehicle and take control of the situation.

After what feels like an eternity, another police car pulls up.

A cop handcuffs Cecilia and puts her in back of the police car. Taylor speaks to a female officer and motions in our direction before crossing the parking lot with the woman and her partner.

"Hello, I'm Officer Grayson. Do you need medical attention?"

I glance at the scratches in the mirror again and shake my head. "I'll live."

"Okay. I'd like to get your statement about what happened." The woman touches the front of her vest. "This is a body cam, so it'll record your statement."

"Is Cecilia under arrest?"

She nods. "Several witnesses confirmed that she attacked you. What is your relationship with Mrs. Novak?"

I frown. "She was my stepmom before my dad died."

"I'm sorry to hear about that. Can you tell me exactly what happened?"

I press my lips together and take a deep breath before recounting everything that happened between me and Cecilia. The officers shoot more questions at me, and then after a while, they ask me to write everything out for them even though they recorded it. They take a few pictures of the scratches on my face and look at me with sympathy.

As the officers wrap up with me, a white taxi pulls up and Aunt Jen and Stacia bolt from it and run in our direction. One of the officers hands me a thick envelope with a pamphlet about being a victim and how I can get help.

Once everything's settled, Aunt Jen pulls me into an embrace. "I'm so sorry, Nora. I swear that woman will be punished to the full extent of the law. I'll see to it myself."

I sigh. "I just want to go back to the hotel and forget all this happened."

She nods. "Deal. The good news is that she won't be coming near you again. This was the last straw."

She's right. I can finally put my past behind me for good and move on. I've never been more ready.

chapter 23

I SIT NEXT to Aunt Jen across from Stacia in her office as she overlooks the details to contest Dad's will. As it turns out, Cecilia not only forged a will, but she had a lawyer, who everyone thought was my dad's lawyer, draw up the paperwork while my dad was dying in the hospital. Her cousin also happened to be a notary and gave the documents his stamp of approval. Two friends of Cecilia's pretended to be witnesses. They were also the ones who verified the signature. A lot of people face legal trouble now that things have come to light, and they're all blaming Cecilia as the mastermind.

"If she even contacts you, her bond will be revoked, and she'll be arrested," Stacia says.

"Think she'll get jail time?" Eli asks from behind me.

Stacia shrugs. "Criminal law isn't my forte, but she'll most likely plea out of it. It was her first offense, and she doesn't have a record—that is, if she has a good lawyer. If the case makes it to trial, you will have to testify, though."

My chest tightens at the thought. "What about the forgery?" I ask. It's hard not to pity Cecilia even after everything. Dad did love her, and he was a forgiving man. But does she deserve my forgiveness? I don't know.

"She's facing up to two years for that and some fines, but I don't want you to worry about any of this. Let my team handle everything." Stacia leans back in her chair. "Just know that we'll get your dad's estate in order, and within the next few months, you can decide what to do. You'll be eighteen soon enough, so your options are open."

Everything is hard to process. His estate is enough to pay for college and give me a fresh start without having to ask Aunt Jen for anything.

I meet Aunt Jen's eyes before turning to Stacia. "I don't know how to thank you, Stacia."

She smiles. "It's my job."

Aunt Jen slides her arms around me and hugs me. I stand and turn to Eli, who hugs me as well. It feels good to finally have control over everything. I'll no longer have to worry about my past being dragged through the media or hiding things I'm embarrassed about. Being in Eli's spotlight has been hard enough. Who knows? Maybe I'll actually enjoy it. Maybe I can use it for something good.

Aunt Jen picks up her purse. "Now that all that's taken care of, why don't we celebrate?"

"Sounds good to me," Eli says.

"I know the perfect place."

I flop on my hotel room bed, still smelling like the scent of barbeque from The Salt Lick, where we met Taylor and her parents for dinner. I wanted to take Eli to another place I loved to go to growing up, and that was the perfect place. It was exactly the same as I remembered it with its giant, circular grill filled with huge slabs of meat, stone walls, wooden bench tables you share with strangers, and twinkling white lights strung along the perimeter. It brought back a lot of good memories with my family. I'm glad I got to share it with Eli since he's shared so much with me.

"Austin really is weird," Eli says, shoving our leftovers into the mini-fridge. "Hugo's not going to believe you can bring your own beer."

I laugh. "It's strange that in LA you don't."

"Good point."

Eli pounces on the bed next to me, sliding his arm under my back to pull me close. I meet his eager lips with mine, tasting the peach cobbler dessert we shared after dinner with every kiss. His hands travel up my shirt, tracing the strap of my bra, and I roll on top of him and lean down to trail my lips down his neck.

This moment couldn't be any more perfect. It's like a weight has been lifted from me. I now see the world with different eyes. I'll cherish every second, because every second counts toward my life—they all add up to who I am and who I want to be. I don't want to be that person Cecilia swore I'd be. I don't want to be anything like Cecilia. And there's only one way I know how.

I pull away from Eli, panting, now distracted.

He frowns. "What's wrong?"

I flip onto my back next to him and stare at the ceiling. "I don't want to be the girl everyone is expecting me to be."

He sits up and pushes my hair out of my face. "I don't understand."

I prop up on my elbows. "I thought I'd be okay after today, but I can't stop thinking about Cecilia."

He leans in and kisses me again. "Let me help you take your mind off her. She doesn't deserve another one of your thoughts."

I gently push him away and shake my head. "Is it crazy that I feel bad for her?"

"Yes, absolutely." His eyes speak the million words that grip my heart.

My rational side fights with my compassion, and I'm not sure which will win. "I think I'm going to help her out."

He grimaces. "Even after everything? You're too good a person, Nora."

A tear slips from my eye. "I'm afraid if I don't do this, I'll end up just like her. People expect me to celebrate and be so happy. But I'm not. I wish that Cecilia never put me in this position."

He touches my face. "She put herself in this position. No one else. This was her doing, and you shouldn't feel bad that she has to deal with the consequences."

I know I should believe him, but the last few months have changed me. I'm not the villain Cecilia thinks I am—the one she thought she was fighting against to save herself in the end. And Cecilia's not the villain of my story, either. She acted in desperation. I can't hate someone I pity.

"My dad was a firm believer in forgiveness. He'd want me to forgive her. He wouldn't want these horrible feelings to haunt me the rest of my life," I say. "They will if I don't show her that I can act the way my dad raised me. Who knows, maybe she'll realize what a fool she's been. Maybe she'll finally get that we're not enemies. We're both just a little lost without the man who thought he'd always be here for us."

"There's no talking you out of this?" he asks.

I shake my head. "Nope." Deep down, I know Cecilia has a good side. It got lost in the tragedy of our bad circumstances. Hopefully with this reality check and my kindness and forgiveness, she'll be able to move on with her life. It's all I've ever wanted, and I'm sure she will, too.

"The tabloids are going to eat this up." He swirls his finger through the air as he writes imaginary words. "Inherited insanity? Nora Novak helps woman who sought to destroy her."

I roll my eyes. "Or maybe it won't say anything at all since this isn't newsworthy."

He grins. "You're right. Maybe we should give them something better to talk about. Should I take Taylor somewhere for fun without you? Or maybe we should fly to Paris?" His shoulders shake with laughter. "Oh, I know what'll really get them talking. How about a trip to a jewelry store?"

I laugh, thinking about all the funny, fake headlines people would come up with. "You'll drive your publicist crazy."

"Have to keep her busy now that things will finally settle."

"I love this—getting to make our own headlines."

He pulls me into an embrace. "You know what I love?"

I press my forehead against his. "What?"

"You."

The fake Christmas tree glows from the corner of my old living room. Today is the last day we're in Austin, and I finally have the chance to go through my parents' belongings. Even though Aunt Jen begged me not to, I'm letting Cecilia stay in the house until she gets her life back in order. I have no idea how everything will work out in court, but with my help, she has a fighting chance. In return, she'll be seeing a psychologist for the help she finally realized she needed.

It's strange—this is my first Christmas without Dad, and the house feels empty without him, yet I somehow manage not to shed any tears. It's almost like he's here with me, Mom too, and they're watching Eli shifting nervously, tapping his foot on the wood floor.

After a minute, he pulls a small wrapped box from his

pocket. "I have something for you."

My heart thumps as I tear the silver paper to reveal a rectangular velvet box. My hands shake so hard that Eli ends up opening it for me, and a diamond and ruby heart glitters on a white gold chain.

I suck in a breath. "It's beautiful, Eli. I love it." I lift my hair so he can clasp it around my neck.

"Like you."

I kiss his cheek and hand him the gift bag by my feet. "My gift is definitely lame."

He chuckles, pulling the blue *Keep Austin Weird* shirt from the bag. I couldn't resist since it's what sparked our first conversation. "I love it, Nora."

He kisses me for a long while, twisting my brown hair between his hands, resting them behind my neck. It takes Aunt Jen clearing her throat to draw our attention away from each other.

"Hey, Nora? Did Cecilia ever show you this?" She holds up a tan, unsealed envelope. "I found it in your dad's safe."

I get off the couch and walk to her. Her gaze drifts to my necklace, and she smiles, handing me the envelope. It's thicker than I expect and contains a dozen or so papers along with a few smaller envelopes. They're all addressed to me. The documents in the envelope are financial statements and other legal documents like mine and my mom's birth certificates as well as her death certificate. My heart hurts looking at them, so I hand those to Aunt Jen and focus on the first envelope with my name on it.

I break the seal, surprised Cecilia didn't do it for me without my knowledge. Tears burst from my eyes when I see the handwritten letter from my dad. I move to sit down on the couch and lean forward to rest my elbows on my knees. Dad dated the letter a month before he died, and I'm angry I didn't get to read it until now.

My Nora,

Nothing in life could have prepared me to accept the knowledge that I won't always be around for you. I still don't believe it, but with all the bad test results and the cancer spreading, I know I must prepare myself for the inevitable. The only comfort I have is that I know you'll be taken care of after I'm gone, and that you're such a strong girl who'll be a beautiful woman soon enough. You're just like your mom was, and I know that you'll pull through this.

I know life ain't always gonna be easy on you, and there will be times that you'll need my advice, and I want to be able to give you that. I want to share everything I learned in life with you, to be able to teach you and guide you as you navigate the world. I know the only way I'll be able to do that is if I write it all down now, because I'm not feeling so hot tonight, and it scares me that I'll leave too many things unsaid.

So, first things first. You gotta know I'm a simple, hardworking man, so try not to be too disappointed with what I'm gonna say next. If life taught me anything, it would be that none of us knows what we're doing. We're just trying to make it by and make the best of what we're given. But that's not what life's about. I've wasted too much time on things I didn't care about when I should've been more focused on doing things I love, even if it didn't amount to anything. What were all those double shifts and late nights worth when I should've been spending them with you and your mom? I even threw myself into work for Cecilia because she always wanted the pretty things in life, and I wanted to make her happy. But I got it wrong. She would've been happier if I'd been around more—and I know you would've liked that, too. I hate that it took me slowly dying to figure out all that. At least in the end, I get to spend my few remaining days with my girls.

Nora, you are the light of my life. You make me want to be a better man because I want you to be proud to be my daughter. I want you to know that I always tried my best for you, and I hope you know that I'm fighting as hard as I can for as many days as I can just to spend them with you.

We're lucky in a way, being able to prepare for good-bye. I used to be so angry that your mom left us like she did. She knew good and well that I couldn't do this alone. But as it turned out, I could. I forgave her, and I hope you'll be able to forgive me one day. You have every right to be angry that I'm dying. But don't hold onto those sour emotions. This life taught me that anger and guilt are worthless. The point is to live and live well. Live and love and enjoy every day, every moment. I want you to keep smiling, because it's the most beautiful smile I've ever laid eyes on. Keep laughing, because it's always been music to my ears. And keep on going, because there's no point in walking backward when you have the whole world in front of you.

I hope that one day you'll find what you're looking for in life like I did. I'm leaving all of my worldly possessions to you to help, Nora, because your mom and I made the decision long ago, that no matter what happened between us, you'd always come first. I trust you'll be there for Cecilia when I'm gone, because she'll need you. You have a big heart and see things in others that people can't even see in themselves.

I love you very much, Nora, and I wish I could write this letter forever, because then I'd never have to leave you. I'd never have to say goodbye for now and until we meet again. You are my sunshine, my sparkling night sky, my universe, my heart.

Forever yours,
Dad

Tears stain Dad's letter as I crinkle the edges and read it a second time. It's like he's here with me now, reading along, and hugging me with his strong arms like he always did every day when he left for work.

"Cecilia knew their entire marriage that Dad was leaving everything to me," I say.

Aunt Jen hugs me. "It's not too late to change your mind about things."

"No. I don't want to be that person who does things out of spite."

Eli hands me a tissue to dry my eyes before pulling me close and kissing my forehead. I hand Eli my dad's letter, wanting to share a piece of him with the one I love, and after a moment, Eli's watery eyes meet mine.

"Your dad was a wise man, Nora," he says.

I nod, letting Dad's letter really sink in. I've been so concerned about the stupid things in my life that I forgot to appreciate all the things that make me happy. All the things that make my life worth living. I want to make Dad proud of me, to show him that he did well raising me. I want the world to see my dad in me through my actions—through my life.

I smile. "He was, wasn't he?" I flip through the other envelopes and notice he scribbled directions on each one. My heart swells, seeing that this one letter isn't all. He left me one for every milestone in my life.

I hold one with, *Your First Love*, written across it. I consider opening it while I'm in private, but I can't wait. I tear the seal and hold onto a plain piece of paper with a small paragraph written on it.

Nora,

Love like it's the first time every time—with a big heart, without worry, and like it's never gonna end. Love as deeply as you can, to the moon, to the stars, to the universe, because love is not to be reasoned with, and it'll sometimes make you crazy, but it's worth it.

Love,
Dad

The doorbell rings, drawing my attention away from my dad's pretty sound advice on love. Aunt Jen crosses the room to let Taylor and her family in.

I tuck the note away without letting Eli or anyone else read it. Dad's right. Even though I've had my ups and downs with Eli, I wouldn't change anything. My love for Eli was unexpected, and like Dad said, I love him to the moon and stars, to the universe, and he does the same. Our love is vast and unending, surprising and never dull. Full of hope and dreams and unrivaled beauty.

I smile, gazing at the people I love on what I think might really be one of the best days of my life since losing my parents. Things have never been clearer.

I know what I want for my future—to live life the best I can with the people I love most in the world. To love life with a big heart, without worry, like it's never going to end—just like I was meant to do.

epilogue

Ready to Take on the Madness

HELLO WORLD,

The last few weeks have been a whirlwind, and I couldn't have asked for better fans than you. Eli thanks you as well, by the way. I'm sure you've read the tabloids lately, and I wanted to make sure y'all know that I'm in a good place. A lot of you have reached out to me across social media, and I do try to read everything you post, but it's easier to answer your questions on a wider scale than individually. So, here goes nothing.

1. Why did you go to Austin when you knew your step-mom was there?

I went because she was there. Ceci hasn't been in a good place, and while I can't discuss the details of my trip, just know that wrongs have been righted, and I forgive her—so you should, too.

2. Are you staying in Beverly Hills?

Yes, I don't plan on going anywhere, unless it's on vacation.

3. I read on some tabloid that someone was making your life into a movie. Is this true?

Nope! Not true at all.

4. I heard that you got offered a part on *Creatures of Slaughter Creek*. That is so cool!

It is cool! I couldn't believe it. It's a very small guest role—literally just two lines—and who knows if I'll even make it into the final cut of the show, but it was such an awesome experience. I can't wait to be able to share more stuff about it.

5. Are you and Elijah getting married?

Whoa! I'm seventeen! So, no. If you saw photos of him at a jewelry store, it was because he bought me a beautiful necklace. You can see it in the picture below.

I know y'all have so many more questions, but I'll have to get to them later. I'm on the way to support Eli on his press tour for his upcoming movie, *The Incredible Life of the Boy with Wings*. I'm super excited about it, and I hope y'all are, too. If you're around in an hour, watch out for our live video from the red carpet. We can't wait to share it with you!

Love always,

Nora

I post the letter to my blog and set my tablet on the leather seat next to me. Eli squeezes my hand, looking sexy in his textured midnight blue suit that matches my floor-length, shimmery gown.

When the limo pulls up in front of the red carpet and the driver opens the door, the screams of fans and the flash of camera lights turn the world into beautiful chaos. Eli shifts in his seat to look at me and smiles.

"You ready to take on the madness?" he asks, lacing his fingers with mine.

I nod. "I'm ready to take on the world."

And I know that I really am.

-The End-

acknowledgements

I HAVE SO many people I want to thank, who have helped me throughout every stage of writing this book. As always, many thanks to my team—Jan Moran, Jamie Hall, Katie Harder-Schauer, and Sarah Collier for your hard work in helping me produce the best book possible. I don't know what I'd do without you all. Jan, your knowledge of Beverly Hills has been such a help. Thanks for giving me the grand tour and introducing me to many inspiring people.

Thank you to Vana Margolese for letting me stay in your home in Beverly Hills, and many thanks to Aly Spencer for sharing some great stories with me and also for recommending places I should go.

Thanks to my husband Eric Moran for all your love and support. Thank you for driving me around both Austin and Beverly Hills because you know how much I hate driving in traffic. Thanks for letting me ditch you and Zoë for a while in Santa Monica so I could wander around and take all the pictures my heart desired. And thanks for being the best. I love you more!

Thanks to everyone who has helped me during some of my most trying times in life that was some of the inspiration behind this story. To my family, both in California and Texas, who are too many to name, for always being there for me. You all are my heroes. Thanks to Mom, Dad, Eddie, Sue, Tami, Jason, Bill, Helen, and Cathy for everything you've done for me. Thanks to Jazmin for your endless encouragement. Thanks for making the trip to visit me in Beverly Hills and for the hilarity that ensued in Whole Foods. Even a year and a half later, I still can't stop laughing. Thanks to Nikki Godwin, Malory Knezha, Amy Holliday, and Nicole Schubert for your friendships. You guys rock! Also, thanks to Lily Millan, who once corrected me while I sang an incorrect song lyric, which I used as the inspiration for Eli's name.

Lastly, thanks to my readers, near and far, for giving me a chance. Without you, these stories would stay locked up forever.

about ginna moran

GINNA MORAN IS a writer living in Austin, Texas originally from sunny Southern California. She started writing poetry as a teenager in a spiral notebook that she still has tucked away on her desk today. Her love of writing grew after she graduated high school and she completed her first unpublished manuscript at age eighteen.

When she realized her love of writing was her life's passion, she studied literature at Mira Costa College in Northern San Diego. Besides writing novels, she was senior editor, content manager, and image coordinator for Crescent House Publishing Inc. for four years.

Aside from Ginna's professional life, she enjoys binge watching television shows, playing pretend with her daughter, and cuddling with her dogs. Some of her favorite things include chocolate, anything that glitters, cheesy jokes, and organizing her bookshelf.

Ginna Moran loves to hear from her readers so visit her online at www.GinnaMoran.com. You can also find her on Facebook, Twitter, Instagram, Snapchat, and Pinterest. To stay up-to-date on new releases, sign up to her newsletter. You'll not only get a FREE short story, but you'll be able to participate in monthly giveaways!

Ginna Moran is currently hard at work on her next novel.

Other Young Adult Novels by Ginna Moran

PARANORMAL

Destined for Dreams Series

Demon Within Series

Finding Nate Series

Going Ghostly Series

Spark of Life Series

When Souls Collide Series

Demon Watcher Series

Call of the Ocean Series

CONTEMPORARY

Falling into Fame Series

Life After Lila